JAMES H. SCHMITZ RESURRECTED

Selected Stories of James H. Schmitz

By James H. Schmitz
Edited by Greg Fowlkes

Includes the Special Bonus Story
AND NOW A MESSAGE . . .
By Greg Fowlkes

JAMES H. SCHMITZ RESURRECTED

© 2010 Resurrected Press
www.ResurrectedPress.com

Published by Intrepid Ink, LLC

Intrepid Ink, LLC provides full publishing services to authors of fiction and non-fiction books, eBooks and websites. From editing to formatting, to publishing, to marketing, Intrepid Ink gets your creative works into the hands of the people who want to read them.
Find out more at www.IntrepidInk.com.

ISBN 13: 978-1-935774-28-0

Printed in the United States of America

FOREWORD

During the 50's and 60's "Space Opera" and James H. Schmitz were almost synonymous. He was famous for his tales of interstellar secret agents and galactic criminals, and particularly for heroines such as Telzey Amberdon and Trigger Argee. Many of these characters had enhanced "psionic" powers that let them use their minds as well as their weapons to foil their enemies. All of them were resourceful in the best heroic tradition.

This collection of his stories does have several examples of this type of tale, with "The Star Hyacinths" and "The Winds of Time" both being in the classic "Space Opera" mold. But it also includes works that demonstrate Schmitz's versatility. This is particularly so in the shorter works, "An Incident on Route 12," "The Other Likeness," "Oneness." and "Ham Sandwich." Each of these stories ends with a twist that would not be out of place in a "Twilight Zone" episode.

"Watch the Sky" is anything but a typical "Space Opera." It features a ragged group of colonists on a backwater planet facing a dubious past and an insecure future. There are no intrepid secret agents, no psi-powers, just a surprising resolution.

On the surface, "Gone Fishing" is the story of a con man who tries to steal a revolutionary invention from a scientist. The story, however, has a much deeper subtext, dealing with what is really important in life, and what do we need to make us happy. It certainly is cosmic in its implications, but in a way completely different than the usual aliens trying to conquer the universe story.

Schmitz's "Space Operas" are certainly fun to read, and he would be remembered if that was all he had written. But he also wrote other types of stories that are equally entertaining in their own ways. I hope you will enjoy the ones collected here.

About The Author

James H. Schmitz (October 11, 1915- April 18, 1981) was born in Hamburg, Germany of American parents where he grew up. During World War II he served in the Pacific as an aerial photographer for the Army Air Corps. His best known novel is *The Witches of Karres*.

Greg Fowlkes
Editor-In-Chief
Resurrected Press
www.ResurrectedPress.com

TABLE OF CONTENTS

An Incident on Route 12

Originally Published in *Worlds of If*, January 1962

He was already a thief, prepared to steal again.
He didn't know that he himself was only booty!

An Incident on Route 12

Phil Garfield was thirty miles south of the little town of Redmon on Route Twelve when he was startled by a series of sharp, clanking noises. They came from under the Packard's hood.

The car immediately began to lose speed. Garfield jammed down the accelerator, had a sense of sick helplessness at the complete lack of response from the motor. The Packard rolled on, getting rid of its momentum, and came to a stop.

Phil Garfield swore shakily. He checked his watch, switched off the headlights and climbed out into the dark road. A delay of even half an hour here might be disastrous. It was past midnight, and he had another hundred and ten miles to cover to reach the small private airfield where Madge waited for him and the thirty thousand dollars in the suitcase on the Packard's front seat.

If he didn't make it before daylight....

He thought of the bank guard. The man had made a clumsy play at being a hero, and that had set off the fool woman who'd run screaming into their line of fire. One dead. Perhaps two. Garfield hadn't stopped to look at an evening paper.

But he knew they were hunting for him.

He glanced up and down the road. No other headlights in sight at the moment, no light from a building showing on the forested hills. He reached back into the car and brought out the suitcase, his gun, a big flashlight and the box of shells which had been standing beside the suitcase. He broke the box open, shoved a handful of shells and the .38 into his coat pocket, then took suitcase and flashlight over to the shoulder of the road and set them down.

There was no point in groping about under the Packard's hood. When it came to mechanics, Phil Garfield was a moron and well aware of it. The car was useless to him now ... except as bait.

But as bait it might be very useful.

Should he leave it standing where it was? No, Garfield decided. To anybody driving past it would merely suggest a necking party, or a drunk sleeping off his load before continuing home. He might have to wait an hour or more before someone decided to stop. He didn't have the time. He reached in through the window, hauled the top of the steering wheel towards him and put his weight against the rear window frame.

The Packard began to move slowly backwards at a slant across the road. In a minute or two he had it in position. Not blocking the road entirely, which would arouse immediate suspicion, but angled across it, lights out, empty, both front doors open and inviting a passerby's investigation.

Garfield carried the suitcase and flashlight across the right-hand shoulder of the road and moved up among the trees and undergrowth of the slope above the shoulder. Placing the suitcase between the bushes, he brought out the .38, clicked the safety off and stood waiting.

Some ten minutes later, a set of headlights appeared speeding up Route Twelve from the direction of Redmon. Phil Garfield went down on one knee before he came within range of the lights. Now he was completely concealed by the vegetation.

The car slowed as it approached, braking nearly to a stop sixty feet from the stalled Packard. There were several people inside it; Garfield heard voices, then a woman's loud laugh. The driver tapped his horn inquiringly twice, moved the car slowly forward. As the headlights went past him, Garfield got to his feet among the bushes, took a step down towards the road, raising the gun.

Then he caught the distant gleam of a second set of headlights approaching from Redmon. He swore under his breath and dropped back out of sight. The car below him reached the Packard, edged cautiously around it, rolled on with a sudden roar of acceleration.

*   *   *   *   *

The second car stopped when still a hundred yards away, the Packard caught in the motionless glare of its lights. Garfield heard the steady purring of a powerful motor.

For almost a minute, nothing else happened. Then the car came gliding smoothly on, stopped again no more than thirty feet to Garfield's left. He could see it now through the screening bushes—a big job, a long, low four-door sedan. The motor continued to purr. After a moment, a door on the far side of the car opened and slammed shut.

A man walked quickly out into the beam of the headlights and started towards the Packard.

Phil Garfield rose from his crouching position, the .38 in his right hand, flashlight in his left. If the driver was alone, the thing was now cinched! But if there was somebody else in the car, somebody capable of fast, decisive action, a slip in the next ten seconds might cost him the sedan, and quite probably his freedom and life. Garfield lined up the .38's sights steadily on the center of the approaching man's head. He let his breath out slowly as the fellow came level with him in the road and squeezed off one shot.

Instantly he went bounding down the slope to the road. The bullet had flung the man sideways to the pavement. Garfield darted past him to the left, crossed the beam of the headlights, and was in darkness again on the far side of the road, snapping on his flashlight as he sprinted up to the car.

The motor hummed quietly on. The flashlight showed the seats empty. Garfield dropped the light, jerked both doors open in turn, gun pointing into the car's interior. Then he stood still for a moment, weak and almost dizzy with relief.

There was no one inside. The sedan was his.

The man he had shot through the head lay face down on the road, his hat flung a dozen feet away from him. Route Twelve still stretched out in dark silence to east and west. There should be time enough to clean up the job before anyone else came along. Garfield brought the suitcase down and put it on the front seat of the sedan, then started back to get his victim off the road and out of sight. He scaled the man's hat into the bushes, bent down, grasped the ankles and started to haul him towards the left side of the road where the ground dropped off sharply beyond the shoulder.

The body made a high, squealing sound and began to writhe violently.

*　　*　　*　　*　　*

Shocked, Garfield dropped the legs and hurriedly took the gun from his pocket, moving back a step. The squealing noise rose in intensity as the wounded man quickly flopped over twice like a struggling fish, arms and legs sawing about with startling energy. Garfield clicked off the safety, pumped three shots into his victim's back.

The grisly squeals ended abruptly. The body continued to jerk for another second or two, then lay still.

Garfield shoved the gun back into his pocket. The unexpected interruption had unnerved him; his hands shook as he reached down again for the stranger's ankles. Then he jerked his hands back, and straightened up, staring.

From the side of the man's chest, a few inches below the right arm, something like a thick black stick, three feet long, protruded now through the material of the coat.

It shone, gleaming wetly, in the light from the car. Even in that first uncomprehending instant, something in its appearance brought a surge of sick disgust to Garfield's throat. Then the stick bent slowly halfway down its length, forming a sharp angle, and its tip opened into what could have been three blunt, black claws which scrabbled clumsily against the pavement. Very faintly, the squealing began again, and the body's back arched up as if another sticklike arm were pushing desperately against the ground beneath it.

Garfield acted in a blur of horror. He emptied the .38 into the thing at his feet almost without realizing he was doing it. Then, dropping the gun, he seized one of the ankles, ran backwards to the shoulder of the road, dragging the body behind him.

In the darkness at the edge of the shoulder, he let go of it, stepped around to the other side and with two frantically savage kicks sent the body plunging over the shoulder and down the steep slope beyond. He heard it crash through the bushes for some seconds, then stop. He turned, and ran back to the sedan, scooping up his gun as he went past. He scrambled into the driver's seat and slammed the door shut behind him.

His hands shook violently on the steering wheel as he pressed down the accelerator. The motor roared into life and the big car surged forward. He edged it past the Packard, cursing aloud in horrified shock, jammed down the accelerator and went flashing up Route Twelve, darkness racing beside and behind him.

*   *   *   *   *

What had it been? Something that wore what seemed to be a man's body like a suit of clothes, moving the body as a man moves, driving a man's car ... roach-armed, roach-legged itself!

Garfield drew a long, shuddering breath. Then, as he slowed for a curve, there was a spark of reddish light in the rear-view mirror.

He stared at the spark for an instant, braked the car to a stop, rolled down the window and looked back.

Far behind him along Route Twelve, a fire burned. Approximately at the point where the Packard had stalled out, where something had gone rolling off the road into the bushes....

Something, Garfield added mentally, that found fiery automatic destruction when death came to it, so that its secrets would remain unrevealed.

But for him the fire meant the end of a nightmare. He rolled the window up, took out a cigarette, lit it, and pressed the accelerator....

In incredulous fright, he felt the nose of the car tilt upwards, headlights sweeping up from the road into the trees.

Then the headlights winked out. Beyond the windshield, dark tree branches floated down towards him, the night sky beyond. He reached frantically for the door handle.

A steel wrench clamped silently about each of his arms, drawing them in against his sides, immobilizing them there. Garfield gasped, looked up at the mirror and saw a pair of faintly gleaming red eyes watching him from the rear of the car. Two of the things ... the second one stood behind him out of sight, holding him. They'd been in what had seemed to be the trunk compartment. And they had come out.

The eyes in the mirror vanished. A moist, black roach-arm reached over the back of the seat beside Garfield, picked up the cigarette he had dropped, extinguished it with rather horribly human motions, then took up Garfield's gun and drew back out of sight.

He expected a shot, but none came.

One doesn't fire a bullet through the suit one intends to wear....

It wasn't until that thought occurred to him that tough Phil Garfield began to scream. He was still screaming minutes later when, beyond the windshield, the spaceship floated into view among the stars.

WATCH THE SKY

ORIGINALLY PUBLISHED IN *ANALOG*, AUGUST 1962

*It's one thing to try to get away with what you
believe to be a lie and be caught at it–
and something different, and far worse
sometimes, to find it isn't a lie ...*

WATCH THE SKY

Uncle William Boles' war-battered old Geest gun gave the impression that at some stage of its construction it had been pulled out of shape and then hardened in that form. What remained of it was all of one piece. The scarred and pitted twin barrels were stubby and thick, and the vacant oblong in the frame behind them might have contained standard energy magazines. It was the stock which gave the alien weapon its curious appearance. Almost eighteen inches long, it curved abruptly to the right and was too thin, knobbed and indented to fit comfortably at any point in a human hand. Over half a century had passed since, with the webbed, boneless fingers of its original owner closed about it, it last spat deadly radiation at human foemen. Now it hung among Uncle William's other collected oddities on the wall above the living room fireplace.

And today, Phil Boles thought, squinting at the gun with reflectively narrowed eyes, some eight years after Uncle William's death, the old war souvenir would quietly become a key factor in the solution of a colonial planet's problems. He ran a finger over the dull, roughened frame, bent closer to study the neatly lettered inscription: GUNDERLAND BATTLE TROPHY, ANNO 2172, SGT. WILLIAM G. BOLES. Then, catching a familiar series of clicking noises from the hall, he straightened quickly and turned away. When Aunt Beulah's go-chair came rolling back into the room, Phil was sitting at the low tea table, his back to the fireplace.

The go-chair's wide flexible treads carried it smoothly down the three steps to the sunken section of the living room, Beulah sitting jauntily erect in it, for all the ninety-six years which had left her the last survivor of the original group of Earth settlers on the world of Roye. She tapped her fingers here and there on the chair's armrests, swinging it deftly about, and brought it to a stop beside the tea table.

"That was Susan Feeney calling," she reported. "And *there* is somebody else for you who thinks I have to be taken care of! Go ahead and finish the pie, Phil. Can't hurt a husky man like you. Got a couple more baking for you to take along."

Phil grinned. "That'd be worth the trip up from Fort Roye all by itself."

Beulah looked pleased. "Not much else I can do for my great-grand nephew nowadays, is there?"

Phil said, after a moment, "Have you given any further thought to—"

"Moving down to Fort Roye?" Beulah pursed her thin lips. "Goodness, Phil, I do hate to disappoint you again, but I'd be completely out of place in a town apartment."

"Dr. Fitzsimmons would be pleased," Phil remarked.

"Oh, him! Fitz is another old worry wart. What he wants is to get me into the hospital. Nothing doing!"

Phil shook his head helplessly, laughed. "After all, working a tupa ranch—"

"Nonsense. The ranch is just enough bother to be interesting. The appliances do everything anyway, and Susan is down here every morning for a chat and to make sure I'm still all right. She won't admit that, of course, but if she thinks something should be taken care of, the whole Feeney family shows up an hour later to do it. There's really no reason for you to be sending a dozen men up from Fort Roye every two months to harvest the tupa."

Phil shrugged. "No one's ever yet invented an easy way to dig up those roots. And the CLU's glad to furnish the men."

"Because you're its president?"

"Uh-huh."

"It really doesn't cost you anything?" Beulah asked doubtfully.

"Not a cent."

*   *   *   *   *

"Hm-m-m. Been meaning to ask you. What made you set up that ... Colonial Labor Union?"

Phil nodded. "That's the official name."

"Why did you set it up in the first place?"

"That's easy to answer," Phil said. "On the day the planetary population here touched the forty thousand mark, Roye became legally entitled to its labor union. Why not take advantage of it?"

"What's the advantage?"

"More Earth money coming in, for one thing. Of the twelve hundred CLU members we've got in Fort Roye now, seventy-six per cent were unemployed this month. We'll have a compensation check from the Territorial Office with the next ship coming in." He smiled at her expression. "Sure, the boys *could* go back to the tupa ranches. But not everyone likes that life as well as you and the Feeneys."

"Earth government lets you get away with it?" Beulah asked curiously. "They used to be pretty tight-fisted."

"They still are—but it's the law. The Territorial Office also pays any CLU president's salary, incidentally. I don't draw too much at the moment, but that will go up automatically with the membership and my responsibilities."

"What responsibilities?"

"We've set up a skeleton organization," Phil explained. "Now, when Earth government decides eventually to establish a big military base here, they can run in a hundred thousand civilians in a couple of months and everyone will be fitted into the pattern on Roye without trouble or confusion. That's really the reason for all the generosity."

Beulah sniffed. "Big base, my eye! There hasn't been six months since I set foot here that somebody wasn't talking about Fort Roye being turned into a Class A military base pretty soon. It'll never happen, Phil. Roye's a farm planet, and that's what it's going to stay."

Phil's lips twitched. "Well, don't give up hope."

"*I'm* not anxious for any changes," Beulah said. "I like Roye the way it is."

She peered at a button on the go-chair's armrest which had just begun to put out small bright-blue flashes of light. "Pies are done," she announced. "Phil, are you sure you can't stay for dinner?"

Phil looked at his watch, shook his head. "I'd love to, but I really have to get back."

"Then I'll go wrap up the pies for you."

Beulah swung the go-chair around, sent it slithering up the stairs and out the door. Phil stood up quickly. He stepped over to the fireplace, opened his coat and detached a flexible, box-shaped object from the inner lining. He laid this object on the mantle, and turned one of three small knobs about its front edge to the right. The box promptly extruded a supporting leg from each of its four corners, pushed itself up from the mantle and became a miniature table. Phil glanced at the door through which Beulah had vanished, listened a moment, then took the Geest gun from the wall, laid it carefully on top of the device and twisted the second dial.

The odd-looking gun began to sink slowly down through the surface of Phil's instrument, like a rock disappearing in mud. Within seconds it vanished completely; then, a moment later, it began to emerge from the box's underside. Phil let the Geest gun drop into his hand, replaced it on the wall, turned the third knob.

The box withdrew its supports and sank down to the mantle. Phil clipped it back inside his coat, closed the coat, and strolled over to the center of the room to wait for Aunt Beulah to return with the pies.

* * * * *

It was curious, Phil Boles reflected as his aircar moved out over the craggy, plunging coastline to the north some while later, that a few bold minds could be all that was needed to change the fate of a world. A few minds with imagination enough to see how circumstances about them might be altered.

On his left, far below, was now the flat ribbon of the peninsula, almost at sea level, its tip widening and lifting into the broad, rocky promontory on which stood Fort Roye—the only thing on the planet bigger and of more significance than the shabby backwoods settlements. And Fort Roye was neither very big nor very significant. A Class F military base around which, over the years, a straggling town had come into existence, Fort Roye was a space-age trading post linking Roye's population to the mighty mother planet, and a station from which the otherwise vacant and utterly unimportant 132nd Segment of the Space Territories was periodically and uneventfully patrolled. It was no more than that. Twice a month, an Earth ship settled down to the tiny port, bringing supplies, purchases, occasional groups of reassigned military and civilians—the latter suspected of being drawn as a rule from Earth's Undesirable classification. The ship would take off some days later, with a return load of the few local products for which there was outside demand, primarily the medically valuable tupa roots; and Fort Roye lay quiet again.

The planet was not at fault. Essentially, it had what was needed to become a thriving colony in every sense. At fault was the Geest War. The war had periods of flare-up and periods in which it seemed to be subsiding. During the past decade it had been subsiding again. One of the early flare-ups, one of the worst, and the one which brought the war closest to Earth itself, was the Gunderland Battle in which Uncle William Boles' trophy gun had been acquired. But the war never came near Roye. The action was all in the opposite section of the giant sphere of the Space Territories, and over the years the war drew steadily farther away.

And Earth's vast wealth—its manpower, materials and money—was pouring into space in the direction the Geest War was moving. Worlds not a tenth as naturally attractive as Roye, worlds where the basic conditions for human life were just above the unbearable point, were settled and held, equipped with everything needed and wanted to turn them into independent giant fortresses, with a population not too dissatisfied with its lot. When Earth government didn't count the expense, life could be made considerably better than bearable almost anywhere.

Those were the circumstances which condemned Roye to insignificance. Not everyone minded. Phil Boles, native son, did mind. His inclinations were those of an operator, and he was not being given an adequate opportunity to exercise them. Therefore, the circumstances would have to be changed, and the precise time to make the change was at hand. Phil himself was not aware of every factor involved, but he was aware of enough of them. Back on Earth, a certain political situation was edging towards a specific point of instability. As a result, an Earth ship which was not one of the regular freighters had put down at Fort Roye some days before. Among its passengers were Commissioner Sanford of the Territorial Office, a well-known politician, and a Mr. Ronald Black, the popular and enterprising owner of Earth's second largest news outlet system. They were on a joint fact-finding tour of the thinly scattered colonies in this remote section of the Territories, and had wound up eventually at the most remote of all—the 132nd Segment and Roye.

That was one factor. Just visible twenty thousand feet below Phil–almost directly beneath him now as the aircar made its third leisurely crossing of the central belt of the peninsula–was another. From here it looked like an irregular brown circle against the peninsula's nearly white ground. Lower down, it would have resembled nothing so much as the broken and half-decayed spirals of a gigantic snail shell, its base sunk deep in the ground and its shattered point rearing twelve stories above it. This structure, known popularly as "the ruins" in Fort Roye, was supposed to have been the last stronghold of a semi-intelligent race native to Roye, which might have become extinct barely a century before the Earthmen arrived. A factor associated with the ruins again was that their investigation was the passionately pursued hobby of First Lieutenant Norman Vaughn, Fort Roye's Science Officer.

Add to such things the reason Roye was not considered in need of a serious defensive effort by Earth's strategists–the vast distances between it and any troubled area, and so the utter improbability that a Geest ship might come close enough to discover that here was another world as well suited for its race as for human beings. And then a final factor: the instrument attached to the lining of Phil's coat–a very special "camera" which now carried the contact impressions made on it by Uncle William's souvenir gun. Put 'em all together, Phil thought cheerily, and they spelled out interesting developments on Roye in the very near future.

He glanced at his watch again, swung the aircar about and started back inland. He passed presently high above Aunt Beulah's tupa ranch and that of the Feeney family two miles farther up the mountain, turned gradually to the east and twenty minutes later was edging back down the ranges to the coast. Here in a wild, unfarmed region, perched at the edge of a cliff dropping nearly nine hundred feet to the swirling tide, was a small, trim cabin which was the property of a small, trim Fort

Roye lady named Celia Adams. Celia had been shipped
out from Earth six years before, almost certainly as an
Undesirable, though only the Territorial Office and Celia
herself knew about that, the Botany Bay aspect of worlds
like Roye being handled with some tact by Earth.

*   *   *   *   *

Phil approached the cabin only as far as was
necessary to make sure that the dark-green aircar parked
before it was one belonging to Major Wayne Jackson, the
Administration Officer and second in command at Fort
Roye–another native son and an old acquaintance. He
then turned away, dropped to the woods ten miles south
and made a second inconspicuous approach under cover
of the trees. There might be casual observers in the area,
and while his meeting with Jackson and Celia Adams
today revealed nothing in itself, it would be better if no
one knew about it.

He grounded the car in the forest a few hundred yards
from the Adams cabin, slung a rifle over his shoulder and
set off along a game path. It was good hunting territory,
and the rifle would explain his presence if he ran into
somebody. When he came within view of the cabin, he
discovered Celia and her visitor on the covered back
patio, drinks standing before them. Jackson was in
hunting clothes. Phil remained quietly back among the
trees for some seconds watching the two, aware of
something like a last-minute hesitancy. A number of
things passed slowly through his mind.

What they planned to do was no small matter. It was
a hoax which should have far-reaching results, on a
gigantic scale. And if Earth government realized it had
been hoaxed, the thing could become very unpleasant.
That tough-minded central bureaucracy did not
ordinarily bother to obtain proof against those it
suspected. The suspicion was enough. Individuals and
groups whom the shadow of doubt touched found

themselves shunted unobtrusively into some backwater of existence and kept there. It was supposed to be very difficult to emerge from such a position again.

In the back of his mind, Phil had been conscious of that, but it had seemed an insignificant threat against the excitement arising from the grandiose impudence of the plan, the perhaps rather small-boyish delight at being able to put something over, profitably, on the greatest power of all. Even now it might have been only a natural wariness that brought the threat up for a final moment of reflection. He didn't, of course, want to incur Earth government's disapproval. But why believe that he might? On all Roye there would be only three who knew—Wayne Jackson, Celia Adams, and himself. All three would benefit, each in a different way, and all would be equally responsible for the hoax. No chance of indiscretion or belated qualms there. Their own interest ruled it out in each case.

And from the other men now involved there was as little danger of betrayal. Their gain would be vastly greater, but they had correspondingly more to lose. They would take every step required to insure their protection, and in doing that they would necessarily take the best of care of Phil Boles.

*　　*　　*　　*　　*

"How did you ever get such a thing smuggled in to Roye?" Phil asked. He'd swallowed half the drink Celia offered him at a gulp and now, a few minutes later, he was experiencing what might have been under different circumstances a comfortable glow, but which didn't entirely erase the awareness of having committed himself at this hour to an irrevocable line of action.

Celia stroked a fluffy lock of red-brown hair back from her forehead and glanced over at him. She had a narrow, pretty face, marred only by a suggestion of hardness about the mouth—which was a little more than ordinarily noticeable just now. Phil decided she felt something like his own tensions, for identical reasons. He was less certain about Major Wayne Jackson, a big, loose-jointed man with an easy-going smile and a pleasantly self-assured voice. The voice might be veering a trifle too far to the hearty side; but that was all.

"I didn't," Celia said. "It belonged to Frank. How he got it shipped in with him—or after him—from Earth I don't know. He never told me. When he died a couple of years ago, I took it over."

Phil gazed reflectively at the row of unfamiliar instruments covering half the table beside her. The "camera" which had taken an imprint of the Geest gun in Aunt Beulah's living room went with that equipment and had become an interior section of the largest of the instruments. "What do you call it?" he asked.

Celia looked irritated. Jackson laughed, said, "Why not tell him? Phil's feeling like we do—this is the last chance to look everything over, make sure nobody's slipped up, that nothing can go wrong. Right, Phil?"

Phil nodded. "Something like that."

Celia chewed her lip. "All right," she said. "It doesn't matter, I suppose—compared with the other." She tapped one of the instruments. "The set's called a duplicator. This one's around sixty years old. They're classified as a forgery device, and it's decidedly illegal for a private person to build one, own one, or use one."

"Why that?"

"Because forgery is ordinarily all they're good for. Frank was one of the best of the boys in that line before he found he'd been put on an outtransfer list."

Phil frowned. "But if it can duplicate any manufactured object—"

"It can. At an average expense around fifty times higher than it would take to make an ordinary reproduction without it. A duplicator's no use unless you want a reproduction that's absolutely indistinguishable from the model."

"I see." Phil was silent a moment. "After sixty years–"

"Don't worry, Phil," Jackson said. "It's in perfect working condition. We checked that on a number of samples."

"How do you know the copies were really indistinguishable?"

Celia said impatiently, "Because that's the way the thing works. When the Geest gun passed through the model plate, it was analyzed down to its last little molecule. The duplicate is now being built up from that analysis. Every fraction of every element used in the original will show up again exactly. Why do you think the stuff's so expensive?"

*   *   *   *   *

Phil grinned. "All right, I'm convinced. How do we get rid of the inscription?"

"The gadget will handle that," Jackson said. "Crack that edge off, treat the cracked surface to match the wear of the rest." He smiled. "Makes an Earth forger's life look easy, doesn't it?"

"It is till they hook you," Celia said shortly. She finished her drink, set it on the table, added, "We've a few questions, too, Phil."

"The original gun," Jackson said. "Mind you, there's no slightest reason to expect an investigation. But after this starts rolling, our necks will be out just a little until we've got rid of that particular bit of incriminating evidence."

Phil pursed his lips. "I wouldn't worry about it. Nobody but Beulah ever looks at Uncle William's collection of oddities. Most of it's complete trash. And probably only she and you and I know there's a Geest gun among the things–William's cronies all passed away before he did. But if the gun disappeared now, Beulah would miss it. And that–since Earth government's made it illegal to possess Geest artifacts–*might* create attention."

Jackson fingered his chin thoughtfully, said, "Of course, there's always a way to make sure Beulah didn't kick up a fuss."

Phil hesitated. "Dr. Fitzsimmons gives Beulah another three months at the most," he said. "If she can stay out of the hospital for even the next eight weeks, he'll consider it some kind of miracle. That should be early enough to take care of the gun."

"It should be," Jackson said. "However, if there does happen to be an investigation before that time–"

Phil looked at him, said evenly, "We'd do whatever was necessary. It wouldn't be very agreeable, but my neck's out just as far as yours."

Celia laughed. "That's the reason we can all feel pretty safe," she observed. "Every last one of us is completely selfish–and there's no more dependable kind of person than that."

Jackson flushed a little, glanced at Phil, smiled. Phil shrugged. Major Wayne Jackson, native son, Fort Roye's second in command, was scheduled for the number one spot and a string of promotions via the transfer of the current commander, Colonel Thayer. Their Earthside associates would arrange for that as soon as the decision to turn Fort Roye into a Class A military base was reached. Phil himself could get by with the guaranteed retention of the CLU presidency, and a membership moving up year by year to the half million mark and beyond–he could get by very, very comfortably, in fact. While Celia Adams would develop a discreetly firm hold on every upcoming minor racket, facilitated by iron-clad protection and an enforced lack of all competitors.

"We're all thinking of Roye's future, Celia," Phil said amiably, "each in his own way. And the future looks pretty bright. In fact, the only possible stumbling block I can still see is right here on Roye, and it's Honest Silas

Thayer. If our colonel covers up the Geest gun find tomorrow—"

Jackson grinned, shook his head. "Leave that to me, my boy—and to our very distinguished visitors from Earth. Commissioner Sanford has arranged to be in Thayer's company on Territorial Office business all day tomorrow. Science Officer Vaughn is dizzy with delight because Ronald Black and most of the newsgathering troop will inspect his diggings in the ruins in the morning, with the promise of giving his theories about the vanished natives of Roye a nice spread on Earth. Black will happen to ask me to accompany the party. Between Black and Sanford—and myself—Colonel Silas Thayer won't have a chance to suppress the discovery of a Geest gun on Roye until the military has had a chance to look into it fully. And the only one he can possibly blame for that will be Science Officer Norm Vaughn—for whom, I'll admit, I feel just a little bit sorry!"

* * * * *

First Lieutenant Norman Vaughn was an intense and frustrated young man whose unusually thick contact lenses and wide mouth gave him some resemblance to a melancholy frog. He suspected, correctly, that a good Science Officer would not have been transferred from Earth to Roye which was a planet deficient in scientific problems of any magnitude, and where requisitions for research purposes were infrequently and grudgingly granted.

The great spiraled ruin on the peninsula of Fort Roye had been Vaughn's one solace. Several similar deserted structures were known to be on the planet, but this was by far in the best condition and no doubt the most recently built. To him, if to no one else, it became clear that the construction had been carried out with conscious plan and purpose, and he gradually amassed great piles of notes to back up his theory that the vanished builders were of near-human intelligence. Unfortunately, their bodies appeared to have lacked hard and durable parts, since nothing that could be construed as their remains was found; and what Lieutenant Vaughn regarded as undeniable artifacts, on the level of very early Man's work, looked to others like chance shards and lumps of the tough, shell-like material of which the ruins were composed.

Therefore, while Vaughn was—as Jackson had pointed out—really dizzy with delight when Ronald Black, that giant of Earth's news media, first indicated an interest in the ruins and his theories about them, this feeling soon became mixed with acute anxiety. For such a chance surely would not come again if the visitors remained unconvinced by what he showed them, and what—actually—did he have to show? In the morning, when the party set out, Vaughn was in a noticeably nervous frame of mind.

Two hours later, he burst into the anteroom of the base commander's office in Fort Roye, where the warrant on duty almost failed to recognize him. Lieutenant Vaughn's eyes glittered through their thick lenses; his face was red and he was grinning from ear to ear. He pounded past the startled warrant, pulled open the door to the inner office where Colonel Thayer sat with the visiting Territorial Commissioner, and plunged inside.

"Sir," the warrant heard him quaver breathlessly, "I have the proof—the undeniable proof! They *were* intelligent beings. They did *not* die of disease. They were exterminated in war! They were ... but see for yourself!" There was a thud as he dropped something on the polished table top between the commissioner and Colonel Thayer. "*That* was dug up just now—among their own artifacts!"

Silas Thayer was on his feet, sucking in his breath for the blast that would hurl his blundering Science Officer back out of the office. What halted him was an odd, choked exclamation from Commissioner Sanford. The colonel's gaze flicked over to the visitor, then followed Sanford's stare to the object on the table.

For an instant, Colonel Thayer froze.

Vaughn was bubbling on. "And, sir, I ..."

"Shut up!" Thayer snapped. He continued immediately, "You say this was found in the diggings in the ruins?"

"Yes, sir–just now! It's ..."

Lieutenant Vaughn checked himself under the colonel's stare, some dawning comprehension of the enormous irregularities he'd committed showing in his flushed face. He licked his lips uncertainly.

"You will excuse me for a moment, sir," Thayer said to Commissioner Sanford. He picked the Geest gun up gingerly by its unmistakably curved shaft, took it over to the office safe, laid it inside and relocked the safe. He then left the office.

*   *   *   *   *

In an adjoining room, Thayer rapped out Major Wayne Jackson's code number on a communicator. He heard a faint click as Jackson's wrist speaker switched on, and said quickly, "Wayne, are you in a position to speak?"

"I am at the moment," Jackson's voice replied cautiously.

Colonel Thayer said, "Norm Vaughn just crashed in here with something he claims was found in the diggings. Sanford saw it, and obviously recognized it. We might be able to keep him quiet. But now some questions. Was that item actually dug up just now?"

"Apparently it was," Jackson said. "I didn't see it happen–I was talking to Black at the moment. But there are over a dozen witnesses who claim they did see it happen, including five or six of the news agency men."

"And they knew what it was?"

"Enough of them did."

Thayer cursed softly. "No chance that one of them pitched the thing into the diggings for an Earthside sensation?"

"I'm afraid not," Jackson said. "It was lying in the sifter after most of the sand and dust had been blown away."

"Why didn't you call me at once?"

"I've been holding down something like a mutiny here, Silas. Vaughn got away before I could stop him, but I grounded the other aircars till you could decide what to do. Our visitors don't like that. Neither do they like the fact that I've put a guard over the section where the find was made, and haven't let them talk to Norm's work crew.

"Ronald Black and his staff have been fairly reasonable, but there's been considerable mention of military highhandedness made by the others. This is the first moment I've been free."

"You did the right thing," Thayer said, "but I doubt it will help much now. Can you get hold of Ronald Black?"

"Yes, he's over there ..."

"Colonel Thayer?" another voice inquired pleasantly a few seconds later.

"Mr. Black," the colonel said carefully, "what occurred in the diggings a short while ago may turn out to be a matter of great importance."

"That's quite obvious, sir."

"And that being the case," the colonel went on, "do you believe it would be possible to obtain a gentleman's agreement from all witnesses to make no mention of this apparent discovery until the information is released through the proper channels? I'm asking for your opinion."

"Colonel Thayer," Ronald Black's voice said, still pleasantly, "my opinion is that the only way you could keep the matter quiet is to arrest every civilian present, including myself, and hold us incommunicado. You have your duty, and we have ours. Ours does not include withholding information from the public which may signal the greatest shift in the conduct of the Geest War in the past two decades."

"I understand," Thayer said. He was silent for some seconds, and perhaps he, too, was gazing during that time at a Fort Roye of the future–a Class A military base under his command, with Earth's great war vessels lined up along the length of the peninsula.

"Mr. Black," he said, "please be so good as to give your colleagues this word from me. I shall make the most thorough possible investigation of what has occurred and forward a prompt report, along with any material evidence obtained, to my superiors on Earth. None of you will receive any other statement from me or from anyone under my command. An attempt to obtain such a statement will, in fact, result in the arrest of the person or persons involved. Is that clear?"

"Quite clear, Colonel Thayer," Ronald Black said softly. "And entirely satisfactory."

*   *   *   *   *

"We have known for the past eight weeks," the man named Cranehart said, "that this was not what it appears to be ... that is, a section of a Geest weapon."

He shoved the object in question across the desk towards Commissioner Sanford and Ronald Black. Neither of the two attempted to pick it up; they glanced at it, then returned their eyes attentively to Cranehart's face.

"It is, of course, an excellent copy," Cranehart went on, "produced with a professional forger's equipment. As I imagine you're aware, that should have made it impossible to distinguish from the original weapon. However ... there's no real harm in telling you this now ... Geest technology has taken somewhat different turns than our own. In their weapons they employ traces of certain elements which we are only beginning to learn to maintain in stable form. That is a matter your government has kept from public knowledge because we don't wish the Geests to learn from human prisoners how much information we are gaining from them.

"The instrument which made this copy naturally did not have such elements at its disposal. So it employed their lower homologues and in that manner successfully produced an almost identical model. In fact, the only significant difference is that such a gun, if it had been a complete model, could not possibly have been fired." He smiled briefly. "But that, I think you will agree, *is* a significant difference! We knew as soon as the so-called Geest gun was examined that it could only have been made by human beings."

"Then," Commissioner Sanford said soberly, "its apparent discovery on Roye during our visit was a deliberate hoax—"

Cranehart nodded. "Of course."

Ronald Black said, "I fail to see why you've kept this quiet. You needn't have given away any secrets. Meanwhile the wave of public criticism at the government's seeming hesitancy to take action on the discovery—that is, to rush protection to the threatened Territorial Segments—has reached almost alarming proportions. You could have stopped it before it began two months ago with a single announcement."

"Well, yes," Cranehart said. "There were other considerations. Incidentally, Mr. Black, we are not unappreciative of the fact that the news media under your own control exercised a generous restraint in the matter."

"For which," Black said dryly, "I am now very thankful."

"As for the others," Cranehart went on, "the government has survived periods of criticism before. That is not important. The important thing is that the Geest War has been with us for more than a human life span now ... and it becomes difficult for many to bear in mind that until its conclusion no acts that might reduce our ability to prosecute it can be tolerated."

Ronald Black said slowly, "So you've been delaying the announcement until you could find out who was responsible for the hoax."

"We were interested," Cranehart said, "only in the important men—the dangerous men. We don't care much who else is guilty of what. This, you see, is a matter of expediency, not of justice." He looked for a moment at the politely questioning, somewhat puzzled faces across the desk, went on, "When you leave this room, each of you will be conducted to an office where you will be given certain papers to sign. That is the first step."

*   *   *   *   *

There was silence for some seconds. Ronald Black took a cigarette from a platinum case, tapped it gently on the desk, put it to his mouth and lit it. Cranehart went on, "It would have been impossible to unravel this particular conspiracy if the forgery had been immediately exposed. At that time, no one had taken any obvious action. Then, within a few days—with the discovery apparently confirmed by our silence—normal maneuverings in industry and finance were observed to be under way. If a major shift in war policy was pending, if one or more key bases were to be established in Territorial Segments previously considered beyond the range of Geest reconnaissance and therefore secure from attack, this would be to somebody's benefit on Earth."

"Isn't it always?" Black murmured.

"Of course. It's a normal procedure, ordinarily of no concern to government. It can be predicted with considerable accuracy to what group or groups the ultimate advantage in such a situation will go. But in these past weeks, it became apparent that somebody else was winning out ... somebody who could have won out only on the basis of careful and extensive preparation for this very situation.

"That was abnormal, and it was the appearance of an abnormal pattern for which we had been waiting. We find there are seven men involved. These men will be deprived of the advantage they have gained."

Ronald Black shook his head, said, "You're making a mistake, Cranehart. I'm signing no papers."

"Nor I," Sanford said thickly.

Cranehart rubbed the side of his nose with a fingertip, said meditatively, "You won't be forced to. Not directly." He nodded at the window. "On the landing flange out there is an aircar. It is possible that this aircar will be found wrecked in the mountains some four hundred miles north of here early tomorrow morning. Naturally, we have a satisfactory story prepared to cover such an eventuality."

Sanford whitened slowly. He said, "So you'd resort to murder!"

Cranehart was silent for a few seconds. "Mr. Sanford," he said then, "you, as a member of the Territorial Office, know very well that the Geest War has consumed over four hundred million human lives to date. That is the circumstance which obliges your government to insist on your co-operation. I advise you to give it."

"But you have no proof! You have nothing but surmises—"

"Consider this," Cranehart said. "A conspiracy of the type I have described constitutes a capital offense under present conditions. Are you certain that you would prefer us to continue to look for proof?"

Ronald Black said in a harsh voice, "And what would the outcome be if we did choose to co-operate?"

"Well, we can't afford to leave men of your type in a position of influence, Mr. Black," Cranehart said amiably. "And you understand, I'm sure, that it would be entirely too difficult to keep you under proper surveillance on Earth—"

*   *   *   *   *

Celia Adams said from outside the cabin door, "I think it is them, Phil. Both cars have started to circle."

Phil Boles came to the door behind her and looked up. It was early evening–Roye's sun just down, and a few stars out. The sky above the sea was still light. After a moment, he made out the two aircars moving in a wide, slow arc far overhead. He glanced at his watch.

"Twenty minutes late," he remarked. "But it couldn't be anyone else. And if they hadn't all come along, they wouldn't have needed two cars." He hesitated. "We can't tell how they're going to take this, Celia, but they may have decided already that they could make out better without us." He nodded towards the edge of the cliff. "Short way over there, and a long drop to the water! So don't let them surprise you."

She said coldly, "I won't. And I've used guns before this."

"Wouldn't doubt it." Phil reached back behind the door, picked up a flarelight standing beside a heavy machine rifle, and came outside. He pointed the light at the cars and touched the flash button briefly three times. After a moment, there were two answering flashes from the leading car.

"So Wayne Jackson's in the front car," Phil said. "Now let's see what they do." He returned the light to its place behind the door and came out again, standing about twelve feet to one side of Celia. The aircars vanished inland, came back at treetop level a few minutes later. One settled down quietly between the cabin and the edge of the cliff, the other following but dropping to the ground a hundred yards away, where it stopped. Phil glanced over at Celia, said softly, "Watch that one!" She nodded almost imperceptibly, right hand buried in her jacket pocket.

The near door of the car before them opened. Major Wayne Jackson, hatless and in hunting clothes, climbed out, staring at them. He said, "Anyone else here?"

"Just Celia and myself," Phil said.

Jackson turned, spoke into the car and two men, similarly dressed, came out behind him. Phil recognized Ronald Black and Sanford. The three started over to the cabin, stopped a dozen feet away.

Jackson said sardonically, "Our five other previous Earthside partners are in the second car. In spite of your insistence to meet the whole group, they don't want you and Celia to see their faces. They don't wish to be identifiable." He touched his coat lapel. "They'll hear what we're saying over this communicator and they could talk to you, but won't unless they feel it's necessary. You'll have to take my word for it that we're all present."

"That's good enough," Phil said.

"All right," Jackson went on, "now what did you mean by forcing us to take this chance? Let me make it plain. Colonel Thayer hasn't been accused of collaborating in the Roye gun hoax, but he got a black eye out of the affair just the same. And don't forget that a planet with colonial status is technically under martial law, which includes the civilians. If Silas Thayer can get his hands on the guilty persons, the situation will become a lot more unpleasant than it already is."

*   *   *   *   *

Phil addressed Ronald Black, "Then how about you two? When you showed up here again on a transfer list, Thayer must have guessed why."

Black shook his head. "Both of us exercised the privilege of changing our names just prior to the outtransfer. He doesn't know we're on Roye. We don't intend to let him find out."

Phil asked, "Did you make any arrangements to get out of Roye again?"

"Before leaving Earth?" Black showed his teeth in a humorless smile. "Boles, you have no idea of how abruptly and completely the government men cut us off from our every resource! We were given no opportunity to draw up plans to escape from exile, believe me."

Phil glanced over at Celia. "In that case," he said, a little thickly, "we'd better see if we can't draw some up together immediately."

Jackson asked, staring, "What are you talking about, Phil? Don't think for a moment Silas Thayer isn't doing what he can to find out who put that trick over on him. I'm not at all sure he doesn't suspect me. And if he can tie it to us, it's our neck. If you have some crazy idea of getting off the planet now, let me tell you that for the next few years we can't risk making a single move! If we stay quiet, we're safe. We–"

"I don't think we'd be safe," Phil said.

On his right, Celia Adams added sharply, "The gentleman in the other car who's just started to lower that window had better raise it again! If he's got good eyesight, he'll see I have a gun pointed at him. Yes, that's much better! Go on, Phil."

"Have you both gone out of your minds?" Jackson demanded.

"No," Celia said. She laughed with a sudden shakiness in her tone, added, "Though I don't know why we haven't! We've thought of the possibility that the rest of you might feel it would be better if Phil and I weren't around any more, Wayne."

"That's nonsense!" Jackson said.

"Maybe. Anyway, don't try it. You wouldn't be doing yourselves a favor even if it worked. Better listen now."

"Listen to what?" Jackson demanded exasperatedly. "I'm telling you it will be all right, if we just don't make any mistakes. The only real pieces of evidence were your duplicator and the original gun. Since we're rid of those–"

"We're not rid of the gun, Wayne," Phil said. "I still have it. I haven't dared get rid of it."

"You ... what do you mean?"

"I was with Beulah in the Fort Roye hospital when she died," Phil said. He added to Ronald Black, "That was two days after the ship brought the seven of you in."

Black nodded, his eyes alert. "Major Jackson informed me."

"She was very weak, of course, but quite lucid," Phil went on. "She talked a good deal–reminiscing, and in a rather happy vein. She finally mentioned the Geest gun, and how Uncle William used to keep us boys ... Wayne and me ... spell-bound with stories about the Gunderland Battle, and how he'd picked the gun up there."

Jackson began, "And what does–"

"He didn't get the gun there," Phil said. "Beulah said Uncle William came in from Earth with the first shipment of settlers and was never off Roye again in his life."

"He ... then–"

Phil said, "Don't you get it? He found the gun right here on Roye. Beulah thought it was awfully funny. William was an old fool, she said, but the best liar she'd ever known. He came in with the thing one day after he'd been traipsing around the back country, and said it looked 'sort of' like pictures of Geest guns he'd seen, and that he was going to put the inscription on it and have some fun now and then." Phil took a deep breath. "Uncle William found it lying in a pile of ashes where someone had made camp a few days before. He figured it would have been a planetary speedster some rich sportsmen from Earth had brought in for a taste of outworld hunting on Roye, and that one of them had dumped the broken oddball gun into the fire to get rid of it.

"That was thirty-six years ago. Beulah remembered it happened a year before I was born."

There was silence for some seconds. Then Ronald Black said evenly, "And what do you conclude, Boles?"

Phil looked at him. "I'd conclude that Norm Vaughn was right about there having been some fairly intelligent creatures here once. The Geests ran into them and exterminated them as they usually do. That might have been a couple of centuries back. Then, thirty-six years ago, one of their scouts slipped in here without being spotted, found human beings on the planet, looked around a little and left again."

He took the Geest gun from his pocket, hefted it in his hand. "We have the evidence here," he said. "We had it all the time and didn't know it."

Ronald Black said dryly, "We may have the evidence. But we have no slightest proof at all now that that's what it is."

"I know it," Phil said. "Now Beulah's gone ... well, we couldn't even prove that William Boles never left the planet, for that matter. There weren't any records to speak of being kept in the early days." He was silent a moment. "Supposing," he said, "we went ahead anyway. We hand the gun in, with the story I just told you—"

Jackson made a harsh, laughing sound. "That would hang us fast, Phil!"

"And nothing else?"

"Nothing else," Black said with finality. "Why should anyone believe the story now? There are a hundred more likely ways in which a Geest gun could have got to Roye. The gun is tangible evidence of the hoax, but that's all."

Phil asked, "Does anybody ... including the cautious gentlemen in the car over there ... disagree with that?"

There was silence again. Phil shrugged, turned towards the cliff edge, drew his arm back and hurled the Geest gun far up and out above the sea. Still without speaking, the others turned their heads to watch it fall towards the water, then looked back at him.

"I didn't think very much of that possibility myself," Phil said unsteadily. "But one of you might have. All right—*we* know the Geests know we're here. But we won't be able to convince anyone else of it. And, these last few years, the war seems to have been slowing down again. In the past, that's always meant the Geests were preparing a big new surprise operation.

"So the other thing now—the business of getting off Roye. It can't be done unless some of you have made prior arrangements for it Earthside. If it had been possible in any other way, I'd have been out of this place ten years ago."

Ronald Black said carefully, "Very unfortunately, Boles, no such arrangements have been made."

"Then there it is," Phil said. "I suppose you see now why I thought this group should get together. The ten masterminds! Well, we've hoaxed ourselves into a massive jam. Now let's find out if there's any possible way—*any possibility at all!*—of getting out of it again."

A voice spoke tinnily from Jackson's lapel communicator. "Major Jackson?"

"Yes?" Jackson said.

"Please persuade Miss Adams that it is no longer necessary to point her gun at this car. In view of the stated emergency, we feel we had better come out now—and join the conference."

*   *   *   *   *

FROM THE RECORDS OF THE TERRITORIAL OFFICE, 2345 A.D.

... It is generally acknowledged that the Campaign of the 132nd Segment marked the turning point of the Geest War. Following the retransfer of Colonel Silas Thayer to Earth, the inspired leadership of Major Wayne Jackson and his indefatigable and exceptionally able assistants, notably CLU President Boles, transformed the technically unfortified and thinly settled key world of Roye within twelve years into a virtual death trap for any invading force. Almost half of the Geest fleet which eventually arrived there was destroyed in the first week subsequent to the landing, and few of the remaining ships were sufficiently undamaged to be able to lift again. The enemy relief fleet, comprising an estimated forty per cent of the surviving Geest space power, was intercepted in the 134th Segment by the combined Earth forces under Admiral McKenna's command and virtually annihilated.

In the following two years ...

THE OTHER LIKENESS

ORIGINALLY PUBLISHED IN *ANALOG SCIENCE FACT & FICTION*,
JULY 1962

*There is a limit to how perfect a counterfeit can be
—a limit that cannot be passed without an odd
phenomenon setting in....*

THE OTHER LIKENESS

When he felt the sudden sharp tingling on his skin
which came from the alarm device under his wrist watch,
Dr. Halder Leorm turned unhurriedly from the culture
tray he was studying, walked past the laboratory
technician to the radiation room, entered it and closed the
door behind him. He slipped the instrument from his
wrist, removed its back plate, and held it up to his eye.

He was looking into the living room of his home, fifty
miles away in another section of Orado's great city of
Draise. A few steps from the entry, a man lay on his back
on the carpeting, eyes shut, face deeply flushed,
apparently unconscious. Halder Leorm's mouth
tightened. The man on the carpet was Dr. Atteo, his new
assistant, assigned to the laboratory earlier in the week.
Beyond Atteo, the entry from the residence's delivery
area and car port stood open.

Fingering the rim of the tiny scanner with practiced
quickness, Halder Leorm shifted the view to other
sections of the house, finally to the car port. An empty
aircar stood in the port; there was no one in sight.

Halder sighed, replaced the instrument on his wrist,
and glanced over at a wall mirror. His face was pale but
looked sufficiently composed. Leaving the radiation room,
he picked up his hat, said to the technician, "Forgot to
mention it, Reef, but I'll have to head over to central
laboratories again."

Reef, a large, red-headed young man, glanced around
in mild surprise.

"They've got a nerve, calling you across town every two days!" he observed. "Whose problem are you supposed to solve now?"

"I wasn't informed. Apparently, something urgent has come up and they want my opinion on it."

"Yeah, I bet!" Reef scratched his head, glanced along the rows of culture trays. "Well ... nothing here at the moment I can't handle, even if Atteo doesn't show up. Will you be back before evening?"

"I wouldn't count on it," Halder said. "You know how those conferences tend to go."

"Uh-huh. Well, Dr. Leorm, if I don't see you before tomorrow, give my love to your beautiful wife."

Halder smiled back at him from the door. "Will do, Reef!" He let the door slide shut behind him, started towards the exit level of the huge pharmaceutical plant. Reef had acted in a completely normal manner. If, as seemed very probable, "Dr. Atteo" was a Federation agent engaged in investigating Dr. Halder Leorm, Halder's co-workers evidently had not been apprised of the fact. Still, Halder thought, he must warn Kilby instantly. It was quite possible that an attempt to arrest him would be made before he left the building.

He stepped into the first ComWeb booth on his route, and dialed Kilby's business number. His wife had a desk job in one of the major fashion stores in the residential section of Draise, and—which was fortunate just now—a private office. Her face appeared almost immediately on the screen before him, a young face, soft-looking, with large, gray eyes. She smiled in pleased surprise. "'Lo, Halder!"

"'Lo, Kilby.... Did you forget?"

Kilby's smile became inquiring. "Forget what?"

"That we're lunching together at Hasmin's today."

Halder paused, watching the color drain quickly from Kilby's cheeks.

"Of course!" she whispered. "I did forget. Got tied up in ... and ... I'll leave right now! All right?"

Halder smiled. She was past the first moment of shock and would be able to handle herself. After all, they had made very precise preparations against the day when they might discover that the Federation's suspicions had turned, however tentatively, in their direction.

"That'll be fine," he said. "I'm calling from the lab and will leave at once"—he paused almost imperceptibly—"if I'm not held up. Meet you at Hasmin's, in any case, in around twenty minutes."

Kilby's eyes flickered for an instant. If Halder didn't make it away, she was to carry out her own escape, as planned. That was the understanding. She gave him a tremulous smile. "And I'm forgiven?"

"Of course." Halder smiled back.

*   *   *   *   *

The guards at the check-out point were not men he knew, but Halder walked through the ID-scanning band without incident, apparently without arousing interest. Beyond, to the left, was a wide one-way portal to a tube station. His aircar was in the executive parking area on the building's roof, but the escape plan called for both of them to abandon their private cars, which were more than likely to be traps, and use the public transportation systems in starting out.

Halder entered the tube station, went to a rented locker, opened it and took out two packages, one containing a complete change of clothing and a mirror, the other half a dozen canned cultures of as many varieties of microlife—highly specialized strains of life, of which the pharmaceutical concern that employed Dr. Halder Leorm knew no more than it did of the methods by which they had been developed.

Halder carried the packages into a ComWeb booth which he locked and shielded for privacy. Then he opened both packages and quickly removed his clothing. Opening the first of the cultures, he dipped one of the needles into it and, watching himself in the mirror, made a carefully measured injection in each side of his face. He laid the needle down and opened the next container, aware of the enzyme reaction that had begun to race through him.

Three minutes later, the mirror showed him a dark-skinned stranger with high cheek bones, heavy jaw, thick nose, slightly slanted eyes, graying hair. Halder disposed of the mirror, the clothes he had been wearing and the remaining contents of the second package. Unchecked, the alien organisms swarming in his blood stream now would have gone on to destroy him in a variety of unpleasant ways. But with their work of disguise completed, they were being checked.

He emerged presently from a tube exit in uptown Draise, on the terrace of a hotel forty stories above the street level. He didn't look about for Kilby, or rather the woman Kilby would turn into on her way here. The plan called for him to arrive first, to make sure he hadn't been traced, and then to see whether she was being followed.

She appeared five minutes later, a slightly stocky lady now, perhaps ten years under Halder's present apparent age, dark-skinned as he was, showing similar racial characteristics. She flashed her teeth at him as she came up, sloe eyes flirting.

"Didn't keep you waiting, did I?" she asked.

Halder growled amiably, "What do you think? Let's grab a cab and get going." Nobody had come out of the tube exit behind her.

Kilby nodded understandingly; she had remembered not to look back. She was talking volubly about some imaginary adventure as they started down the terrace stairs towards a line of aircabs, playing her part, high-piled golden hairdo bobbing about. A greater contrast to the slender, quiet, gray-eyed girl, brown hair falling softly to her shoulders, with whom Halder had talked not more than twenty minutes ago would have been difficult to devise. The disguises might have been good enough, he thought, to permit them to remain undetected in Draise itself.

But the plan didn't call for that. There were too many things at stake.

Kilby slipped into the cab ahead of him without a break in her chatter.

Her voice stopped abruptly as Halder closed the cab door behind him, activating the vehicle's one-way vision shield. Kilby was leaning across the front seat beside the driver, turning off the comm box. She straightened, dropped down into the back seat beside Halder, biting her lip. The driver's head sagged sideways as if he had fallen asleep; then he slid slowly down on the seat and vanished from Halder's sight.

"Got him instantly, eh?" Halder asked, switching on the passenger controls.

"Hm-m-m!" Kilby opened her purse, slipped the little gun which had been in the palm of her left hand into it, reached out and gripped Halder's hand for an instant. "You drive, Halder," she said. "I'm so nervous I could scream! I'm scared cold! What happened?"

*   *   *   *   *

Halder lifted the cab out from the terrace, swung it skywards. "We were right in wondering about Dr. Atteo," he said. "Half an hour ago, he attempted to go through our home in our absence. We'll have to assume he's a Federation agent. The entry trap knocked him out, but the fat's probably in the fire now. The Federation may not have been ready to make an arrest yet, but after this there'll be no hesitation. We'll have to move fast if we intend to keep ahead of Atteo's colleagues."

Kilby drew in an unsteady breath. "You warned Rane and Santin?"

Halder nodded. "I sent the alert signal to their apartment ComWeb in the capital. Under the circumstances, I didn't think a person-to-person call would be advisable. They'll have time to pack and get out to the ranch before we arrive. We'll give them the details then."

"Did you reset the trap switch at the house entry?"

Halder slowed the cab, turning it into one of the cross-city traffic lines above Draise. "No," he said. "Knocking out a few more Federation agents wouldn't give us any advantage. It'll be eight or nine hours before Atteo will be able to talk; and, with any luck at all, we'll be clear of the planet by that time."

The dark woman who was Kilby and a controlled devil's swarm of microlife looked over at him and asked in Kilby's voice, "Halder, do you think we should still go on trying to find the others now?"

"Of course. Why stop?"

Kilby hesitated, said, "It took you three months to find me. Four months later, we located Rane Rellis ... and Santin, at almost the same time. Since then we've drawn one blank after another. A year and a half gone, and a year and a half left."

She paused, and Halder said nothing, knowing she was fighting to keep her voice steady. After a few seconds, Kilby went on. "Almost twelve hundred still to find, scattered over a thousand worlds. Most of them probably in hiding, as we were. And with the Federation on our trail ... even if we get away this time, what chance is there now of contacting the whole group before time runs out?"

Halder said patiently, "It's not an impossibility. We've been forced to spend most of the past year and a half gathering information, studying the intricate functioning of this gigantic civilization—so many things that our mentors on Kalechi either weren't aware of or chose not to tell us. And we haven't done too badly, Kilby. We're prepared now to conduct the search for the group in a methodical manner. Nineteen hours in space, and we'll be on another world, under cover again, with new identities. Why shouldn't we continue with the plan until ..."

Kilby interrupted without change of expression. "Until we hear some day that billions of human beings are dying on the Federation's worlds?"

Halder kept his eyes fixed on the traffic pattern ahead. "It won't come to that," he said.

"Won't it? How can you be sure?" Kilby asked tonelessly.

"Well," Halder asked, "what else can we do? You aren't suggesting that we give ourselves up–"

"I've thought of it."

"And be picked apart mentally and physically in the Federation's laboratories?" Halder shook his head. "In their eyes we'd be Kalechi's creatures ... monsters. Even if we turn ourselves in, they'll think it's some trick, that we'd realized we'd get caught anyway. We couldn't expect much mercy. No, if everything fails, we'll see to it that the Federation gets adequate warning. But not, if we can avoid it, at the expense of our own lives." He glanced over at her, his eyes troubled. "We've been over this before, Kilby."

"I know." Kilby bit her lip. "You're right, I suppose."

Halder let the cab glide out of the traffic lane, swung it around towards the top of a tall building three miles to their left. "We'll be at the club in a couple of minutes," he said. "If you're too disturbed, it would be better if you stayed in the car. I'll pick up our flighthiking outfits and we can take the cab on to the city limits before we dismiss it."

Kilby shook her head. "We agreed we shouldn't change any details of the escape plan unless it was absolutely necessary. I'll straighten out. I've just let this situation shake me too much."

*   *   *   *   *

They set the aircab to traffic-safe random cruise control before getting out of it at their club. It lifted quietly into the air again as soon as the door had closed, was out of sight beyond the building before they reached the club entrance. The driver's records had indicated that his shift would end in three hours. Until that time he would not be missed. More hours would pass after the cab was located before the man returned to consciousness. What he had to say then would make no difference.

In one of the club rooms, rented to a Mr. and Mrs. Anley, they changed to shorts and flighthiking equipment, then took a tube to the outskirts of Draise where vehicleless flight became possible. Forest parks interspersed with small residential centers stretched away to the east. They set their flight harnesses to Draise's power broadcast system, moved up fifty feet and floated off into the woods, energizing drive and direction units with the measured stroking motion which made flighthiking one of the most relaxing and enjoyable of sports. And one—so Halder had theorized—which would be considered an improbable occupation for a couple attempting to escape from the Federation's man-hunting systems.

For an hour and a half, they held a steady course eastwards, following the contours of the rolling forested ground, rarely emerging into the open. Other groups of vehicleless fliers passed occasionally; as members of a sporting fraternity, they exchanged waves and shouted greetings. At last, a long, wild valley opened ahead, showing no trace of human habitation; at its far end began open land, dotted with small tobacco farms where automatic cultivators moved unhurriedly about. Kilby, glancing back over her shoulder at Halder for a moment, swung around towards one of the farms, gliding down close to the ground, Halder twenty feet behind her. They settled down beside a hedge at the foot of a slope covered with tobacco plants. A small gate in the hedge immediately swung open.

"All clear here, folks!" a voice curiously similar to Halder's addressed them from the gate speaker.

Rane Rellis, a lanky, red-headed man with a wide-boned face, was striding down the slope towards them as they moved through the gate. "We got your alert," he said, "but as it happens, we'd already realized that something had gone wrong."

Kilby gave him a startled glance. "Somebody has been checking on you, too?"

"Not that ... at least as far as we know. Come on up to the shed. Santin's already inside the mountain." As they started along the narrow path between the rows of plants, Rellis went on, "The first responses to our inquiries came in today. One of them looked very promising. Santin flew her car to Draise immediately to inform you about it. She scanned your home as usual before calling, discovered three strange men waiting inside."

"When was this?" Halder interrupted.

"A few minutes after one o'clock. Santin checked at once at your place of work and Kilby's, learned you both were absent, deduced you were still at large and probably on your way here. She called to tell me about it. Your alert signal sounded almost before she'd finished talking."

Halder glanced at Kilby. "We seem to have escaped arrest by something like five minutes," he remarked dryly. "Were you able to bring the records with you, Rane?"

"Yes, everything. If we get clear of Orado, we can pick up almost where we left off." Rane Rellis swung the door of the cultivator shed open and followed them in, closing and locking the door behind him. They crossed quickly through the small building to an open wall portal at the far end. Beyond the portal a large, brightly lit room was visible, comfortably furnished, windowless. Between that room and the shed the portal spanned a distance of seven miles, a vital point in the organization of their escape route. If they were traced this far, the trail would end—temporarily, at least—at the ranch.

They stepped over into the room, and Rane Rellis pulled down a switch. Behind them the portal entry vanished. Back in the deserted ranch building, its mechanisms were bursting into flames, would burn fiercely for a few seconds and fuse to dead slag.

*   *   *   *   *

Rane said tightly, "I feel a little better now ... just a little! The Fed agents are good, but I haven't yet heard of detection devices that could drive through five hundred yards of solid rock to spot us inside a mountain." He paused as a tall girl with black hair, dark-brown eyes, came in from an adjoining room. Santin Rellis was the only one of the four who was not employing a biological disguise at the moment. In spite of the differences in their appearance, she might have been taken for Kilby's sister.

Halder told them what had occurred in Draise, concluded, "I'd believed that suspicion was more likely to center first on one of you. Particularly, of course, on Santin, working openly in Orado's Identification Center."

Santin grinned. "And, less openly, copying out identity-patterns!" she added. Her face sobered quickly again. "There's no indication of what did attract attention to you?"

Halder shook his head. "I can only think it's the microbiological work I've been doing. That, of course, would suggest that they already have an inkling of Kalechi's three-year plan to destroy the Federation."

Rane added, "And that at least one of the group already has been captured!"

"Probably."

There was silence for a moment. Santin said evenly, "That isn't a pleasant thought. Halder, everything we've learned recently at the Identification Center indicates that Rane's theory is correct ... every one of the twelve hundred members of the Kalechi group probably can be analyzed down to the same three basic identity-patterns, reshuffled in endless variation. The Federation wouldn't have to capture many of us before discovering the fact. It will then start doing exactly what we're trying to do—use it to identify the rest of the group."

Halder nodded. "I've thought of that."

"You still intend to use the Senla Starlight Cruisers to get out into space?" Rane asked.

"Kilby and I will," Halder said. "But now, of course, you two had better select one of the alternate escape routes."

"Why that?" Santin asked sharply.

Halder looked at her. "That's obvious, isn't it? There's a good chance you're still completely in the clear."

"That's possible. But it isn't a good enough reason for splitting up. We're a working team, and we should stay together, regardless of circumstances. What do you say, Rane?"

Her husband said, "I agree with you." He smiled briefly at Halder. "We'll be waiting for you on the north shore of Lake Senla ten minutes before the Starlight Cruise lifts. Now, is there anything else to discuss?"

"Not at the moment." Halder paused, dissatisfied, then went on. "All right. We still don't know just what the Federation is capable of ... one move might as easily be wrong as the other. We'll pick you up, as arranged. Kilby and I are flighthiking on to Senla, so we might as well start immediately."

They went into the second room of the underground hideout. Rane turned to the exit portal's controls, asked, "Where shall I let you out?"

"We'll take the river exit," Halder said. "Six miles from here, nine from the ranch ... that should be far enough. We'll be lost in an army of vacationers from Draise and the capital thirty seconds after we emerge."

* * * * *

It was dusk when Halder and Kilby turned into the crowded shore walk of the lake resort of Senla, moving

unhurriedly towards a bungalow Halder had bought
under another name some months before. Halder's
thoughts went again over the details of the final stage of
their escape from Orado. Essentially, the plan was
simple. An hour from now they would slide their small
star cruiser out of the bungalow's yacht stall, pick up
Rane and Santin on the far shore of the lake, then join
the group of thirty or so private yachts which left the
resort area nightly for a two-hour flight to a casino ship
stationed off the planet. A group cruise was unlikely to
draw official scrutiny even tonight; and after reaching the
casino, they should be able to slip on unobserved into
space.

There was, however, no way of knowing with
certainty that the plan ... or any other plan ... would
work. It was only during the past few months that the
four of them had begun to understand in detail the extent
to which the vast, apparently loose complex of the
Federation's worlds was actually organized. How long
they had been under observation, how much the
Federation suspected or knew about them—those
questions were, at the moment, unanswerable. So Halder
walked on in alert silence, giving his attention to
anything which might be a first indication of danger in
the crowds surging quietly past them along Senla's shore
promenade in the summer evening. It was near the peak
of the resort's season; a sense of ease and relaxation came
from the people he passed, their voices seeming to blend
into a single, low-pitched, friendly murmur. Well, and in
time, Halder told himself, if everything went well, he and
Kilby might be able to mingle undisguised, unafraid, with
just such a crowd. But tonight they were hunted.

He laid his hand lightly on Kilby's arm, said, "Let's
rest on that bench over there for a moment."

She smiled up at him, said, "All right," turned and led
the way towards an unoccupied bench set back among the
trees above the walk. They sat down, and Halder quickly
slipped the watch off his wrist and removed the scanner's

cover plate. The bungalow was a few hundred yards away now, on a side path which led down to the lake. It was showing no lights, but as the scanner reached into it, invisible radiation flooded the dark rooms and hallway, disclosing them to the instrument's inspection. For two or three minutes, Halder studied the bungalow's interior carefully; then he shifted the view to the grounds outside, finally to the yacht stall and the little star cruiser. Twice Kilby touched him warningly as somebody appeared about to approach the bench, and Halder put down his hand. But the strangers went by without pausing.

At last, he replaced the instrument on his wrist. He had discovered no signs of intrusion in the bungalow; and, at any rate, it was clear that no one was waiting there now, either in the little house itself or in the immediate vicinity. He stood up, and put out his hand to assist Kilby to her feet.

"We'll go on," he said.

A few minutes later, they came along a narrow garden path to the bungalow's dark side entrance. There was to be no indication tonight that the bungalow had occupants. Halder unlocked the door quietly, and after Kilby had slipped inside, he stepped in behind her and secured the door.

For an instant, as they moved along the short, lightless passage to the front rooms, a curious sensation touched Halder—a terrifying conviction that some undefinable thing had just gone wrong. And with that, his whole body was suddenly rigid, every muscle locking in mid-motion. He felt momentum topple him slowly forwards; then he was no longer falling but stopped, tilted off-balance at a grotesque angle, suspended in a web of forces he could not feel. Not the slightest sound had come from Kilby, invisible in the blackness ahead of him.

Halder threw all his will and strength into the effort to force motion back into his body. Instead, a wave of cold numbness washed slowly up through him. It welled into his brain, and for a time all thought and sensation ended.

*   *   *   *   *

His first new awareness was a feeling of being asleep and not knowing how to wake up. There was no disturbance associated with it. All about was darkness, complete and quiet.

With curious deliberation, Halder's senses now began bringing other things to his attention. He was seated, half reclining, in a deep and comfortable chair, his back against it. He seemed unable to move. His arms were secured in some manner to the chair's armrests; but, beyond that, he also found it impossible to lift his body forwards or, he discovered next, to turn his head in any direction. He was breathing normally, and he could open and shut his eyes and glance about in unchanging darkness. But that was all.

Still with a dreamlike lack of concern, Halder began to ask himself what had happened; and in that instant, with a rush of hot terror, his memory opened out. They had been trapped ... some undetectable trick of Federation science had waited for them in the bungalow at Lake Senla. He had been taken somewhere else.

What had they done with Kilby?

Immediately, almost as if in answer to his question, the darkness seemed to lighten. But the process was gradual; seconds passed before Halder gained the impression of a very large room of indefinite proportions. Twenty feet away was the rim of a black, circular depression in the flooring. At first, his chair seemed the only piece of furnishing here; then, as the area continued to brighten, Halder became aware of several objects at some distance on his right.

For an instant, he strained violently to turn his head towards them. That was still impossible, but the objects were there, near the edge of his vision. Again the great room grew lighter, and for seconds Halder could distinguish three armchairs like his own, spaced perhaps twenty feet apart along the rim of the central pit. Each chair had an occupant; in the nearest was Kilby, restored to her natural appearance, motionless, pale face turned forwards, eyes open. Suddenly the light vanished.

Halder sat shocked, realizing he had tried to speak to Kilby and that no sound had come from his throat. Neither speech nor motion was allowed them here. But he didn't doubt that Kilby was awake, or that Santin and Rane Rellis were in the farther chairs, though he hadn't seen either of them clearly. Their captors had given them a brief glimpse of one another, perhaps to let them know all had been caught. Then, as the light disappeared, Halder's glance had shifted for an instant to his right hand lying on the armrest—long enough to see that the dark tinge was gone from his skin, as it was from Kilby's, that he, too, had been deprived of the organisms which disguised him.

And that, his studies in Draise had showed clearly, was something the Federation's science would be a century away from knowing how to do unless it learned about Kalechi's deadly skills.

Once more, it was almost as if the thought were being given an answer. In the darkness of the room a bright image appeared, three-dimensional, not quite a sphere in form, tiger-striped in orange and black, balanced on a broad, bifurcated swimming tail. Stalked eyes protruded from the top of the sphere; their slit pupils seemed to be staring directly at Halder. Down both sides ran a row of ropy arms.

*   *   *   *   *

Simultaneously with the appearance of this projection, a man's voice began to speak, not loudly but distinctly. Dreamlike again, the voice seemed to have no specific source, as if it were coming from every direction at once; and a numbing conviction arose in Halder that their minds were being destroyed in this room, that a methodical dissecting process had begun which would continue move by move and hour by hour until the Federation's scientists were satisfied that no further scraps of information could be drained from the prisoners. The investigation might be completely impersonal; but the fact that they were being ignored here as sentient beings, were not permitted to argue their case or offer an explanation, seemed more chilling than deliberate brutality. And yet, Halder told himself, he couldn't really blame anyone for the situation they were in. The Kalechi group represented an urgent and terrible threat. The Federation could not afford to make any mistakes in dealing with it.

"This image," the voice was saying, "represents a Great Satog, the oxygen-breathing, water-dwelling native of the world of Kalechi. There are numerous type-variations of the species. Shown here is the dominant form. It is highly intelligent; approximately a third of a Satog's body space is occupied by its brain.

"Kalechi's civilization is based on an understanding of biological processes and the means of their manipulation which is well in advance of our own. This specialized interest appears to have developed from the Satogs' genetic instability, a factor which they have learned to control and to use to their advantage. At present, they have established themselves on at least a dozen other worlds, existing on each in a modified form which is completely adapted to the new environment.

"Our occasional contacts with Kalechi and its colonies during the past two centuries have been superficially friendly, but it appears now that the Great Satogs have regarded our technological and numerical superiority with alarm and have cast about for a method to destroy the Federation without risk to themselves. A weapon was on hand–their great skill and experience in altering genetic patterns in established life forms to produce desired changes. They devised the plan of distributing Kalechi agents secretly throughout the Federation. These were to develop and store specific strains of primitive organisms which, at an indicated later date, would sweep our major worlds simultaneously with an unparalleled storm of plagues.

"The most audacious part of the Kalechi scheme follows. Ninety-two years ago, a Federation survey ship disappeared in that sector of the galaxy. Aboard it was a man named Ohl Cantrall, an outstanding scientist of the period. We know now that this ship was captured by the Great Satogs, and that Cantrall, his staff, and his crew, were subjected to extensive experimentation by them, and eventually were killed.

"The experimentation had been designed to provide Kalechi's master-biologists with models towards which to work. They proposed to utilize the high mutability of their species to develop a Satog type that would be the exact physical counterpart of a human being and could live undetected on our worlds for the several years required to prepare for the attack. They were amazingly successful. Each group of cells in the long series which began moving towards an approximation of the human pattern was developed only far enough to initiate the greatest favorable shift possible at that point in its genetic structure. Cell generations may have followed each other within hours in this manner, for over six decades.

"The goal of the experiment, the last generation issued in Kalechi's laboratories, were Satog copies of embryonic human beings. This stage was comprised of approximately twelve hundred individuals who were now permitted to mature and were schooled individually in complete isolation by Satog teachers. They were indoctrinated with their purpose in life ... the destruction of our populations ... and trained fully in the manner of accomplishing it.

"Eventually, each was shipped to a Federation world. Cover identities as obscure Federation citizens with backgrounds and records had been prepared. The final instructions given these agents were simple. They were to do nothing to draw attention to themselves, make no attempt to contact one another. They were to create their stocks of lethal organisms, provide methods of distribution and, on a selected day, three Federation years away, release the floods of death."

*   *   *   *   *

The voice paused briefly, went on. "It is a sobering reflection that this plan–an attack by a comparatively minor race with one specialized skill on the greatest human civilization in history–might very well have been appallingly successful. But the Great Satogs failed, in part because of the very perfection of their work.

"From the human beings on board Ohl Cantrall's captured survey ship the Satog scientists selected Cantrall himself and two female technicians on his staff as the models to be followed in developing Kalechi's pseudohumanity. In the twelve hundred members of the group sent to the Federation ninety years later, these three identity-patterns are recognizable. They appear in varying degrees of combination, but an occasional individual will show only one or the other of the three patterns involved.

"Ohl Cantrall was regarded as a great man in his time, and his identification pattern is on record. That was the detail which first revealed the plot. When three duplicates of that particular pattern–and a considerable number of approximate duplicates–turned up simultaneously in identification banks at widely separated points in the Federation, it aroused more than scientific curiosity. Our security system has learned to look with suspicion on apparent miracles. The unsuspecting 'Cantralls' were located and apprehended at once; the threat to the Federation was disclosed; and an intensive though unpublicized search for the scattered group of Kalechi agents began immediately...."

The voice paused again.

The Satog image above the pit vanished. A clear light sprang up in the big room. Simultaneously, Halder felt the nightmare immobility draining from him and the sensation of dreamlike unreality fade from his mind. He turned to the right, found Kilby's eyes already on him, saw the Rellis couple sitting beyond her ... Rane, no longer disguised, looking like a mirror image of Halder.

They were still fastened to their chairs. Halder's gaze shifted back quickly to the center of the room. Where the pit had been, the flooring was now level, carrying a massive, polished table. Behind the table sat a heavily built, white-haired man with a strong face, harsh mouth, in the formal black and gold robes of a Councilman of the Federation.

"I am Councilman Mavig." The voice was the one that had spoken in the dark; it came now from the man at the table. "I am in charge of the operation against the Kalechi agents, and it is my duty to inform them, after their arrest and examination, of the disposition that must be made of them."

He hesitated, twisting his mouth thoughtfully, almost as if unwilling to continue. "You four have been thoroughly examined," he stated at last. "Most of the work has been done while you were still unconscious. A final check of your emotional reactions was being made throughout the stress situation just ended, in which you listened to a replay of a report on the Kalechi matter. That part is now concluded."

Mavig paused, scowled, cleared his throat. "I find," he went on, "that some aspects of this affair still strain my credulity! More than half of your group have been captured by now; the remainder are at large but under observation. The danger is past. The activities of the Great Satogs of Kalechi will receive our very close scrutiny for generations to come. They shall be given no opportunity to repeat such a trick; nor—after they have been made aware of the measures we are preparing against them—will they feel the slightest inclination to try it.

"Now, as to yourselves. After we had tracked down the first dozen or so of you, a startling pattern began to emerge. You were not following Kalechi's careful instructions. In one way and another—in often very ingenious ways—you were attempting primarily to establish contact with one another. When captured and examined while unconscious by the various interrogation instruments of our psychologists you told us your reasons for doing this."

Councilman Mavig shook his head. "The interrogation machines are supposed to be infallible," he remarked. "Possibly they are. But I am not a psychologist, and for a long time I refused to accept the reports they returned. But still ..."

He sighed. "Well, as to what is to happen with you. You will be sent to join the previously arrested members of your group, and will remain with them until the last of you is in our hands, has been examined, and ..."

Mavig paused again.

"You see, we can accuse you of no crime!" he said irritably. "As individuals and as a group, your intention from the beginning has been to prevent the crime against the Federation from being committed. The Great Satogs simply did too good a job. You have been given the most searching physical examinations possible. They show uniformly that your genetic pattern is stable, and that in no detail can it be distinguished from a wholly human one of high order.

"You appreciate, I imagine, where that leaves the Federation! When imitation is carried to the point of identity ..." Federation Councilman Mavig shook his head once more, concluded, "It is utterly absurd, in direct contradiction to everything we have understood to date! You've regarded yourselves as human beings, and believed that your place was among us. And we can only agree."

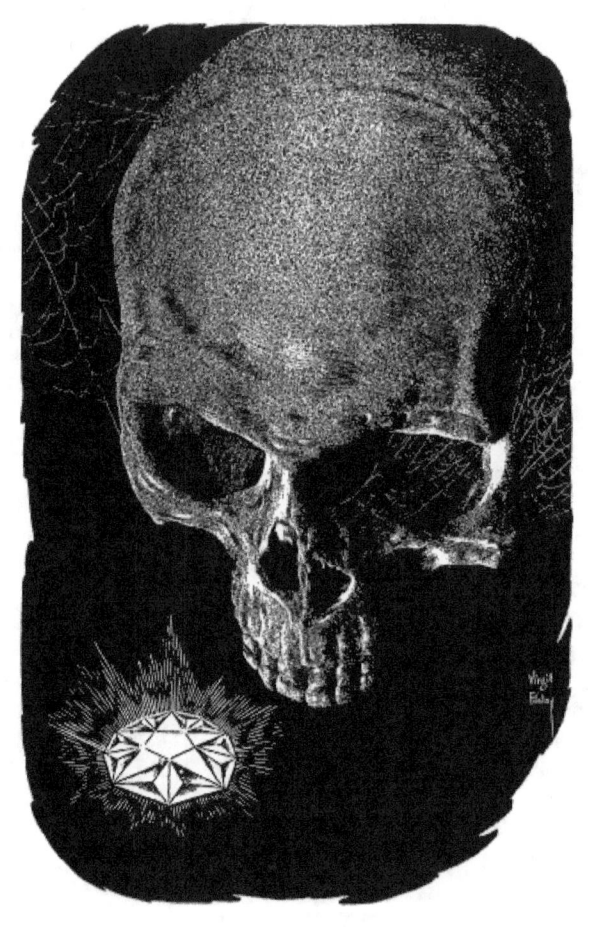

THE STAR HYACINTHS

ORIGINALLY PUBLISHED IN *AMAZING STORIES*, DECEMBER 1961

On a bleak, distant unchartered world two ships lay wrecked and a lone man stared at a star hyacinth. Its brilliance burned into his retina ... and he knew that men could easily kill and kill for that one beauty alone.

THE STAR HYACINTHS

The robbery of the Dosey Asteroids Shipping Station in a remote and spottily explored section of space provided the newscasting systems of the Federation of the Hub with one of the juiciest crime stories of the season. In a manner not clearly explained, the Dosey Asteroids Company had lost six months' production of gem-quality cut star hyacinths valued at nearly a hundred million credits. It lost also its Chief Lapidary and seventy-eight other company employees who had been in the station dome at the time.

All these people appeared at first to have been killed by gunfire, but a study of their bodies revealed that only in a few instances had gun wounds been the actual cause of death. For the most part the wounds had been inflicted on corpses, presumably in an attempt to conceal the fact that disaster in another and unknown form had befallen the station.

The raiders left very few clues. It appeared that the attack on the station had been carried out by a single ship, and that the locks to the dome had been opened from within. The latter fact, of course, aroused speculation, but led the investigators nowhere.

Six years later the great Dosey Asteroids robbery remained an unsolved mystery.

*   *   *   *   *

The two wrecked spaceships rested almost side by side near the tip of a narrow, deep arm of a great lake.

The only man on the planet sat on a rocky ledge three miles uphill from the two ships, gazing broodingly down at them. He was a big fellow in neatly patched shipboard clothing. His hands were clean, his face carefully shaved. He had two of the castaway's traditional possessions with him; a massive hunting bow rested against the rocks, and a minor representative of the class of life which was this world's equivalent of birds was hopping about near his feet. This was a thrush-sized creature with a jaunty bearing and bright yellow eyes. From the front of its round face protruded a short, narrow tube tipped with small, sharp teeth. Round, horny knobs at the ends of its long toes protected retractile claws as it bounded back and forth between the bow and the man, giving a quick flutter of its wings on each bound. Finally it stopped before the man, stretching its neck to stare up at him, trying to catch his attention.

He roused from his musing, glanced irritably down at it.

"Not now, Birdie," he said. "Keep quiet!"

The man's gaze returned to the two ships, then passed briefly along a towering range of volcanos on the other side of the lake, and lifted to the cloudless blue sky. His eyes probed on, searching the sunlit, empty vault above him. If a ship ever came again, it would come from there, the two wrecks by the lake arm already fixed in its detectors; it would not come gliding along the surface of the planet....

Birdie produced a sharp, plaintive whistle. The man looked at it.

"Shut up, stupid!" he told it.

He reached into the inner pocket of his coat, took out a small object wrapped in a piece of leather, and unfolded the leather.

Then it lay in his cupped palm, and blazed with the brilliance of twenty diamonds, seeming to flash the fires of the spectrum furiously from every faceted surface, without ever quite subduing the pure violet luminance which made a star hyacinth impossible to imitate or, once seen, to forget. The most beautiful of gems, the rarest, the most valuable. The man who was a castaway stared at it for long seconds, his breath quickening and his hand beginning to tremble. Finally he folded the chip of incredible mineral back into the leather, replaced it carefully in his pocket.

When he looked about again, the sunlit air seemed brighter, the coloring of lake and land more vivid and alive. Once during each of this world's short days, but no oftener, he permitted himself to look at the star hyacinth. It was a ritual adhered to with almost religious strictness, and it had kept him as sane as he was ever likely to be again, for over six years.

It might, he sometimes thought, keep him sane until a third ship presently came along to this place. And then ...

The third ship was coming along at the moment, still some five hours' flight out from the system. She was a small ship with lean, rakish lines, a hot little speedster, gliding placidly through subspace just now, her engines throttled down.

Aboard her, things were less peaceful.

*   *   *   *   *

The girl was putting up a pretty good fight but getting nowhere with it against the bull-necked Fleetman who had her pinned back against the wall.

Wellan Dasinger paused in momentary indecision at the entrance to the half-darkened control section of the speedboat. The scuffle in there very probably was none of his business. The people of the roving Independent Fleets had their own practices and mores and resented interference from uninformed planet dwellers. For all Dasinger knew, their blue-eyed lady pilot enjoyed roughhousing with the burly members of her crew. If the thing wasn't serious....

He heard the man rap out something in the Willata Fleet tongue, following the words up with a solid thump of his fist into the girl's side. The thump hadn't been playful, and her sharp gasp of pain indicated no enjoyment whatever. Dasinger stepped quickly into the room.

He saw the girl turn startled eyes toward him as he came up behind the man. The man was Liu Taunus, the bigger of the two crew members ... too big and too well muscled by a good deal, in fact, to make a sportsmanlike suggestion to divert his thumpings to Dasinger look like a sensible approach. Besides Dasinger didn't know the Willata Fleet's language. The edge of his hand slashed twice from behind along the thick neck; then his fist brought the breath whistling from Taunus's lungs before the Fleetman had time to turn fully towards him.

It gave Dasinger a considerable starting advantage. During the next twenty seconds or so the advantage seemed to diminish rapidly. Taunus's fists and boots had scored only near misses so far, but he began to look like the hardest big man to chop down Dasinger had yet run into. And then the Fleetman was suddenly sprawling on the floor, face down, arms flung out limply, a tough boy with a thoroughly bludgeoned nervous system.

Dasinger was straightening up when he heard the *thunk* of the wrench. He turned sharply, discovered first the girl standing ten feet away with the wrench in her raised hand, next their second crew member lying on the carpet between them, finally the long, thin knife lying near the man's hand.

"Thanks, Miss Mines!" he said, somewhat out of breath. "I really should have remembered Calat might be somewhere around."

Duomart Mines gestured with her head at the adjoining control cabin. "He was in there," she said, also breathlessly. She was a long-legged blonde with a limber way of moving, pleasing to look at in her shaped Fleet uniform, though with somewhat aloof and calculating eyes. In the dim light of the room she seemed to be studying Dasinger now with an expression somewhere between wariness and surprised speculation. Then, as he took a step forward to check on Calat's condition, she backed off slightly, half lifting the wrench again.

Dasinger stopped and looked at her. "Well," he said, "make up your mind! Whose side are you on here?"

Miss Mines hesitated, let the wrench down. "Yours, I guess," she acknowledged. "I'd better be, now! They'd murder me for helping a planeteer."

*   *   *   *   *

Dasinger went down on one knee beside Calat, rather cautiously though the Fleetman wasn't stirring, and picked up the knife. Miss Mines turned up the room's lights. Dasinger asked, "What was this ... a mutiny? You're technically in charge of the ship, aren't you?"

"Technically," she agreed, added, "We were arguing about a Fleet matter."

"I see. We'll call it mutiny." Dasinger checked to be sure Calat wasn't faking unconsciousness. He inquired, "Do you really need these boys to help you?"

Duomart Mines shook her blond head. "Not at all. Flying the Mooncat is a one-man job."

"I did have a feeling," Dasinger admitted, "that Willata's Fleet was doing a little featherbedding when they said I'd have to hire a crew of three to go along with their speedboat."

"Uh-huh." Her tone was non-committal. "They were. What are you going to do with them?"

"Anywhere they can be locked up safely?"

"Not safely. Their own cabin's as good as anything. They can batter their way out of here if they try hard enough. Of course we'd hear them doing it."

"Well, we can fix that." Dasinger stood up, fished his cabin key out of a pocket and gave it to her. "Tan suitcase standing at the head of my bunk," he said. "Mind bringing that and the little crane from the storeroom up here?"

Neither of the Fleetmen had begun to stir when Duomart Mines came riding a gravity crane back in through the door a couple of minutes later, the suitcase dangling in front of her. She halted the crane in the center of the room, slid out of its saddle with a supple twist of her body, and handed Dasinger his cabin key.

"Thanks." Dasinger took the suitcase from the crane, unlocked and opened it. He brought out a pair of plastic handcuffs, aware that Miss Mines stood behind him making an intent scrutiny of what could be seen of the suitcase's contents. He didn't blame her for feeling curious; she was looking at a variety of devices which might have delighted the eyes of both a professional burglar and military spy. She offered no comment.

Neither did Dasinger. He hauled Liu Taunus over on his back, fastened handcuffs about the Fleetman's wrists, then rolled him over on his face again. He did the same for Calat, hung the suitcase back in the crane, slung a leg across the crane's saddle and settled into it.

Miss Mines remarked, "I'd look their cabin over pretty closely for guns and so on before leaving them there."

"I intend to. By the way, has Dr. Egavine mentioned how close we are to our destination?" Dasinger maneuvered the crane over to Taunus, lowered a beam to the small of the Fleetman's back and hoisted him up carefully, arms, head and legs dangling.

The blond girl checked her watch. "He didn't tell me exactly," she said, "but there's what seems to be a terraprox in the G2 system ahead. If that's it, we'll get there in around five hours depending on what subspace conditions in the system are. Dr. Egavine's due up here in thirty minutes to give me the final figures." She paused, added curiously, "Don't you know yourself just where we're going?"

"No," Dasinger said. "I'm financing the trip. The doctor is the man with the maps and other pertinent information."

"I thought you were partners."

"We are. Dr. Egavine is taciturn about some things. I'll bring him back here with me as soon as I have these two locked away." Dasinger finished picking up Calat, swung the crane slowly towards the door, the unconscious Fleetmen suspended ahead of him.

*   *   *   *   *

Dr. Egavine stood at the open door to his stateroom as Dasinger came walking back up the passage from the crew quarters and the storage. Quist, the doctor's manservant, peered out of the stateroom behind him.

"What in heaven's name were you doing with those two men?" Egavine inquired, twitching his eyebrows disapprovingly up and down. The doctor was a tall, thin man in his forties, dressed habitually in undertaker black, with bony features and intense dark eyes. He added, "They appeared to be unconscious ... and fettered!"

"They were both," Dasinger admitted. "I've confined them to their cabin."

"Why?"

"We had a little slugfest in the control section a few minutes ago. One of the boys was beating around on our pilot, so I laid him out, and she laid out the other one when he tried to get into the act with a knife. She says the original dispute was a Fleet matter ... in other words, none of our business. However, I don't know. There's something decidedly fishy about the situation."

"In what way?" Egavine asked.

Dasinger said, "I checked over the crew quarters for weapons just now and found something which suggests that Willata's Fleet is much more interested in what we're doing out here than we thought."

Egavine looked startled, peered quickly along the passage to the control section. "I feel," he said, lowering his voice, "that we should continue this discussion behind closed doors...."

"All right." Quist, a bandy-legged, wiry little man with a large bulb of a nose and close-set, small eyes, moved back from the door. Dasinger went inside. Egavine pulled the door shut behind them and drew a chair out from the cabin table. Dasinger sat down opposite him.

"What did you find?" Dr. Egavine asked.

Dasinger said, "You know Miss Mines is supposed to be the only Fleet member on board who speaks the Federation's translingue. However, there was a listening device attached to the inside of the cabin communicator in the crew quarters. Its settings show that the Willata Fleet people have bugged each of the Mooncat's other cabins, and also—which I think is an interesting point—the control section. Have you and Quist discussed our project in any detail since coming aboard?"

"I believe we did, on several occasions," Egavine said hesitantly.

"Then we'd better assume Taunus and Calat knew that we're looking for the wreck of the Dosey Asteroids raider, and ..."

Egavine put a cautioning finger to his lips. "Should we...?"

"Oh, no harm in talking now," Dasinger assured him. "I pulled the instrument out and dropped it in my cabin. Actually, the thing needn't be too serious if we stay on guard. But of course we shouldn't go back to the Fleet station after we have the stuff. Gadgetry of that kind suggests bad intentions ... also a rather sophisticated level of criminality for an I-Fleet. We'll return directly to the Hub. We might have to go on short rations for a few weeks, but we'll make it. And we'll keep those two so-called crew members locked up."

The doctor cleared his throat. "Miss Mines ..."

"She doesn't appear to be personally involved in any piratical schemes," Dasinger said. "Otherwise they wouldn't have bugged her cabin and the control rooms. If we dangle a few star hyacinths before her eyes, she should be willing to fly us back. If she balks, I think I can handle the Mooncat well enough to get us there."

Dr. Egavine tugged pensively at his ear lobe. "I see." His hand moved on toward his right coat lapel. "What do you think of ..."

"Mind watching this for a moment, doctor?" Dasinger interrupted. He nodded at his own hand lying on the table before him.

"Watch...?" Egavine began questioningly. Then his eyes went wide with alarm.

Dasinger's hand had turned suddenly sideways from the wrist, turned up again. There was a small gun in the hand now, its stubby muzzle pointing up steadily at Egavine's chest.

"Dasinger! What does ..."

"Neat trick, eh?" Dasinger commented. "Sleeve gun. Now keep quiet and hold everything just as it is. If you move or Quist over there moves before I tell you to, you've had it, doctor!"

*　　*　　*　　*　　*

He reached across the table with his left hand, slipped it beneath Egavine's right coat lapel, tugged sharply at something in there, and brought out a flat black pouch with a tiny spray needle projecting from it. He dropped the pouch in his pocket, said, "Keep your seat, doctor," stood up and went over to Quist. Quist darted an anxious glance at his employer, and made a whimpering sound in his throat.

"You're not getting hurt," Dasinger told him. "Just put your hands on top of your head and stand still. Now let's take a look at the thing you started to pull from your pocket a moment ago ... Electric stunsap, eh? That wasn't very nice of you, Quist! Let's see what else—

"Good Lord, Egavine," he announced presently, "your boy's a regular armory! Two blasters, a pencil-beam, a knife, and the sap ... All right, Quist. Go over and sit down with the doctor." He watched the little man move dejectedly to the table, then fitted the assorted lethal devices carefully into one of his coat pockets, brought the pouch he had taken from Egavine out of the other pocket.

"Now, doctor," he said, "let's talk. I'm unhappy about this. I discovered you were carrying this thing around before we left Mezmiali, and I had a sample of its contents analyzed. I was told it's a hypnotic with an almost instantaneous effect both at skin contact and when inhaled. Care to comment?"

"I do indeed!" Egavine said frigidly. "I have no intention of denying that the instrument is a hypnotic spray. As you know, I dislike guns and similar weapons, and we are engaged in a matter in which the need to defend myself against a personal attack might arise. Your assumption, however, that I intended to employ the spray on you just now is simply ridiculous!"

"I might be chuckling myself," Dasinger said, "if Quist hadn't had the sap halfway out of his pocket as soon as you reached for your lapel. If I'd ducked from the spray, I'd have backed into the sap, right? There's a little too much at stake here, doctor. You may be telling the truth, but just in case you're nourishing unfriendly ideas—and that's what it looks like to me—I'm taking a few precautions."

Dr. Egavine stared at him, his mouth set in a thin, bitter line. Then he asked, "What kind of precautions?"

Dasinger said, "I'll keep the hypnotic and Quist's bag of dirty tricks until we land. You might need those things on the planet but you don't need them on shipboard. You and I'll go up to the control section now to give Miss Mines her final flight directions. After that, you and Quist stay in this cabin with the door locked until the ship has set down. I don't want to have anything else to worry about while we're making the approach. If my suspicions turn out to be unjustified, I'll apologize ... after we're all safely back in the Hub."

* * * * *

"What was your partner looking so sour about?" Duomart Mines inquired a little later, her eyes on the flight screens. "Have a quarrel with him?"

Dasinger, standing in the entry to the little control cabin across from her, shrugged his shoulders.

"Not exactly," he said. "Egavine tried to use a hypno spray on me."

"Hypno spray?" the young woman asked.

"A chemical which induces an instantaneous hypnotic trance in people. Leaves them wide open to suggestion. Medical hypnotists make a lot of use of it. So do criminals."

She turned away from the control console to look at him. "Why would your partner want to hypnotize you?"

"I don't know," Dasinger said. "He hasn't admitted that he intended to do it."

"Is he a criminal?"

"I wouldn't say he isn't," Dasinger observed judiciously, "but I couldn't prove it."

Duomart puckered her lips, staring at him thoughtfully. "What about yourself?" she asked.

"No, Miss Mines, I have a very high regard for the law. I'm a simple businessman."

"A simple businessman who flies his own cruiser four weeks out from the Hub into I-Fleet territory?"

"That's the kind of business I'm in," Dasinger explained. "I own a charter ship company."

"I see," she said. "Well, you two make an odd pair of partners...."

"I suppose we do. Incidentally, has there been any occasion when you and Dr. Egavine—or you and Dr.

Egavine and his servant—were alone somewhere in the ship together? For example, except when we came up here to give you further flight instructions, did he ever enter the control room?"

She shook her blond head. "No. Those are the only times I've seen him."

"Certain of that?" he asked.

Duomart nodded without hesitation. "Quite certain!"

Dasinger took an ointment tube from his pocket, removed its cap, squeezed a drop of black, oily substance out on a fingertip. "Mind rolling up your sleeve a moment?" he asked. "Just above the elbow...."

"What for?"

"It's because of the way those hypno sprays work," Dasinger said. "Give your victim a dose of the stuff, tell him what to do, and it usually gets done. And if you're being illegal about it, one of the first things you tell him to do is to forget he's ever been sprayed. This goop is designed for the specific purpose of knocking out hypnotic commands. Just roll up your sleeve like a good girl now, and I'll rub a little of it on your arm."

"You're not rubbing anything on my arm, mister!" Duomart told him coldly.

Dasinger shrugged resignedly, recapped the tube, and dropped it in his pocket. "Have it your way then," he remarked. "I was only ..."

He lunged suddenly towards her.

Duomart gave him quite a struggle. A minute or two later, he had her down on the floor, her body and one arm clamped between his knees, while he unzipped the cuff on the sleeve of the other arm and pulled the sleeve up. He brought out the tube of antihypno ointment and rubbed a few drops of the ointment into the hollow of Duomart's elbow, put the tube back in his pocket, then went on holding her down for nearly another minute. She was gasping for breath, blue eyes furious, muscles tensed.

*   *   *   *   *

Suddenly he felt her relax. An expression of stunned surprise appeared on her face. "Why," she began incredulously, "he *did* ..."

"Gave you the spray treatment, eh?" Dasinger said, satisfied. "I was pretty sure he had."

"Why, that– At his beck and call, he says! Well, we'll just see about ... let me up, Dasinger! Just wait till I get my hands on that bony partner of yours!"

"Now take it easy."

"Take it easy! Why should I? I ..."

"It would be better," Dasinger explained, "if Egavine believes you're still under the influence."

She scowled up at him; then her face turned thoughtful. "Ho! You feel it isn't that he's a depraved old goat, that he's got something more sinister in mind?"

"It's a definite possibility. Why not wait and find out? The ointment will immunize you against further tricks."

Miss Mines regarded him consideringly for a few seconds, then nodded. "All right! You can let me up now. What do you think he's planning?"

"Not easy to say with Dr. Egavine. He's a devious man." Dasinger got himself disentangled, came to his feet, and reached down to help her scramble up.

"They certainly wrap you up with that hypno stuff, don't they!" she observed wonderingly.

Dasinger nodded. "They certainly do!" Then he added, "I'm keeping the doctor and his little sidekick locked up, too, until we get to the planet. That leaves you and me with the run of the ship."

Duomart looked at him. "So it does," she agreed.

"Know how to use a gun?"

"Of course. But I'm not allow– I don't have one with me on this trip."

*   *   *   *   *

He reached into his coat, took out a small gun in a fabric holster. Duomart glanced at it, then her eyes went back to his face.

"Might clip it to your belt," Dasinger said. "It's a good little shocker, fifty-foot range, safe for shipboard use. It's got a full load, eighty shots. We may or may not run into emergencies. If we don't, you'll still be more comfortable carrying it."

Duomart holstered the gun and attached the holster to her belt. She slid the tip of her tongue reflectively out between her lips, drew it back, blinked at the flight screens for a few seconds, then looked across at Dasinger and tapped the holster at her side.

"That sort of changes things, too!" she said.

"Changes what?"

"Tell you in a minute. Sit down, Dasinger. Manual course corrections coming up...." She slid into the pilot seat, moved her hands out over the controls, and appeared to forget about him.

Dasinger settled into a chair to her left, lit a cigarette, smoked and watched her, glancing occasionally at the screens. She was jockeying the Mooncat deftly in and out of the fringes of a gravitic stress knot, presently brought it into the clear, slapped over a direction lever and slid the palm of her right hand along a row of speed control buttons depressing them in turn.

*　　*　　*　　*　　*

"Nice piece of piloting," Dasinger observed.

Duomart lifted one shoulder in a slight shrug. "That's my job." Her face remained serious. "Are you wondering why I edged us through that thing instead of going around it?"

"Uh-huh, a little," Dasinger admitted.

"It knocked half an hour off the time it should take us to get to your planet," she said. "That is, if you'll still want to go there. We're being followed, you see."

"By whom?"

"They call her the Spy. After the Mooncat she's the fastest job in the Fleet. She's got guns, and her normal complement is twenty armed men."

"The idea being to have us lead them to what we're after, and then take it away from us?" Dasinger asked.

"That's right. I'm not supposed to know about it. You know what a Gray Fleet is?"

Dasinger nodded. "An Independent that's turned criminal."

"Yes. Willata's Fleet was a legitimate outfit up to four years ago. Then Liu Taunus and Calat and their gang took over. That happened to be the two Fleet bosses you slapped handcuffs on, Dasinger. We're a Gray Fleet now. So I had some plans of my own for this trip. If I can get to some other I-Fleet or to the Hub, I might be able to do something about Taunus. After we were down on the planet, I was going to steal the Mooncat and take off by myself."

"Why are you telling me?"

Miss Mines colored a little. "Well, you gave me the gun," she said. "And you clobbered Taunus, and got me out of that hypno thing ... I mean, I'd have to be pretty much of a jerk to ditch you now, wouldn't I? Anyway, now that I've told you, you won't be going back to Willata's Fleet, whatever you do. I'll still get to the Hub." She paused. "So what do you want to do now? Beat it until the coast's clear, or make a quick try for your loot before the Spy gets there?"

"How far is she behind us?" Dasinger asked.

Duomart said, "I don't know exactly. Here's what happened. When we started out, Taunus told me not to let the Mooncat travel at more than three-quarters speed for any reason. I figured then the Spy was involved in whatever he was planning; she can keep up with us at that rate, and she has considerably better detector reach than the Cat. She's stayed far enough back not to register on our plates throughout the trip.

"Late yesterday we hit some extensive turbulence areas, and I started playing games. There was this little cluster of three sun systems ahead. One of them was our target, though Dr. Egavine hadn't yet said which. I ducked around a few twisters, doubled back, and there was the Spy coming the other way. I beat it then–top velocity. The Spy dropped off our detectors two hours later, and she can't have kept us on for more than another hour herself.

"So they'll assume we're headed for one of those three systems, but they don't know which one. They'll have to look for us. There's only one terraprox in the system we're going to. There may be none in the others, or maybe four or five. But the terraprox worlds is where they'll look because the salvage suits you're carrying are designed for ordinary underwater work. After the way I ran from them, they'll figure something's gone wrong with Taunus's plans, of course."

*   *   *   *   *

Dasinger rubbed his chin. "And if they're lucky and follow us straight in to the planet?"

"Then," Miss Mines said, "you might still have up to six or seven hours to locate the stuff you want, load it aboard and be gone again."

"Might have?"

She shrugged. "We've got a lead on them, but just how big a lead we finally wind up with depends to a considerable extent on the flight conditions they run into behind us. They might get a break there, too. Then there's another very unfortunate thing. The system Dr. Egavine's directed us to now is the one we were closest to when I broke out of detection range. They'll probably decide to look there first. You see?"

"Yes," Dasinger said. "Not so good, is it?" He knuckled his jaw again reflectively. "Why was Taunus pounding around on you when I came forward?"

"Oh, those two runches caught me flying the ship at top speed. Taunus was furious. He couldn't know whether the Spy still had a fix on us or not. Of course he didn't tell me that. The lumps he was preparing to hand out were to be for disregarding his instructions. He does things like that." She paused. "Well, are you going to make a try for the planet?"

"Yes," Dasinger said. "If we wait, there's entirely too good a chance the Spy will run across what we're after while she's snooping around for us there. We'll try to arrange things for a quick getaway in case our luck doesn't hold up."

Duomart nodded. "Mind telling me what you're after?"

"Not at all. Under the circumstances you should be told...."

*   *   *   *   *

"Of course," Dasinger concluded a minute or two later, "all we'll have a legal claim to is the salvage fee."

Miss Mines glanced over at him, looking somewhat shaken. "You *are* playing this legally?"

"Definitely."

"Even so," she said, "if that really is the wreck of the Dosey Asteroids raider, and the stones are still on board ... you two will collect something like ten million credits between you!"

"Roughly that," Dasinger agreed. "Dr. Egavine learned about the matter from one of your Willata Fleetmen."

Her eyes widened. "He what!"

"The Fleet lost a unit called Handing's Scout about four years ago, didn't it?"

"Three and a half," she said. She paused. "Handing's Scout is the other wreck down there?"

"Yes. There was one survivor ... as far as we know. You may recall his name. Leed Farous."

Duomart nodded. "The little kwil hound. He was assistant navigator. How did Dr. Egavine...?"

Dasinger said, "Farous died in a Federation hospital on Mezmiali two years ago, apparently of the accumulative effects of kwil addiction. He'd been picked up in Hub space in a lifeboat which we now know was one of the two on Handing's Scout."

"In Hub space? Why, it must have taken him almost a year to get that far in one of those tubs!"

"From what Dr. Egavine learned," Dasinger said, "it did take that long. The lifeboat couldn't be identified at the time. Neither could Farous. He was completely addled with kwil ... quite incoherent, in fact already apparently in the terminal stages of the addiction. Strenuous efforts were made to identify him because a single large star hyacinth had been found in the lifeboat ... there was the possibility it was one of the stones the Dosey Asteroids Company had lost. But Farous died some months later without regaining his senses sufficiently to offer any information.

"Dr. Egavine was the physician in charge of the case, and eventually also the man who signed the death certificate. The doctor stayed on at the hospital for another year, then resigned, announcing that he intended to go into private research. Before Farous died, Egavine had of course obtained his story from him."

Miss Mines looked puzzled. "If Farous never regained his senses ..."

"Dr. Egavine is a hypnotherapist of exceptional ability," Dasinger said. "Leed Farous wasn't so far gone that the information couldn't be pried out of him with an understanding use of drug hypnosis."

"Then why didn't others ..."

"Oh, it was attempted. But you'll remember," Dasinger said, "that I had a little trouble getting close to you with an antihypnotic. The good doctor got to Farous first, that's all. Instead of the few minutes he spent on you, he could put in hour after hour conditioning Farous.

Later comers simply didn't stand a chance of getting through to him."

*   *   *   *   *

Duomart Mines was silent a moment, then asked, "Why did you two come out to the Willata Fleet station and hire one of our ships? Your cruiser's a lot slower than the Mooncat but it would have got you here."

Dasinger said, "Dr. Egavine slipped up on one point. One can hardly blame him for it since interstellar navigation isn't in his line. The reference points on the maps he had Farous make up for him turned out to be meaningless when compared with Federation star charts. We needed the opportunity to check them against your Fleet maps. They make sense then."

"I see." Duomart gave him a sideways glance, remarked, "You know, the way you've put it, the thing's still pretty fishy."

"In what manner?"

"Dr. Egavine finished off old Farous, didn't he?"

"He may have," Dasinger conceded. "It would be impossible to prove it now. You can't force a man to testify against himself. It's true, of course, that Farous died at a very convenient moment, from Dr. Egavine's point of view."

"Well," she said, "a man like that wouldn't be satisfied with half a salvage fee when he saw the chance to quietly make away with the entire Dosey Asteroids haul."

"That could be," Dasinger said thoughtfully. "On the other hand, a man who had committed an unprovable murder to obtain a legal claim to six million credits might very well decide not to push his luck any farther. You know the space salvage ruling that when a criminal act or criminal intent can be shown in connection with an operation like this, the guilty person automatically forfeits any claim he has to the fee."

"Yes, I know ... and of course," Miss Mines said, "you aren't necessarily so lily white either. That's another possibility. And there's still another one. You don't happen to be a Federation detective, do you?"

Dasinger blinked. After a moment he said, "Not a bad guess. However, I don't work for the Federation."

"Oh? For whom do you work?"

"At the moment, and indirectly, for the Dosey Asteroids Company."

"Insurance?"

"No. After Farous died, Dosey Asteroids employed a detective agency to investigate the matter. I represent the agency."

"The agency collects on the salvage?"

"That's the agreement. We deliver the goods or get nothing."

"And Dr. Egavine?"

Dasinger shrugged. "If the doctor keeps his nose clean, he stays entitled to half the salvage fee."

"What about the way he got the information from Farous?" she asked.

"From any professional viewpoint, that was highly unethical procedure. But there's no evidence Egavine broke any laws."

Miss Mines studied him, her eyes bright and quizzical. "I had a feeling about you," she said. "I ..."

A warning burr came from the tolerance indicator; the girl turned her head quickly, said, "Cat's complaining ... looks like we're hitting the first system stresses!" She slid back into the pilot seat. "Be with you again in a while...."

*   *   *   *   *

When Dasinger returned presently to the control section Duomart sat at ease in the pilot seat with coffee and a sandwich before her.

"How are the mutineers doing?" she asked.

"They ate with a good appetite, said nothing, and gave me no trouble," Dasinger said. "They still pretend they don't understand Federation translingue. Dr. Egavine's a bit sulky. He wanted to be up front during the prelanding period. I told him he could watch things through his cabin communicator screen."

Miss Mines finished her sandwich, her eyes thoughtful. "I've been wondering, you know ... how can you be sure Dr. Egavine told you the truth about what he got from Leed Farous?"

Dasinger said, "I studied the recordings Dr. Egavine made of his sessions with Farous in the hospital. He may have held back on a few details, but the recordings were genuine enough."

"So Farous passes out on a kwil jag," she said, "and he doesn't even know they're making a landing. When he comes to, the scout's parked, the Number Three drive is smashed, the lock is open, and not another soul is aboard or in sight.

"Then he notices another wreck with its lock open, wanders over, sees a few bones and stuff lying around inside, picks up a star hyacinth, and learns from the ship's records that down in the hold under sixty feet of water is a sealed compartment with a whole little crateful of the stones...."

"That's the story," Dasinger agreed.

"In the Fleets," she remarked, "if we heard of a place where a couple of ship's crews seemed to have vanished into thin air, we'd call it a spooked world. And usually we'd keep away from it." She clamped her lower lip lightly between her teeth for a moment. "Do you think Dr. Egavine has considered the kwil angle?"

Dasinger nodded. "I'm sure of it. Of course it's only a guess that the kwil made a difference for Farous. The stuff has no known medical value of any kind. But when the only known survivor of two crews happens to be a kwil-eater, the point has to be considered."

"Nobody else on Handing's Scout took kwil," Duomart said. "I know that. There aren't many in the Fleet who do." She hesitated. "You know, Dasinger, perhaps I should try it again! Maybe if I took it straight from the needle this time ..."

Dasinger shook his head. "If the little flake you nibbled made you feel drowsy, even a quarter of a standard shot would put you out cold for an hour or two. Kwil has that effect on a lot of people. Which is one reason it isn't a very popular drug."

"What effect does it have on you?" she asked.

"Depends to some extent on the size of the dose. Sometimes it slows me down physically and mentally. At other times there were no effects that I could tell until the kwil wore off. Then I'd have hallucinations for a while–that can be very distracting, of course, when there's something you have to do. Those hangover hallucinations seem to be another fairly common reaction."

He concluded, "Since you can't take the drug and stay awake, you'll simply remain inside the locked ship. It will be better anyway to keep the Mooncat well up in the air and ready to move most of the time we're on the planet."

"What about Taunus and Calat?" she asked.

"They come out with us, of course. If kwil is what it takes to stay healthy down there, I've enough to go around. And if it knocks them out, it will keep them out of trouble."

*   *   *   *   *

"Looks like there's a firemaker down there!" Duomart's slim forefinger indicated a point on the ground-view plate. "Column of smoke starting to come up next to that big patch of trees!... Two point nine miles due north and uphill of the wrecks."

From a wall screen Dr. Egavine's voice repeated sharply, "Smoke? Then Leed Farous was not the only survivor!"

Duomart gave him a cool glance. "Might be a native animal that knows how to make fire. They're not so unusual." She went on to Dasinger. "It would take a hand detector to spot us where we are, but it does look like a distress signal. If it's men from one of the wrecks, why haven't they used the scout's other lifeboat?"

"Would the lifeboat still be intact?" Dasinger asked.

Duomart spun the ground-view plate back to the scout. "Look for yourself," she said. "It *couldn't* have been damaged in as light a crash as that one was. Those tubs are built to stand a really solid shaking up! And what else could have harmed it?"

"Farous may have put it out of commission before he left," Dasinger said. "He wanted to come back from the Hub with an expedition to get the hyacinths, so he wouldn't have cared for the idea of anyone else getting away from the planet meanwhile." He looked over at the screen. "How about it, doctor? Did Farous make any mention of that?"

Dr. Egavine seemed to hesitate an instant. "As a matter of fact, he did. Farous was approximately a third of the way to the Hub when he realized he might have made a mistake in not rendering the second lifeboat unusable. But by then it was too late to turn back, and of course he was almost certain there were no other survivors."

"So that lifeboat should still be in good condition?"

"It was in good condition when Farous left here."

"Well, whoever's down there simply may not know how to handle it."

Duomart shook her blond head decidedly. "That's out, too!" she said. "Our Fleet lifeboats all came off an old Grand Commerce liner which was up for scrap eighty, ninety years ago. They're designed so any fool can tell what to do, and the navigational settings are completely automatic. Of course if it *is* a native firemaker–with mighty keen eyesight–down there, that could be different! A creature like that mightn't think of going near the scout. Should I start easing the Cat in towards the smoke, Dasinger?"

"Yes. We'll have to find out what the signal means before we try to approach the wrecks. Doctor, are you satisfied now that Miss Mines's outworld biotic check was correct?"

"The analysis appears to be fairly accurate," Dr. Egavine acknowledged, "and all detectable trouble sources are covered by the selected Fleet serum."

*　　*　　*　　*　　*

Dasinger said, "We'll prepare for an immediate landing then. There'll be less than an hour of daylight left on the ground, but the night's so short we'll disregard that factor." He switched off the connection to Egavine's cabin, turned to Duomart. "Now our wrist communicators, you say, have a five-mile range?"

"A little over five."

"Then," Dasinger said, "we'll keep you and the Cat stationed at an exact five-mile altitude ninety-five per cent of the time we spend on the planet. If the Spy arrives while you're up there, how much time will we have to clear out?"

She shrugged. "That depends of course on how they arrive. My detectors can pick the Spy up in space before their detectors can make out the Cat against the planet. If we spot them as they're heading in, we'll have around fifteen minutes.

"But if they show up on the horizon in atmosphere, or surface her out of subspace, that's something else. If I don't move instantly then, they'll have me bracketed ... and BLOOIE!"

Dasinger said, "Then those are the possibilities you'll have to watch for. Think you could draw the Spy far enough away in a chase to be able to come back for us?"

"They wouldn't follow me that far," Duomart said. "They know the Cat can outrun them easily once she's really stretched out, so if they can't nail her in the first few minutes they'll come back to look around for what we were interested in here." She added, "And if I *don't* let the Cat go all out but just keep a little ahead of them, they'll know that I'm trying to draw them away from something."

Dasinger nodded. "In that case we'll each be on our own, and your job will be to keep right on going and get the information as quickly as possible to the Kyth detective agency in Orado. The agency will take the matter from there."

*   *   *   *   *

Miss Mines looked at him. "Aren't you sort of likely to be dead before the agency can do anything about the situation?"

"I'll try to avoid it," Dasinger said. "Now, we've assumed the worst as far as the Spy is concerned. But things might also go wrong downstairs. Say I lose control of the group, or we all get hit down there by whatever hit the previous landing parties and it turns out that kwil's no good for it. It's understood that in any such event you again head the Cat immediately for the Hub and get the word to the agency. Right?"

Duomart nodded.

He brought a flat case of medical hypodermics out of his pocket, and opened it.

"Going to take your shot of kwil before we land?" Miss Mines asked.

"No. I want you to keep one of these needles on hand, at least until we find out what the problem is. It'll knock you out if you have to take it, but it might also keep you alive. I'm waiting myself to see if it's necessary to go on kwil. The hallucinations I get from the stuff afterwards could hit me while we're in the middle of some critical activity or other, and that mightn't be so good." He closed the case again, put it away. "I think we've covered everything. If you'll check the view plate, something–or somebody–has come out from under the trees near the column of smoke. And unless I'm mistaken it's a human being."

Duomart slipped the kwil needle he'd given her into a drawer of the instrument console. "I don't think you're mistaken," she said. "I've been watching him for the last thirty seconds."

"It is a man?"

"Pretty sure of it. He moves like one."

Dasinger stood up. "I'll go talk with Egavine then. I had a job in mind for him and his hypno sprays if we happened to run into human survivors."

"Shall I put the ship down next to this one?"

"No. Land around five hundred yards to the north, in the middle of that big stretch of open ground. That should keep us out of ambushes. Better keep clear of the airspace immediately around the wrecks as you go down."

Duomart looked at him. "Darn right I'll keep clear of that area!"

Dasinger grinned. "Something about the scout?"

"Sure. No visible reason at all why the scout should have settled hard enough to buckle a drive. Handing was a good pilot."

"Hm-m-m." Dasinger rubbed his chin. "Well, I've been wondering. The Dosey Asteroids raiders are supposed to have used an unknown type of antipersonnel weapon in their attack on the station, you know. Nothing in sight on their wreck that might be, say, an automatic gun but ... well, just move in carefully and stay ready to haul away very fast at the first hint of trouble!"

*   *   *   *   *

The Mooncat slid slowly down through the air near the point where the man stood in open ground, a hundred yards from the clump of trees out of which smoke still billowed thickly upwards. The man watched the speedboat's descent quietly, making no further attempt to attract the attention of those on board to himself.

Duomart had said that the man was not a member of Handing's lost crew but a stranger. He was therefore one of the Dosey Asteroids raiders.

Putting down her two land legs, the Mooncat touched the open hillside a little over a quarter of a mile from the woods, stood straddled and rakish, nose high. The storeroom lock opened, and a slender ramp slid out. Quist showed in the lock, dumped two portable shelters to the ground, came scrambling nimbly down the ramp. Dr. Egavine followed, more cautiously, the two handcuffed Fleetmen behind him. Dasinger came out last, glancing over at the castaway who had started across the slope towards the ship.

"Everyone's out," he told his wrist communicator. "Take her up."

The ramp snaked soundlessly back into the lock, the lock snapped shut and the Mooncat lifted smoothly and quickly from the ground. Liu Taunus glanced after the rising speedboat, looked at Calat, and spoke loudly and emphatically in Fleetlingue for a few seconds, his broad face without expression. Dasinger said, "All right, Quist, break out the shelter."

When the shelter was assembled, Dasinger motioned the Fleetmen towards the door with his thumb. "Inside, boys!" he said. "Quist, lock the shelter behind them and stay on guard here. Come on, doctor. We'll meet our friend halfway...."

*　　*　　*　　*　　*

The castaway approached unhurriedly, walking with a long, easy stride, the bird thing on his shoulder craning its neck to peer at the strangers with round yellow eyes. The man was big and rangy, probably less heavy by thirty pounds than Liu Taunus, but in perfect physical condition. The face was strong and intelligent, smiling elatedly now.

"I'd nearly stopped hoping this day would arrive!" he said in translingue. "May I ask who you are?"

"An exploration group." Dasinger gripped the extended hand, shook it, as Dr. Egavine's right hand went casually to his coat lapel. "We noticed the two wrecked ships down by the lake," Dasinger explained, "then saw your smoke signal. Your name?"

"Graylock. Once chief engineer of the Antares, out of Vanadia on Aruaque." Graylock turned, still smiling, towards Egavine.

Egavine smiled as pleasantly.

"Graylock," he observed, "you feel, and will continue to feel, that this is the conversation you planned to conduct with us, that everything is going exactly in accordance with your wishes." He turned his head to Dasinger, inquired, "Would you prefer to question him yourself, Dasinger?"

Dasinger hesitated, startled; but Graylock's expression did not change. Dasinger shook his head. "Very smooth, doctor!" he commented. "No, go ahead. You're obviously the expert here."

"Very well ... Graylock," Dr. Egavine resumed, "you will cooperate with me fully and to the best of your ability now, knowing that I am both your master and friend. Are any of the other men who came here on those two ships down by the water still alive?"

There was complete stillness for a second or two. Then Graylock's face began to work unpleasantly, all color draining from it. He said harshly, "No. But I ... I don't ..." He stammered incomprehensibly, went silent again, his expression wooden and set.

"Graylock," Egavine continued to probe, "you can remember everything now, and you are not afraid. Tell me what happened to the other men."

Sweat covered the castaway's ashen face. His mouth twisted in agonized, silent grimaces again. The bird thing leaped from his shoulder with a small purring sound, fluttered softly away.

Dr. Egavine repeated, "You are not afraid. You can remember. What happened to them? How did they die?"

And abruptly the big man's face smoothed out. He looked from Egavine to Dasinger and back with an air of brief puzzlement, then explained conversationally, "Why, Hovig's generator killed many of us as we ran away from the Antares. Some reached the edges of the circle with me, and I killed them later."

Dr. Egavine flicked another glance towards Dasinger but did not pause.

"And the crew of the second ship?" he asked.

"Those two. They had things I needed, and naturally I didn't want them alive here."

"Is Hovig's generator still on the Antares?"

"Yes."

"How does the generator kill?"

Sweat suddenly started out on Graylock's face again, but now he seemed unaware of any accompanying emotions. He said, "It kills by fear, of course...."

*　　*　　*　　*　　*

The story of the Dosey Asteroids raider and of Hovig's fear generators unfolded quickly from there. Hovig had developed his machines for the single purpose of robbing the Dosey Asteroids Shipping Station. The plan then had been to have the Antares cruise in uncharted space with the looted star hyacinths for at least two years, finally to approach the area of the Federation from a sector far removed from the Dosey system. That precaution resulted in disaster for Hovig. Chief Engineer Graylock had time to consider that his share in the profits of the raid would be relatively insignificant, and that there was a possibility of increasing it.

Graylock and his friends attacked their shipmates as the raider was touching down to the surface of an uncharted world to replenish its water supply. The attack succeeded but Hovig, fatally wounded, took a terrible revenge on the mutineers. He contrived to set off one of his grisly devices, and to all intents and purposes everyone still alive on board the Antares immediately went insane with fear. The ship crashed out of control at the edge of a lake. Somebody had opened a lock and a number of the frantic crew plunged from the ramp and fell to their death on the rocks below. Those who reached the foot of the ramp fled frenziedly from the wreck, the effects of Hovig's machine pursuing them but weakening gradually as they widened the distance between themselves and the Antares. Finally, almost three miles away, the fear impulses faded out completely....

But thereafter the wreck was unapproachable. The fear generator did not run out of power, might not run out of power for years.

Dasinger said, "Doctor, let's hurry this up! Ask him why they weren't affected by their murder machines when they robbed Dosey Asteroids. Do the generators have a beam-operated shut-off, or what?"

Graylock listened to the question, said, "We had taken kwil. The effects were still very unpleasant, but they could be tolerated."

There was a pause of a few seconds. Dr. Egavine cleared his throat. "It appears, Dasinger," he remarked, "that we have failed to consider a very important clue!"

Dasinger nodded. "And an obvious one," he said drily. "Keep it moving along, doctor. How much kwil did they take? How long had they been taking it before the raid?"

Dr. Egavine glanced over at him, repeated the questions.

Graylock said Hovig had begun conditioning the crew to kwil a week or two before the Antares slipped out of Aruaque for the strike on the station. In each case the dosage had been built up gradually to the quantity the man in question required to remain immune to the generators. Individual variations had been wide and unpredictable.

Dasinger passed his tongue over his lips, nodded. "Ask him ..."

*   *   *   *   *

He checked himself at a soft, purring noise, a shadowy fluttering in the air. Graylock's animal flew past him, settled on its master's shoulder, turned to stare at Dasinger and Egavine. Dasinger looked at the yellow owl-eyes, the odd little tube of a mouth, continued to Egavine, "Ask him where the haul was stored in the ship."

Graylock confirmed Leed Farous's statement of what he had seen in the Antares's records. All but a few of the star hyacinths had been placed in a vault-like compartment in the storage, and the compartment was sealed. Explosives would be required to open it. Hovig kept out half a dozen of the larger stones, perhaps as an antidote to boredom during the long voyage ahead. Graylock had found one of them just before Hovig's infernal instrument went into action.

"And where is that one now?" Dr. Egavine asked.

"I still have it."

"On your person?"

"Yes."

Dr. Egavine held out his hand, palm upward. "You no longer want it, Graylock. Give it to me."

Graylock looked bewildered; for a moment he appeared about to weep. Then he brought a knotted piece of leather from his pocket, unwrapped it, took out the gem and placed it in Egavine's hand. Egavine picked it up between thumb and forefinger of his other hand, held it out before him.

There was silence for some seconds while the star hyacinth burned in the evening air and the three men and the small winged animal stared at it. Then Dr. Egavine exhaled slowly.

"Ah, now!" he said, his voice a trifle unsteady. "Men might kill and kill for that one beauty alone, that is true!... Will you keep it for now, Dasinger? Or shall I?"

Dasinger looked at him thoughtfully.

"You keep it, doctor," he said.

*   *   *   *   *

"Dasinger," Dr. Egavine observed a few minutes later, "I have been thinking...."

"Yes?"

"Graylock's attempted description of his experience indicates that the machine on the Antares does not actually broadcast the emotion of terror, as he believes. The picture presented is that of a mind in which both the natural and the acquired barriers of compartmentalization are temporarily nullified, resulting in an explosion of compounded insanity to an extent which would be inconceivable without such an outside agent. As we saw in Graylock, the condition is in fact impossible to describe or imagine! A diabolical device...."

He frowned. "Why the drug kwil counteracts such an effect remains unclear. But since we now know that it does, I may have a solution to the problem confronting us."

Dasinger nodded. "Let's hear it."

"Have Miss Mines bring the ship down immediately," Egavine instructed him. "There is a definite probability that among my medical supplies will be an effective substitute for kwil, for this particular purpose. A few hours of experimentation, and ..."

"Doctor," Dasinger interrupted, "hold it right there! So far there's been no real harm in sparring around. But we're in a different situation now ... we may be running out of time very quickly. Let's quit playing games."

Dr. Egavine glanced sharply across at him. "What do you mean?"

"I mean that we both have kwil, of course. There's no reason to experiment. But the fact that we have it is no guarantee that we'll be able to get near that generator. Leed Farous's tissues were soaked with the drug. Graylock's outfit had weeks to determine how much each of them needed to be able to operate within range of the machines and stay sane. We're likely to have trouble enough without trying to jockey each other."

Dr. Egavine cleared his throat. "But I ..."

Dasinger interrupted again. "Your reluctance to tell me everything you knew or had guessed is understandable. You had no more reason to trust me completely than I had to trust you. So before you say anything else I'd like you to look at these credentials. You're familiar with the Federation seal, I think."

Dr. Egavine took the proffered identification case, glanced at Dasinger again, then opened the case.

"So," he said presently. "You're a detective working for the Dosey Asteroids Company...." His voice was even. "That alters the situation, of course. Why didn't you tell me this?"

"That should be obvious," Dasinger said. "If you're an honest man, the fact can make no difference. The company remains legally bound to pay out the salvage fee for the star hyacinths. They have no objection to that. What they didn't like was the possibility of having the gems stolen for the second time. If that's what you had in mind, you wouldn't, of course, have led an agent of the company here. In other words, doctor, in cooperating with me you're running no risk of being cheated out of your half of the salvage rights."

Dasinger patted the gun in his coat pocket. "And of course," he added, "if I happened to be a bandit in spite of the credentials, I'd be eliminating you from the partnership right now instead of talking to you! The fact that I'm not doing it should be a sufficient guarantee that I don't intend to do it."

Dr. Egavine nodded. "I'm aware of the point."

"Then let's get on with the salvage," Dasinger said. "For your further information, there's an armed Fleet ship hunting for us with piratical intentions, and the probability is that it will find us in a matter of hours...."

*   *   *   *   *

He described the situation briefly, concluded, "You've carried out your part of the contract by directing us here. You can, if you wish, minimize further personal risks by using the Fleet scout's lifeboat to get yourself and Quist off the planet, providing kwil will get you to the scout. Set a normspace course for Orado then, and we'll pick you up after we've finished the job."

Dr. Egavine shook his head. "Thank you, but I'm staying. It's in my interest to give you what assistance I can ... and, as you've surmised, I do have a supply of kwil. What is your plan?"

"Getting Hovig's generator shut off is the first step," Dasinger said. "And since we don't know what dosage of the drug is required for each of us, we'd be asking for trouble by approaching the Antares in the ship. Miss Mines happens to be a kwil-sensitive, in any case. So it's going to take hiking, and I'll start down immediately now. Would Graylock and the Fleetmen obey hypnotic orders to the extent of helping out dependably in the salvage work?"

Egavine nodded. "There is no question of that."

"Then you might start conditioning them to the idea now. From the outer appearance of the Antares, it may be a real job to cut through inside her to get to the star hyacinths. We have the three salvage suits. If I can make it to the generator, shut it off, and it turns out then that I need some hypnotized brawn down there, Miss Mines will fly over the shelter as a signal to start marching the men down."

"Why march? At that point, Miss Mines could take us to the wreck within seconds."

Dasinger shook his head. "Sorry, doctor. Nobody but Miss Mines or myself goes aboard the Mooncat until we either wind up the job or are forced to clear out and run. I'm afraid that's one precaution I'll have to take. When you get to the Antares we'll give each of the boys a full shot of kwil. The ones that don't go limp on it can start helping."

Dr. Egavine said reflectively, "You feel the drug would still be a requirement?"

"Well," Dasinger said, "Hovig appears to have been a man who took precautions, too. We know he had three generators and that he set off one of them. The question is where the other two are. It wouldn't be so very surprising, would it, if one or both of them turned out to be waiting for intruders in the vault where he sealed away the loot?"

* * * * *

The night was cool. Wind rustled in the ground vegetation and the occasional patches of trees. Otherwise the slopes were quiet. The sky was covered with cloud layers through which the Mooncat drifted invisibly. In the infrared glasses Dasinger had slipped on when he started, the rocky hillside showed clear for two hundred yards, tinted green as though bathed by a strange moonlight; beyond was murky darkness.

"Still all right?" Duomart's voice inquired from the wrist communicator.

"Uh-huh!" Dasinger said. "A little nervous, but I'd be feeling that way in any case, under the circumstances."

"I'm not so sure," she said. "You've gone past the two and a half mile line from the generator. From what that Graylock monster said, you should have started to pick up its effects. Why not take your shot, and play safe?"

"No," Dasinger said. "If I wait until I feel something that can be definitely attributed to the machine, I can keep the kwil dose down to what I need. I don't want to load myself up with the drug any more than I have to."

A stand of tall trees with furry trunks moved presently into range of the glasses, thick undergrowth beneath. Dasinger picked his way through the thickets with some caution. The indications so far had been that local animals had as much good reason to avoid the vicinity of Hovig's machine as human beings, but if there was any poisonous vermin in the area this would be a good place for it to be lurking. Which seemed a fairly reasonable apprehension. Other, equally definite, apprehensions looked less reasonable when considered objectively. If he stumbled on a stone, it produced a surge of sharp alarm which lingered for seconds; and his breathing had quickened much more than could be accounted for by the exertions of the downhill climb.

*   *   *   *   *

Five minutes beyond the wood Dasinger emerged from the mouth of a narrow gorge, and stopped short with a startled exclamation. His hand dug hurriedly into his pocket for the case of kwil needles.

"What's the matter?" Duomart inquired sharply.

Dasinger produced a somewhat breathless laugh. "I've decided to take the kwil. At once!"

"You're feeling ... things?" Her voice was also shaky.

"I'll say! Not just a matter of feeling it, either. For example, a couple of old friends are walking towards me at the moment. Dead ones, as it happens."

"Ugh!" she said faintly. "Hurry up!"

Dasinger shoved the needle's plunger a quarter of the way down on the kwil solution, pulled the needle out of his arm. He stood still for some seconds, filled his lungs with the cool night air, let it out in a long sigh.

"That did it!" he announced, his voice steadying again. "The stuff works fast. A quarter shot...."

"Why did you wait so long?"

"It wasn't too bad till just now. Then suddenly ... that generator can't be putting out evenly! Anyway, it hit me like a rock. I doubt you'd be interested in details."

"I wouldn't," Duomart agreed. "I'm crawly enough as it is up here. I wish we were through with this!"

"With just a little luck we should be off the planet in an hour."

By the time he could hear the lapping of the lake water on the wind, he was aware of the growing pulse of Hovig's generator ahead of him, alive and malignant in the night. Then the Fleet scout came into the glasses, a squat, dark ship, its base concealed in the growth that had sprung up around it after it piled up on the slope. Dasinger moved past the scout, pushing through bushy aromatic shrubbery which thickened as he neared the water. He felt physically sick and sluggish now, was aware, too, of an increasing reluctance to go on. He would need more of the drug before attempting to enter the Antares.

To the west, the sky was partly clear, and presently he saw the wreck of the Dosey Asteroids raider loom up over the edge of the lake arm, blotting out a section of stars. Still beyond the field of the glasses, it looked like an armored water animal about to crawl up on the slopes. Dasinger approached slowly, in foggy unwillingness, emerged from the bushes into open ground, and saw a broad ramp furred with a thick coat of moldlike growth rise steeply towards an open lock in the upper part of the Antares. The pulse of the generator might have been the beating of the maimed ship's heart, angry and threatening. It seemed to be growing stronger. And had something moved in the lock? Dasinger stood, senses swimming sickly, dreaming that something huge rose slowly, towered over him like a giant wave, leaned forwards....

*   *   *   *   *

"Still all right?" Duomart inquired.

The wave broke.

"*Dasinger! What's happened?*"

"Nothing," Dasinger said, his voice raw. He pulled the empty needle out of his arm, dropped it. "But something nearly did! The kwil I took wasn't enough. I was standing here waiting to let that damned machine swamp me when you spoke."

"You should have heard what you sounded like over the communicator! I thought you were ..." her voice stopped for an instant, began again. "Anyway," she said briskly, "you're loaded with kwil now, I hope?"

"More than I should be, probably." Dasinger rubbed both hands slowly down along his face. "Well, it couldn't be helped. That was pretty close, I guess! I don't even remember getting the hypo out of the case."

He looked back up at the looming bow of the Antares, unbeautiful enough but prosaically devoid of menace and mystery now, though the pulsing beat still came from there. A mechanical obstacle and nothing else. "I'm going on in now."

From the darkness within the lock came the smell of stagnant water, of old decay. The mold that proliferated over the ramp did not extend into the wreck. But other things grew inside, pale and oily tendrils festooning the walls. Dasinger removed his night glasses, brought out a pencil light, let the beam fan out, and moved through the lock.

The crash which had crumpled the ship's lower shell had thrust up the flooring of the lock compartment, turned it into what was nearly level footing now. On the

right, a twenty-foot black gap showed between the ragged
edge of the deck and the far bulkhead from which it had
been torn. The oily plant life spread over the edges of the
flooring and on down into the flooded lower sections of the
Antares. The pulse of Hovig's generator came from above
and the left where a passage slanted steeply up into the
ship's nose. Dasinger turned towards the passage, began
clambering up.

*   *   *   *   *

There was no guesswork involved in determining
which of the doors along the passage hid the machine in
what, if Graylock's story was correct, had been Hovig's
personal stateroom. As Dasinger approached that point,
it was like climbing into silent thunder. The door was
locked, and though the walls beside it were warped and
cracked, the cracks were too narrow to permit entry.
Dasinger dug out a tool which had once been the prized
property of one of Orado's more eminent safecrackers,
and went to work on the lock. A minute or two later he
forced the door partly back in its tilted frame, scrambled
through into the cabin.

Not enough was left of Hovig after this span of time to
be particularly offensive. The generator lay in a lower
corner, half buried under other molded and
unrecognizable debris. Dasinger uncovered it, feeling as if
he were drowning in the invisible torrent pouring out
from it, knelt down and placed the light against the wall
beside him.

The machine matched Graylock's description. A
pancake-shaped heavy plastic casing eighteen inches
across, two thick studs set into its edge, one stud
depressed and flush with the surface, the other extended.
Dasinger thumbed experimentally at the extended stud,
found it apparently immovable, took out his gun.

"How is it going, Dasinger?" Miss Mines asked.

"All right," Dasinger said. He realized he was speaking with difficulty. "I've found the thing! Trying to get it shut off now. Tell you in a minute...."

He tapped the extended stud twice with the butt of the gun, then slashed heavily down. The stud flattened back into the machine. Its counterpart didn't move. The drowning sensations continued.

Dasinger licked his lips, dropped the gun into his pocket, brought out the lock opener. He had the generator's cover plate pried partway back when it shattered. With that, the thunder that wasn't sound ebbed swiftly from the cabin. Dasinger reached into the generator, wrenched out a power battery, snapping half a dozen leads.

He sat back on his heels, momentarily dizzy with relief, then climbed to his feet with the smashed components of Hovig's machine, and turned to the door. Something in the debris along the wall flashed dazzlingly in the beam of his light.

Dasinger stared at the star hyacinth for an instant, then picked it up. It was slightly larger than the one Graylock had carried out of the Antares with him, perfectly cut. He found four others of similar quality within the next minute, started back down to the lock compartment with what might amount to two million credits in honest money, around half that in the Hub's underworld gem trade, in one of his pockets.

"Yes?"

"Got the thing's teeth pulled now."

"Thank God! Coming right down...."

The Mooncat was sliding in from the south as Dasinger stepped out on the head of the ramp. "Lock's open," Duomart's voice informed him. "I'll come aft and help."

*   *   *   *   *

It took four trips with the gravity crane to transfer the salvage equipment into the Antares's lock compartment. Then Miss Mines sealed the Mooncat and went back upstairs. Dasinger climbed into one of the three salvage suits, hung the wrist communicator inside the helmet, snapped on the suit's lights and went over to the edge of the compartment deck. Black water reflected the lights thirty feet below. He checked the assortment of tools attached to his belt, nudged the suit's gravity cutoff to the right, energized magnetic pads on knees, boot tips and wrists, then fly-walked rapidly down a bulkhead and dropped into the water.

"No go, Duomart!" he informed the girl ten minutes later, his voice heavy with disappointment. "It's an ungodly twisted mess down here ... worse than I thought it might be! Looks as if we'll have to cut all the way through to that vault. Give Egavine the signal to start herding the boys down."

Approximately an hour afterwards, Miss Mines reported urgently through the communicator, "They'll reach the lock in less than four minutes now, Dasinger! Better drop it and come up!"

"I'm on my way." Dasinger reluctantly switched off the beam-saw he was working with, fastened it to the belt of the salvage suit, turned in the murky water and started back towards the upper sections of the wreck. The job of getting through the tangled jungle of metal and plastic to the gem vault appeared no more than half completed, and the prospect of being delayed over it until the Spy discovered them here began to look like a disagreeably definite possibility. He clambered and floated hurriedly up through the almost vertical passage he'd cleared, found daylight flooding the lock compartment, the system's yellow sun well above the horizon. Peeling off the salvage suit, he restored the communicator to his wrist and went over to the head of the ramp.

*   *   *   *   *

The five men came filing down the last slopes in the morning light, Taunus and Calat in the lead, Graylock behind them, the winged animal riding his shoulder and lifting occasionally into the air to flutter about the group. Quist and Egavine brought up the rear. Dasinger took the gun from his pocket.

"I'll clip my gun to the suit belt when I go back down in the water with the boys," he told the communicator. "If the doctor's turning any tricks over in his mind, that should give him food for thought. I'll relieve Quist of his weapon as he comes in."

"What about the guns in Graylock's hut?" Duomart asked.

"No charge left in them. If I'm reasonably careful, I really don't see what Dr. Egavine can do. He knows he loses his half-interest in the salvage the moment he pulls any illegal stunts."

A minute or two later, he called out, "Hold it there, doctor?"

The group shuffled to a stop near the foot of the ramp, staring up at him.

"Yes, Dasinger?" Dr. Egavine called back, sounding a trifle winded.

"Have Quist come up first and alone, please." Dasinger disarmed the little man at the entrance to the lock, motioned him on to the center of the compartment. The others arrived then in a line, filed past Dasinger and joined Quist.

"You've explained the situation to everybody?" Dasinger asked Egavine. There was an air of tenseness about the little group he didn't like, though tension might be understandable enough under the circumstances.

"Yes," Dr. Egavine said. "They feel entirely willing to assist us, of course." He smiled significantly.

"Fine." Dasinger nodded. "Line them up and let's get going! Taunus first. Get ..."

There was a momentary stirring of the air back of his head. He turned sharply, jerking up the gun, felt twin needles drive into either side of his neck.

His body instantly went insensate. The lock appeared to circle about him, then he was on his back and Graylock's pet was alighting with a flutter of wings on his chest. It craned its head forward to peer into his face, the tip of its mouth tube open, showing a ring of tiny teeth. Vision and awareness left Dasinger together.

The other men hadn't moved. Now Dr. Egavine, his face a little pale, came over to Dasinger, the birdlike creature bounding back to the edge of the lock as he approached. Egavine knelt down, said quietly, his mouth near the wrist communicator, "Duomart Mines, you will obey me."

There was silence for a second or two. Then the communicator whispered, "Yes."

Dr. Egavine drew in a long, slow breath.

"You feel no question, no concern, no doubt about this situation," he went on. "You will bring the ship down now and land it safely beside the Antares. Then come up into the lock of the Antares for further instructions." Egavine stood up, his eyes bright with triumph.

$$* \quad * \quad * \quad * \quad *$$

In the Mooncat three miles overhead, Duomart switched off her wrist communicator, sat white-faced, staring at the image of the Antares in the ground-view plate.

"Sweet Jana!" she whispered. "How did he ... now what do I ..."

She hesitated an instant, then opened a console drawer, took out the kwil needle Dasinger had left with her and slipped it into a pocket, clipped the holstered shocker back to her belt, and reached for the controls. A vast whistling shriek smote the Antares and the ears of those within as the Mooncat ripped down through atmosphere at an unatmospheric speed, leveled out smoothly and floated to the ground beside the wreck.

There was no one in sight in the lock of the Antares as Duomart came out and sealed the Mooncat's entry behind her. She went quickly up the broad, mold-covered ramp. The lock remained empty. From beyond it came the sound of some metallic object being pulled about, a murmur of voices. Twelve steps from the top, she took out the little gun, ran up to the lock and into it, bringing the gun up. She had a glimpse of Dr. Egavine and Quist standing near a rusty bench in the compartment, of Graylock half into a salvage suit, Dasinger on the floor ... then a flick of motion to right and left.

The tips of two space lines lashed about her simultaneously, one pinning her arms to her sides, the other clamping about her ankles and twitching her legs out from beneath her. She fired twice blindly to the left as the lines snapped her face down to the floor of the compartment. The gun was clamped beneath her stretched-out body and useless.

*   *   *   *   *

"What made that animal attack me anyway?" Dasinger asked wearily. He had just regained consciousness and been ordered by Calat to join the others on a rusted metal bench in the center of the lock compartment; Duomart to his left, Egavine on his right, Quist on the other side of Egavine. Calat stood watching them fifteen feet away, holding Dasinger's gun in one hand while he jiggled a few of Hovig's star hyacinths gently about in the other.

Calat's expression was cheerful, which made him the exception here. Liu Taunus and Graylock were down in the hold of the ship, working sturdily with cutter beams and power hoists to get to the sealed vault and blow it open. How long they'd been at it, Dasinger didn't know.

"You can thank your double-crossing partner for what happened!" Duomart informed him. She looked pretty thoroughly mussed up though still unsubdued. "Graylock's been using the bird-thing to hunt with," she said. "It's a bloodsucker ... nicks some animal with its claws and the animal stays knocked out while the little beast fills its tummy. So the intellectual over there had Graylock point you out to his pet, and it waited until your back was turned...." She hesitated, went on less vehemently, "Sorry about not carrying out orders, Dasinger. I assumed Egavine really was in control here, and I could have handled *him*. I walked into a trap." She fished the shards of a smashed kwil needle out of her pocket, looked at them, and dropped them on the floor before her. "I got slammed around a little," she explained.

Calat laughed, said something in the Fleet tongue, grinning at her. She ignored him.

Egavine said, "My effects were secretly inspected while we were at the Fleet station, Dasinger, and the Fleetmen have been taking drugs to immunize themselves against my hypnotic agents. They disclosed this when Miss Mines brought the speedboat down. There was nothing I could do. I regret to say that they intend to murder us. They are waiting only to assure themselves that the star hyacinths actually are in the indicated compartment."

"Great!" Dasinger groaned. He put his hands back in a groping gesture to support himself on the bench.

"Still pretty feeble, I suppose?" Miss Mines inquired, gentle sympathy in her voice.

"I'm poisoned," he muttered brokenly. "The thing's left me paralyzed...." He sagged sideways a little, his hand moving behind Duomart. He pinched her then in a markedly unparalyzed and vigorous manner.

Duomart's right eyelid flickered for an instant.

*   *   *   *   *

"Somebody wrung the little monster's neck before I got here," she remarked. "But there're other necks *I'd* sooner wring! Your partner's, for instance. Not that he's necessarily the biggest louse around at the moment." She nodded at Calat. "The two runches who call themselves Fleetmen don't intend to share the star hyacinths even with their own gang! They're rushing the job through so they can be on their way to the Hub before the Spy arrives. And don't think Liu Taunus trusts that muscle-bound foogal standing there, either! He's hanging on to the key of the Mooncat's console until he comes back up."

Calat smiled with a suggestion of strain, then said something in a flat, expressionless voice, staring at her.

"Oh, sure," she returned. "With Taunus holding me, I suppose?" She looked at Dasinger. "They're not shooting *me* right off, you know," she told him. "They're annoyed with me, so they're taking me along for something a little more special. But they'll have to skip the fun if the Spy shows up, or I'll be telling twenty armed Fleetmen exactly what kind of thieving cheats they have leading them!" She looked back at Calat, smiled, placed the tip of her tongue lightly between her lips for an instant, then pronounced a few dozen Fleet words in a clear, precise voice.

It must have been an extraordinarily unflattering comment. Calat went white, then red. Half-smart tough had been Duomart's earlier description of him. It began to look like an accurate one ... Dasinger felt a surge of pleased anticipation. His legs already were drawn well back beneath the bench; he shifted his weight slowly forwards now, keeping an expression of anxious concern on his face. Calat spoke in Fleetlingue again, voice thickening with rage.

Miss Mines replied sweetly, stood up. The challenge direct.

The Fleetman's face worked in incredulous fury. He shifted the gun to his left hand and came striding purposefully towards Miss Mines, right fist cocked. Then, as Dasinger tensed his legs happily, a muffled thump from deep within the wreck announced the opening of the star hyacinth vault.

The sound was followed by instant proof that Hovig had trapped the vault.

Duomart and Calat screamed together. Dasinger drove himself forward off the bench, aiming for the Fleetman's legs, checked and turned for the gun which Calat, staggering and shrieking, his face distorted with lunatic terror, had flung aside. Dr. Egavine, alert for this contingency, already was stooping for the gun, hand outstretched, when Dasinger lunged against him, bowling him over.

* * * * *

Dasinger came up with the gun, Quist pounding at his shoulders, flung the little man aside, turned back in a frenzy of urgency. Duomart twisted about on the floor near the far end of the compartment, arms covering her face. The noises that bubbled out from behind her arms set Dasinger's teeth on edge. She rolled over convulsively twice, stopped dangerously close to the edge of the jagged break in the deck, was turning again as Dasinger dropped beside her and caught her.

Immediately there was a heavy, painful blow on his shoulder. He glanced up, saw Quist running toward him, a rusted chunk of metal like the one he had thrown in his raised hand, and Egavine peering at both of them from the other side of the compartment. Dasinger flung a leg across Duomart, pinning her down, pulled out the gun, fired without aiming. Quist reversed his direction almost in mid-stride. Dasinger fired again, saw Egavine dart towards the lock, hesitate there an instant, then disappear down the ramp, Quist sprinting out frantically after him.

A moment later he drove one of the remaining kwil needles through the cloth of Duomart's uniform, and rammed the plunger down.

The drug hit hard and promptly. Between one instant and the next, the plunging and screaming ended; she drew in a long, shuddering breath, went limp, her eyes closing slowly. Dasinger was lifting her from the floor when the complete silence in the compartment caught his attention. He looked around. Calat was not in sight. And only then did he become aware of a familiar sensation ... a Hovig generator's pulsing, savage storm of seeming nothingness, nullified by the drug in his blood.

He laid the unconscious girl on the bench, went on to the lock.

Dr. Egavine and Quist had vanished; the thick shrubbery along the lake bank stirred uneasily at twenty different points but he wasn't looking for the pair. With the Mooncat inaccessible to them, there was only one place they could go. Calat's body lay doubled up in the rocks below the ramp, almost sixty feet down, where other human bodies had lain six years earlier. Dasinger glanced over at the Fleet scout, went back into the compartment.

He was buckling himself into the third salvage suit when he heard the scout's lifeboat take off. At a guess Hovig's little private collection of star hyacinths was taking off with it. Dasinger decided he couldn't care less.

He snapped on the headpiece, then hesitated at the edge of the deck, looking down. A bubble of foggy white light was rising slowly through the water of the hold, and in a moment the headpiece of one of the other suits broke the oily surface, stayed there, bobbing gently about. Dasinger climbed down, brought Liu Taunus's body back up to the lock compartment, and recovered the Mooncat's master key.

He found Graylock floating in his suit against a bulkhead not far from the shattered vault where Hovig's two remaining generators thundered.

Dasinger silenced the machines, fastened them and a small steel case containing nearly a hundred million credits' worth of star hyacinths to the salvage carrier, and towed it all up to the lock compartment.

A very few minutes later, the Mooncat lifted in somewhat jerky, erratic fashion from the planet's surface. As Dasinger had suspected, he lacked, and by a good deal, Miss Mines's trained sensitivity with the speedboat's controls; but he succeeded in wrestling the little ship up to a five-mile altitude where a subspace dive might be carried out in relative safety.

He was attempting then to get the Mooncat's nose turned away from the distant volcano ranges towards which she seemed determined to point when the detector needles slapped flat against their pins and the alarm bell sounded. A strange ship stood outlined in the Mooncat's stern screen.

*   *   *   *   *

The image vanished as Dasinger hit the dive button, simultaneously flattening the speed controls with a slam of his hand. The semisolid subspace turbulence representing the mountain ranges beyond the lake flashed instantly past below him ... within yards, it seemed. Another second put them beyond the planet's atmosphere. Then the Spy reappeared in subspace, following hard. A hammering series of explosions showed suddenly in the screens, kept up for a few hair-raising moments, began to drop back. Five minutes later, with the distance between them widening rapidly, the Spy gave up the chase, swung around and headed back towards the planet.

Dasinger shakily reduced his ship's speed to relatively sane level, kept her moving along another twenty minutes, then surfaced into normspace and set a general course for the Hub. He was a very fair yachtsman for a planeteer. But after riding the Mooncat for the short time he'd turned her loose to keep ahead of the Spy through the G2's stress zone, he didn't have to be told that in Fleet territory he was outclassed. He mopped his forehead, climbed gratefully out of the pilot seat and went to the cot he had hauled into the control room, to check on Duomart Mines.

She was still unconscious, of course; the dose he'd given her was enough to knock a kwil-sensitive out for at least a dozen hours. Dasinger looked down at the filth-smudged, pale face, the bruised cheeks and blackened left eye for a few seconds, then opened Dr. Egavine's medical kit to do what he could about getting Miss Mines patched up again.

Fifteen hours later she was still asleep, though to all outer appearances back in good repair. Dasinger happened to be bemusedly studying her face once more when she opened her eyes and gazed up at him.

"We made it! You ..." She smiled, tried to sit up, looked startled, then indignant. "What's the idea of tying me down to this thing?"

Dasinger nodded. "I guess you're all there!" He reached down to unfasten her from the cot. "After what happened, I wasn't so sure you'd be entirely rational when the kwil wore off and you woke up."

Duomart paled a little. "I hadn't imagined ..." She shook her blond head. "Well, let's skip that! I'll have nightmares for years.... What happened to the others?"

$$*\quad*\quad*\quad*\quad*$$

Dasinger told her, concluded, "Egavine may have run into the Spy, but I doubt it. He'll probably show up in the Hub eventually with the gems he took from Calat, and if he doesn't get caught peddling them he may wind up with around a million credits ... about the sixth part of what he would have collected if he'd stopped playing crooked and trying to get everything. I doubt the doctor will ever quit kicking himself for that!"

"Your agency gets the whole salvage fee now, eh?"

"Not exactly," Dasinger said. "Considering everything that's happened, the Kyth Interstellar Detective Agency would have to be extremely ungrateful if it didn't feel you'd earned the same split we were going to give Dr. Egavine."

Miss Mines gazed at him in startled silence, flushed excitedly. "Think you can talk the Kyth people into *that*, Dasinger?"

"I imagine so," Dasinger said, "since I own the agency. That should finance your Willata Fleet operation very comfortably and still leave a couple of million credits over for your old age. I doubt we'll clear anything on Hovig's generators...."

Miss Mines looked uncomfortable. "Do you have those things aboard?"

"At the moment. Disassembled of course. Primarily I didn't want the Fleet gang to get their hands on them. We might lose them in space somewhere or take them back to the Federation for the scientists to poke over. We'll discuss that on the way. Now, do you feel perky enough to want a look at the stuff that's cost around a hundred and fifty lives before it ever hit the Hub's markets?"

"Couldn't feel perkier!" She straightened up expectantly. "Let's see them...."

Dasinger turned away towards the wall where he had put down the little steel case with the loot of the Dosey Asteroids robbery.

Behind him, Duomart screamed.

He spun back to her, his face white. "What's the matter?"

Duomart was staring wide-eyed past him towards the instrument console, the back of one hand to her mouth. "That ... the thing!"

"Thing?"

"Big ... yellow ... wet ... *ugh*! It's ducked behind the console, Dasinger! It's lurking there!"

"Oh!" Dasinger said, relaxing. He smiled. "That's all right. Don't worry about it."

"Don't worry about ... are you crazy?"

"Not in the least. I thought you were for a second, but it's very simple. You've worked off the kwil and now you're in the hangover period. You get hallucinations then, just as I usually do. For the next eight or nine hours, you'll be seeing odd things around from time to time. So what? They're not real."

*   *   *   *   *

"All right, they're not real, but they seem real enough while they're around," Duomart said. "I don't want to see them." She caught her breath and her hand flew up to her mouth again. "Dasinger, please, don't you have something that will put me back to sleep till I'm past the hangover too?"

Dasinger reflected. "One of Doc Egavine's hypno sprays will do it. I know enough of the mumbo jumbo to send you to dreamland for another ten hours." He smiled evilly. "Of course, you realize that means you're putting yourself completely in my power."

Duomart's eyes narrowed for an instant. She considered him, grinned.

"I'll risk it," she said.

Oneness

Originally Published In *Analog Science Fact & Fiction*, May 1963

*At that, you know the power to enforce the
Golden Rule would make a terrible weapon!*

ONENESS

Menesee felt excitement surge like a living tide about
him as he came with the other directors into the vast
Tribunal Hall. Sixty years ago, inexcusable carelessness
had deprived Earth of its first chance to obtain a true
interstellar drive. Now, within a few hours, Earth, or
more specifically, the upper echelons of that great
political organization called the Machine which had
controlled the affairs of Earth for the past century and a
half, should learn enough of the secrets of the drive to
insure that it would soon be in their possession.

Menesee entered his box between those of Directors
Cornelius and Ojeda, immediately to the right of the
Spokesman's Platform and with an excellent view of the
prisoner. When Administrator Bradshaw and Spokesman
Dorn had taken their places on the platform, Menesee
seated himself, drawing the transcript of the day's
proceedings towards him. However, instead of glancing
over it at once, he spent some seconds in a study of the
prisoner.

The fellow appeared to be still young. He was a
magnificent physical specimen, tall and strongly muscled,
easily surpassing in this respect any of the hard-trained
directors present. His face showed alert intelligence,
giving no indication of the fact that for two of the three
days since his capture he had been drugged and subject to
constant hypnotic suggestion. He had given his name as
Rainbolt, acknowledged freely that he was a member of
the group of malcontent deserters known in the records of
the Machine as the Mars Convicts, but described himself
as being a "missionary of Oneness" whose purpose was to

bring the benefits of some of the principles of "Oneness" to Earth. He had refused to state whether he had any understanding of the stardrive by the use of which the Mars Convicts had made their mass escape from the penal settlements of the Fourth Planet sixty years before, though the drive obviously had been employed in bringing him out of the depths of interstellar space to the Solar System and Earth. At the moment, while the significance of the bank of torture instruments on his right could hardly have escaped him, his expression was serious but not detectably concerned.

"Here is an interesting point!" Director Ojeda's voice said on Menesee's right.

Menesee glanced over at him. Ojeda was tapping the transcript with a finger.

"This Rainbolt," he said, "hasn't slept since he was captured! He states, furthermore, that he has never slept since he became an adult—"

Menesee frowned slightly, failing to see any great significance in the fact. That the fellow belonged to some curious cult which had developed among the Mars Convicts following their flight from the Solar System was already known. Earth's science had methods of inducing permanent sleeplessness but knew, too, that in most instances the condition eventually gave rise to very serious side effects which more than offset any advantages to be gained from it.

He picked up his transcript, indicating that he did not wish to be drawn into conversation. His eyes scanned quickly over the pages. Most of it was information he already had. Rainbolt's ship had been detected four days earlier, probing the outermost of the multiple globes of force screens which had enclosed Earth for fifty years as a defense both against faster-than-light missiles and Mars Convict spies. The ship was alone. A procedure had been planned for such an event, and it was now followed. The ship was permitted to penetrate the first two screens which were closed again behind it.

Rainbolt's ship, for all its incredible speed, was then a prisoner. Unhurriedly, it was worked closer to Earth until it came within range of giant scanners. For an instant, a large section of its interior was visible to the instruments of the watchers on Earth; then the picture blurred and vanished again. Presumably automatic anti-scanning devices had gone into action.

The photographed view was disappointing in that it revealed no details of the engines or their instruments. It did show, however, that the ship had been designed for the use of one man, and that it was neither armored or armed. Its hull was therefore bathed with paralytics, which in theory should have left the pilot helpless, and ships of the Machine were then sent up to tow the interstellar captive down to Earth.

At that point, the procedure collapsed. The ship was in atmosphere when an escape capsule was suddenly ejected from it, which later was found to contain Rainbolt, alert and obviously not affected by the paralysis beams. A moment later, the ship itself became a cloud of swiftly dissipating hot gas.

The partial failure of the capture might have been unavoidable in any case. But the manner in which it occurred still reflected very poorly, Menesee thought, on the thoroughness with which the plans had been prepared. The directors who had been in charge of the operation would not be dealt with lightly—

He became aware suddenly that the proceedings of the day had begun and hastily put down the transcript.

*   *   *   *   *

Spokesman Dorn, the Machine's executive officer, sitting beside Administrator Bradshaw at a transparent desk on the raised platform to Menesee's left, had enclosed the area about the prisoner with a sound block and was giving a brief verbal resume of the background of the situation. Few of the directors in the Tribunal Hall would have needed such information; but the matter was being carried on the Grand Assembly Circuit, and in hundreds of auditoriums on Earth the first and second echelons of the officials of the Machine had gathered to witness the interrogation of the Mars Convict spy.

The penal settlements on Mars had been established almost a century earlier, for the dual purpose of mining the mineral riches of the Fourth Planet and of utilizing the talents of political dissidents with a scientific background too valuable to be wasted in research and experimental work considered either too dangerous to be conducted on Earth or requiring more space than could easily be made available there. One of these projects had been precisely the development of more efficient spacedrives to do away with the costly and tedious manoeuverings required for travel even among the inner planets.

Work of such importance, of course, was supposed to be carried out only under close guard and under the direct supervision of reliable upper-echelon scientists of the Machine. Even allowing for criminal negligence, the fact that the Mars Convicts were able to develop and test their stardrive under such circumstances without being detected suggested that it could not be a complicated device. They did, at any rate, develop it, armed themselves and the miners of the other penal settlements and overwhelmed their guards in surprise attack. When the next ship arrived from Earth, two giant ore carriers and a number of smaller guard ships had been outfitted with the drive, and the Mars Convicts had disappeared in them. Their speed was such that only the faintest and briefest of disturbances had been registered on the tracking screens of space stations near Mars, the cause of which remained unsuspected until the news came out.

Anything which could have thrown any light on the nature of the drive naturally had been destroyed by the deserters before they left; and the few Machine scientists who had survived the fighting were unable to provide information though they were questioned intensively for several years before being executed. What it added up to was that some eighteen thousand sworn enemies of the Machine had disappeared into space, equipped with an instrument of unknown type which plainly could be turned into one of the deadliest of all known weapons.

The superb organization of the Machine swung into action instantly to meet the threat, though the situation became complicated by the fact that rumors of the manner in which the Mars Convicts had disappeared filtered out to the politically dissatisfied on Earth and set off an unprecedented series of local uprisings which took over a decade to quell. In spite of such difficulties, the planet's economy was geared over to the new task; and presently defenses were devised and being constructed which would stop missiles arriving at speeds greater than that of light. Simultaneously, the greatest research project in history had begun to investigate the possibilities of either duplicating the fantastic drive some scientific minds on Mars had come upon–chiefly, it was concluded, by an improbable stroke of good luck–or of matching its effects through a different approach. Since it had been demonstrated that it could be done, there was no question that in time the trained men of the Machine would achieve their goal. Then the armed might of the Machine would move into space to take control of any colony established by the Mars Convicts and their descendants.

That was the basic plan. The task of developing a stardrive remained a huge one because of the complete lack of information about the direction organized research should take. That difficulty would be overcome easily only by a second unpredictable twist of fortune–unless one of the Mars Convicts' FTL ships ventured close enough to Earth to be captured.

The last had now happened. The ship had been destroyed before it could be investigated, so that advantage was again lost. The ship's pilot, however, remained in their hands. The fact that he disclaimed having information pertinent to the drive meant nothing. So far as he knew, he might very well be speaking the truth. But he had piloted a ship that employed the stardrive, was familiar with instruments which controlled it, had been schooled in their use. A detailed investigation of his memories could not fail to provide literally hundreds of meaningful clues. And the Machine's scientists, in their superficially still fruitless search for the nature of the drive, had, in fact, covered basic possibilities with such comprehensive thoroughness that a few indisputably valid clues would show them now what it *must* be.

*   *   *   *   *

The prisoner, still demonstrating an extraordinary degree of obliviousness to what lay in store for him, appeared to welcome the opportunity to be heard by the directors of the Machine. Menesee, leaning back in his chair, studied the man thoughtfully, giving only partial attention to what was said. This was the standard opening stage of a Tribunal interrogation, an underplayed exchange of questions and answers. Innocuous as it seemed, it was part of a procedure which had become refined almost to an unvarying ritual–a ritual of beautiful and terrible precision which never failed to achieve its goals. Every man watching and listening in the Machine's auditoriums across the world was familiar with the swift processes by which a normal human being was transformed into a babbling puppet, his every significant thought becoming available for the upper echelons to regard and evaluate.

They would, of course, use torture. It was part of the interlocking mechanisms of interrogation, no more to be omitted than the preliminary conditioning by drug and hypnosis. Menesee was not unduly squeamish, but he felt some relief that it would not be the crude instruments ranked beside the prisoner which would be used. They were reserved as a rule for offending members of the organization, providing a salutary warning for any others who might be tempted to act against the interests of the Machine or fail culpably in their duties. This prisoner, as an individual, meant nothing to the Machine. He was simply a source of valuable information. Therefore, only direct nerve stimulation would be employed, in the manipulation of which Spokesman Dorn was a master.

So far the Spokesman had restricted himself to asking the prisoner questions, his voice and manner gravely courteous. To Menesee's surprised interest, he had just inquired whether two men of the last Earth ship to visit Mars, who had disappeared there, might not have been captured by Mars Convicts operating secretly within the Solar System.

"Yes, sir," Rainbolt replied readily, "they were. I'm happy to say that they're still alive and well."

Menesee recalled the incident now. After the mass escape of the Mars Convicts, the penal settlements had been closed down and the mining operations abandoned. To guard the desert planet against FTL raiders as Earth was guarded was technically infeasible. But twice each decade a patrol ship went there to look for signs that the Mars Convicts had returned. The last of these patrols had been conducted two years before. The missing men were believed to have been inspecting a deserted settlement in a ground vehicle when they vanished, but no trace of them or the vehicle could be discovered.

Administrator Bradshaw, seated to the spokesman's left, leaned forward as if to speak, but then sat back again. Menesee thought that Rainbolt's blunt admission had angered him. Bradshaw, white-haired and huge in build, had been for many years the nominal head of the Machine; but in practice the powers of the administrator were less than those of the spokesman, and it would have been a breach of protocol for Bradshaw to intervene in the interrogation.

Dorn appeared to have noticed nothing. He went on. "What was the reason for capturing these men?" "It was necessary," Rainbolt explained, "to find out what the conditions on Earth were like at present. At the time we didn't want to risk discovery by coming too close to Earth itself. And your two men were able to tell us all we needed to know."

"What was that?" the spokesman said.

Rainbolt was silent a moment, then said, "You see, sir, most of the past sixty years have been spent in finding new worlds on which human beings can live without encountering too many difficulties. But then–"

Dorn interrupted quietly, "You found such worlds?"

"Yes, sir, we did," Rainbolt said. "We're established, in about equal numbers, on planets of three star systems. Of course, I'm not allowed to give you more precise information on that at present."

"Quite understandable," the spokesman agreed dryly.

Menesee was conscious of a stir of intense interest among the listening directors in the hall. This was news, indeed! Mingled with the interest was surprised amusement at the prisoner's artless assumption that he had any choice about what he would or would not tell.

"But now that we're established," Rainbolt went on, apparently unaware of the sensation he had created, "our next immediate concern is to resume contact with Earth. Naturally, we can't do that freely while your Machine remains in political control of the planet. We found out from the two captured men that it still is in control. We'd hoped that after sixty years government in such a form would have become obsolete here."

*   *   *   *   *

Menesee heard an astonished murmuring from the director boxes on his right, and felt himself that the fellow's impudent last remark might well have been answered by a pulse of nerve stimulation. Spokesman

Dorn, however, replied calmly that the Machine happened to be indispensable to Earth. A planetary economy, and one on the verge of becoming an interplanetary and even interstellar economy, was simply too intricate and precariously balanced a structure to maintain without the assistance of a very tightly organized governing class.

"If the Machine were to vanish today," he explained, "Earth would approach a state of complete chaos before the month was out. In a year, a billion human beings would be starving to death. There would be fighting ... wars–" He shrugged, "You name it. No, my friend, the Machine is here to stay. And the Mars Convicts may as well resign themselves to the fact."

Rainbolt replied earnestly that he was not too well informed in economics, that not being his field. However, he had been told and believed that while the situation described by the spokesman would be true today, it should not take many years to train the populations of Earth to run their affairs quite as efficiently as the Machine had done, and without loss of personal and political liberties.

At any rate, the Mars Convicts and their descendants did not intend to give up the independence they had acquired. On the other hand, they had two vital reasons for wanting to come to an agreement with Earth. One was that they might waste centuries in attempting to accomplish by themselves what they could now do immediately if Earth's vast resources were made available to them. And the other, of course, was the obvious fact that Earth would not remain indefinitely without a stardrive of its own. If an unfriendly government was in control when it obtained one, the Mars Convicts would be forced either to abandon their newly settled planets and retreat farther into the galaxy or submit to Earth's superior strength.

Meanwhile, however, they had developed the principles of Oneness.

Oneness was in essence a philosophy, but it had many practical applications; and it was in such practical applications that he, Rainbolt, was a trained specialist. He had, therefore, been dispatched to Earth to introduce the principles, which would in time bring about the orderly disintegration of the system of the Machine, to be followed by the establishment of an Earth government with which the Mars Convicts could deal without detriment to themselves.

Menesee had listened with a sense of growing angry incredulity. The fellow couldn't be as much of a fool as he seemed! Therefore, he had devised this hoax after he realised he would be captured, to cover up his real purpose which could only be that of a spy. Menesee saw that Administrator Bradshaw was saying something in a low voice to the spokesman, his face stony. Dorn glanced over at him, then looked back at the prisoner and said impassively, "So the goal of your missionary work here is the disintegration of the Machine?"

Rainbolt nodded, with an air almost of eagerness. "Yes, sir, it is! And if I will now be permitted to—"

"I am afraid you will be permitted to do nothing," Spokesman Dorn said dryly, "except, of course, to answer the number of questions we intend to ask you."

Rainbolt checked himself, looking startled. The spokesman's hand had moved very slightly on the desk before him and Rainbolt had just had his first experience with direct nerve stimulation. He stood kneading his right hand with his left, staring up at the spokesman, mouth half open.

Menesee smiled in grim amusement. It would have been a low-level pulse, of course; but even a low-level pulse, arriving unexpectedly, was a very unpleasant surprise. He had foreseen the spokesman's action, had, in fact, felt a sympathetic imaginary twinge in his own right hand as the pulse reached the prisoner.

Rainbolt swallowed, said in a changed voice, "Sir, we heard from the two captured men that the Machine has retained its practice of torture during interrogations. It isn't necessary to convince me that you are serious about this. Do the questions you referred to have to do with the stardrive?"

The spokesman nodded. "Of course."

Rainbolt said stubbornly, "Then, sir, it can do you no good at all to torture me. I simply don't have such information. We do plan to make the stardrive freely available to Earth. But not while Earth is ruled by the organization of the Machine."

This time, Menesee did not observe the motion of the spokesman's hand. Instead he saw Rainbolt jerk violently to the right. At the same moment, a blast of intense, fiery, almost unbearable pain shot up his own arm. As he grasped his arm, sweat spurting out on his face, he heard screams from the box on his left and realized it was Director Cornelius who screamed.

There were answering screams from around the hall.

Then the pain suddenly subsided.

*   *   *   *   *

Menesee started about, breathing raggedly. The pain-reaction had been severe enough to affect his vision; the great hall looked momentarily darker than it should have been. And although the actual pain had ended, the muscles of his arm and shoulder were still trying to cramp into knots.

There was no more screaming. From the right came Director Ojeda's gasping voice. "What happened? Did something go wrong with the stimulating devices? We might all have been killed—!"

Menesee didn't reply. Wherever he looked, he saw faces whitened with shock. Apparently everyone in the Tribunal Hall, from the administrator and Spokesman Dorn on down to the directors' attendants and the two guards flanking the prisoner's area, had felt the same thing. Here and there, men who had collapsed were struggling awkwardly back to their feet. He heard a hoarse whisper behind him. "Sir, Director Cornelius appears to have fainted!"

Menesee glanced around, saw Cornelius' attendant behind the box, then Cornelius himself, slumped forward, face down and motionless, sprawling half across his table. "Let him lie there and keep quiet, fool!" Menesee ordered the man sharply. He returned his attention to the center of the hall as Spokesman Dorn announced in a voice which held more of an edge than was normal but had lost none of its strength and steadiness, "Before any moves are suggested, I shall tell you what has been done.

"The Tribunal Hall has been sealed and further events in it will be monitored from without. No one will be able to leave until the matter with which we are now concerned here has been settled to the satisfaction of the Machine.

"Next, any of you who believe that an instrument failure was involved in the experience we shared can disabuse themselves. The same effect was reported immediately from two other auditoriums on the Great Circuit, and it is quite possible that it was repeated in all of them."

Rainbolt, grimacing and massaging his right arm vigorously, nodded. "It was repeated in all of them, sir!"

The spokesman ignored him, went on. "The Tribunal Hall has, therefore, been cut out of the Grand Assembly Circuit. How circuit energies could have been employed to transmit such physical sensations is not clear. But they will not be used in that manner again."

Menesee felt a flash of admiration. His own thoughts had been turning in the same direction, but he couldn't have approached Spokesman Dorn's decisive speed of action.

Dorn turned his attention now to Rainbolt. "What happened," he said, "apparently was caused by yourself."

Rainbolt nodded. "Yes, sir. It was. It was an application of Oneness. At present, I'm acting as a focal point of Oneness. Until that condition is changed, whatever I experience here will be simultaneously experienced by yourselves."

Menesee thought that the effects of the Machine's discipline became splendidly apparent at that point. No one stirred in the great hall though it must have been obvious to every man present that Rainbolt's words might have doomed them along with himself.

Rainbolt went on, addressing Spokesman Dorn.

"There is only one mistake in your reasoning, sir. The demonstrated effect of Oneness is not carried by the energies of the Grand Assembly Circuit, though I made use of those energies in establishing an initial connection with the other auditoriums and the people in them.

"You see, sir, we learned from the two men captured on Mars about your practice of having the two highest echelons of your organization attend significant hearings in the Tribunal Hall through the Assembly Circuit. Our plan was based on that. We knew that if anything was to be accomplished with the Oneness principles on Earth, it would have to be through a situation in which they could be applied simultaneously to the entire leadership of the Machine. That has now been done, and the fact that you had the Tribunal Hall taken out of the Assembly Circuit did not change the Oneness contact. It remains in full effect."

Spokesman Dorn stared at him for an instant, said, "We can test the truth of that statement immediately, of course; and we shall!" His hand moved on the desk.

*　　*　　*　　*　　*

Menesee felt pain surge through his left arm. It was not nearly as acute a sensation as the previous pulse had been, but it lasted longer—a good ten seconds. Menesee let his breath out carefully as it again ebbed away.

He heard the spokesman saying, "Rainbolt's claim appears to be verified. I've received a report that the pulse was being experienced in one of the auditoriums ... and, yes ... now in several."

Rainbolt nodded. "It was a valid claim, believe me, sir!" he said earnestly. "The applications of our principles have been very thoroughly explored, and the effects are invariable. Naturally, our strategem would have been useless if I'd been able to maintain contact only long enough to provide you with a demonstration of Oneness. Such a contact can be broken again, of course. But until I act deliberately to break it, it maintains itself automatically.

"To make that clear, I should explain that distance, direction and intervening shielding materials do not change the strength of the contact. Distance at least does not until it is extended to approximately fifty thousand miles."

"And what happens then?" the spokesman asked, watching him.

"At that point," Rainbolt acknowledged, "Oneness contacts do become tenuous and begin to dissolve." He added, almost apologetically, "However, that offers you no practical solution to your problem."

"Why not?" Dorn asked. He smiled faintly. "Why shouldn't we simply lock you into a spaceship and direct the ship through the defense fields and out into the solar system on automatic control?"

"I sincerely hope you don't try it, sir! Experiments in dissolving contacts in that manner have been invariably fatal to all connected individuals."

The spokesman hesitated. "You and every member of the Machine with whom you are now in contact would die together if that were done?"

"Yes, sir. That is certain what the results of those experiments show."

Administrator Bradshaw, who had been staring coldly at Rainbolt, asked in a hard, flat voice, "If you do nothing to break the contact, how long will this situation continue?"

Rainbolt looked at him. "Indefinitely, sir," he said. "There is nothing I need to do about it. It is a static condition."

"In that case," Bradshaw said icily, "*this* should serve to break the contact through you!"

As his hand came up, leveling a gun, Menesee was half out of his chair, hands raised in alarmed protest. "Stop him!" Menesee shouted.

But Administrator Bradshaw already was sagging sideways over the armrest of this chair, head lolling backwards. The gun slid from his hand, dropped to the platform.

"Director Menesee," Dorn said coolly from beside Bradshaw, "I thank you for your intended warning! Since the administrator and the spokesman are the only persons permitted to bear arms in the Tribunal Hall, I was naturally prepared to paralyze Administrator Bradshaw if he showed intentions of resorting to thoughtless action." He looked down at Rainbolt. "Are Director Menesee and I correct in assuming that if you died violently the persons with whom you are in contact would again suffer the same experience?"

"Yes, sir," Rainbolt said. "That is implicit in the principles of Oneness." He shrugged. "Under most circumstances, it is a very undesirable effect. But here we have made use of it—"

*   *   *   *   *

"The situation," Spokesman Dorn told the directors in the Tribunal Hall some minutes later, "is then this. There has been nothing haphazard about the Mars Convicts' plan to coerce us into accepting their terms. Considering the probable quality of the type of minds which developed both the stardrive and the extraordinary 'philosophy' we have encountered today, that could be taken for granted from the start. We cannot kill their emissary here, or subject him to serious pain or injury, since we would pay a completely disproportionate penalty in doing it.

"However, that doesn't mean that we should surrender to the Mars Convicts. In fact, for all their cleverness, they appear to be acting out of something very close to desperation. They have gained no essential advantage through their trick, and we must assume they made the mistake of underestimating us. This gentleman they sent to Earth has been given thorough physical examinations. They show him to be in excellent health. He is also younger by many years than most of us.

"So he will be confined to quarters where he will be comfortable and provided with whatever he wishes ... but where he will not be provided with any way of doing harm to himself. And then, I believe, we can simply forget about him. He will receive the best of attention, including medical care. Under such circumstances, we can expect his natural life span to exceed our own.

"Meanwhile, we shall continue our program of developing our own spacedrive. As the Mars Convicts themselves foresee, we'll gain it eventually and will then be more than a match for them. Until then the defense fields around Earth will remain closed. No ship will leave Earth and no ship will be admitted to it. And in the long run we will win."

The spokesman paused, added, "If there are no other suggestions, this man will now be conducted to the hospital of the Machine where he is to be detained for the remainder of his days."

Across the hall from Menesee, a figure arose deliberately in one of the boxes. A heavy voice said, "Spokesman Dorn, I very definitely do have a suggestion."

Dorn looked over, nodded warily. "Go ahead, Director Squires!"

Menesee grimaced in distaste. He had no liking for Squires, a harsh, arrogant man, notorious for his relentless persecution of any director or officer who, in Squires' opinion, had become slack in his duties to the

Machine. But he had a large following in the upper echelons, and his words carried weight.

Squires folded his arms, said unhurriedly as if savoring each word, "As you pointed out, Spokesman Dorn, we cannot hurt the person of this prisoner. His immediate accomplices also remain beyond our reach at present. However, our hands are not–as you seem to imply–so completely tied that we cannot strike back at these rascals at once. There are camps on Earth filled with people of the same political stripe–potential supporters of the Mars Convicts who would be in fullest sympathy with their goals if they learned of them.

"I suggest that these people serve now as an object lesson to show the Mars Convicts the full measure of our determination to submit to no threats of force! Let this prisoner and the other convicts who doubtless are lurking in nearby space beyond Earth's defense fields know that *for every day* their obscene threat against the high officers of the Machine continues hundreds of malcontents who would welcome them on Earth will be painfully executed! Let them–"

Pain doubled Menesee abruptly over the table before him. A savage, compressing pain, very different from the fiery touch of the nerve stimulators, which held him immobile, unable to cry out or draw breath.

It relaxed almost as instantaneously as it had come on. Menesee slumped back in his chair, shaken and choking, fighting down bitter nausea. His eyes refocused painfully on Rainbolt, gray-faced but on his feet, in the prisoner's area.

"You will find," Rainbolt was saying, "that Director Squires is dead. And so, I'm very much afraid, is every other member of the upper echelons whose heart was in no better condition than his. This was a demonstration I had not intended to give you. But since it has been given, it should serve as a reminder that while it is true we could not force you directly to do as we wish, there are things we are resolved not to tolerate."

Ojeda was whispering shakily near Menesee, "He controls his body to the extent that he was able to bring on a heart attack in himself and project it to all of us! He counted on his own superb physical condition to pull him through it unharmed. *That* is why he didn't seem frightened when the administrator threatened him with a gun. Even if the spokesman hadn't acted, that gun never would have been fired.

"Menesee, no precautions we could take will stop that monster from killing us all whenever he finally chooses— simply by committing suicide through an act of will!"

Spokesman Dorn's voice seemed to answer Ojeda.

"Director Squires," Dorn's voice said, still thinned by pain but oddly triumphant, "became a victim of his own pointless vindictiveness. It was a mistake which, I am certain, no member of the Machine will care to repeat.

"Otherwise, this incident has merely served to confirm that the Mars Convicts operate under definite limitations. They *could* kill us but can't afford to do it. If they are to thrive in space, they need Earth, and Earth's resources. They are aware that if the Machine's leadership dies, Earth will lapse into utter anarchy and turn its tremendous weapons upon itself.

"The Mars Convicts could gain nothing from a ruined and depopulated planet. Therefore, the situation as it stands remains a draw. We shall devote every effort to turn it into a victory for us. The agreement we come to eventually with the Mars Convicts will be on our terms— and there is essentially nothing they or this man, with all his powers, can do to prevent it."

*   *   *   *   *

The Missionary of Oneness swung his bronzed, well-muscled legs over the side of the hammock and sat up. With an expression of great interest, he watched Spokesman Dorn coming across the sun room towards him from the entrance corridor of his hospital suite. It was the first visit he'd had from any member of the organization of the Machine in the two years he had been confined here.

For Spokesman Dorn it had been, to judge by his appearance, a strenuous two years. He had lost weight and there were dark smudges of fatigue under his eyes. At the moment, however, his face appeared relaxed. It might have been the relaxation a man feels who has been emptied out by a hard stint of work, but knows he has accomplished everything that could possibly have been done.

Dorn came to a stop a dozen feet from the hammock. For some seconds, the two men regarded each other without speaking.

"On my way here," Dorn remarked then, "I was wondering whether you mightn't already know what I've come to tell you."

Rainbolt shook his head.

"No," he said. "I think I could guess what it is—I pick up generalized impressions from outside—but I don't really know."

Spokesman Dorn considered that a moment, chewing his lower lip reflectively. Then he shrugged.

"So actual mind-reading doesn't happen to be one of your talents," he said. "I was rather sure of that, though others had a different opinion. Of course, considering what you are able to do, it wouldn't really make much difference.

"Well ... this morning we sent out a general call by space radio to any Mars Convict ships which might be in the Solar System to come in. The call was answered. Earth's defense fields have been shut down, and the first FTL ships will land within an hour."

"For what purpose?" Rainbolt said curiously.

"There's a strong popular feeling," Spokesman Dorn said, "that your colleagues should take part in deciding what pattern Earth's permanent form of government will take. In recent months we've handled things in a rather provisional and haphazard manner, but the situation is straightened out well enough now to permit giving attention to such legalistic details. Incidentally, you will naturally be free to leave when I do. Transportation is available for you if you wish to welcome your friends at the spaceport."

"Thank you," said Rainbolt. "I believe I will."

Spokesman Dorn shrugged. "What could we do?" he said, almost disinterestedly. "You never slept. In the beginning you were drugged a number of times, as you probably know, but we soon discovered that drugging you seemed to make no difference at all."

"It doesn't," Rainbolt agreed.

"Day after day," Dorn went on, "we'd find thoughts and inclinations coming into our minds we'd never wanted there. It was an eerie experience–though personally I found it even more disconcerting to awaken in the morning and discover that my attitudes had changed in some particular or other, and as a rule changed irrevocably."

Rainbolt said, "In a sense, those weren't really your attitudes, you know. They were results of the conditioning of the Machine. It was the conditioning I was undermining."

"Perhaps it was that," Dorn said. "It seems to make very little difference now." He paused, frowned. "When the first talk of initiating change began in the councils, there were numerous executions. I know now that we were badly frightened men. Then those of us who had ordered the executions found themselves wanting similar changes. Presently we had a majority, and the changes began to be brought about. Reforms, you would call them–and reforms I suppose they actually were. There was considerable general disturbance, of course, but we retained the organization to keep that within reasonable bounds."

"We expected that you would," Rainbolt said.

"It hasn't really been too bad," Spokesman Dorn said reflectively. "It was simply an extraordinary amount of work to change the structure of things that had been imposed on Earth by the Machine for the past century and a half. And the curious part of it is, you know, that now it's done we don't even feel resentment! We actually wouldn't want to go back to what we had before. You've obtained an incredible hold on our minds—and frankly I expect that when at last you do relinquish your control, we'll commit suicide or go mad."

Rainbolt shook his head. "There's been just one mistake in what you've said," he remarked.

Spokesman Dorn looked at him with tired eyes. "What's that?" he asked.

"I said I was undermining the conditioning of the Machine. I did—and after that I did nothing. You people simply have been doing what most of you always would have preferred to do, Spokesman. I relinquished control of the last of you over six months ago."

THE WINDS OF TIME

ORIGINALLY PUBLISHED IN *ANALOG*, SEPTEMBER 1962

*He contracted for a charter trip–but the man
who hired his spacer wasn't quite a man, it
turned out–and he wanted more than service!*

THE WINDS OF TIME

Gefty Rammer came along the narrow passages
between the *Silver Queen's* control compartment and the
staterooms, trying to exchange the haggard look on his
face for one of competent self-assurance. There was
nothing to gain by letting his two passengers suspect that
during the past few minutes their pilot, the owner of
Rammer Spacelines, had been a bare step away from
plain and fancy gibbering.

He opened the door to Mr. Maulbow's stateroom and
went inside. Mr. Maulbow, face very pale, eyes closed, lay
on his back on the couch, still unconscious. He'd been
knocked out when some unknown forces suddenly started
batting the *Silver Queen's* turnip-shape around as the
Queen had never been batted before in her eighteen years
of spacefaring. Kerim Ruse, Maulbow's secretary, knelt
beside her employer, checking his pulse. She looked
anxiously up at Gefty.

"What did you find out?" she asked in a voice that was
not very steady.

Gefty shrugged. "Nothing definite as yet. The ship
hasn't been damaged–she's a tough tub. That's one good
point. Otherwise ... well, I climbed into a suit and took a
look out the escape hatch. And I saw the same thing there
that the screens show. Whatever that is."

"You've no idea then of what's happened to us, or
where we are?" Miss Ruse persisted. She was a rather
small girl with large, beautiful gray eyes and thick blue-
black hair. At the moment, she was barefoot and in a
sleeping outfit which consisted of something soft wrapped

around her top, soft and floppy trousers below. The black hair was tousled and she looked around fifteen. She'd been asleep in her stateroom when something smacked the *Queen*, and she was sensible enough then not to climb out of the bunk's safety field until the ship finally stopped shuddering and bucking about. That made her the only one of the three persons aboard who had collected no bruises. She was scared, of course, but taking the situation very well.

Gefty said carefully, "There're a number of possibilities. It's obvious that the *Queen* has been knocked out of normspace, and it may take some time to find out how to get her back there. But the main thing is that the ship's intact. So far, it doesn't look too bad."

Miss Ruse seemed somewhat reassured. Gefty could hardly have said the same for himself. He was a qualified normspace and subspace pilot. He had put in a hitch with the Federation Navy, and for the past eight years he'd been ferrying his own two ships about the Hub and not infrequently beyond the Federation's space territories, but he had never heard of a situation like this. What he saw in the viewscreens when the ship steadied enough to let him pick himself off the instrument room floor, and again, a few minutes later and with much more immediacy, from the escape hatch, made no sense— seemed simply to have no meaning. The pressure meters said there was a vacuum outside the *Queen's* skin. That vacuum was dark, even pitch-black but here and there came momentary suggestions of vague light and color. Occasional pinpricks of brightness showed and were gone. And there had been one startling phenomenon like a distant, giant explosion, a sudden pallid glare in the dark, which appeared far ahead of the *Queen* and, for the instant it remained in sight, seemed to be rushing directly towards them. It had given Gefty the feeling that the ship itself was plowing at high speed through this eerie medium. But he had cut the *Queen's* drives to the merest idling pulse as soon as he staggered back to the control console and got his first look at the screens, so it must have been the light that had moved.

But such details were best not discussed with a passenger. Kerim Ruse would be arriving at enough disquieting speculations on her own; the less he told her, the better. There was the matter of the ship's location instruments. The only set Gefty had been able to obtain any reading on were the direction indicators. And what they appeared to indicate was that the *Silver Queen* was turning on a new heading something like twenty times a second.

Gefty asked, "Has Mr. Maulbow shown any signs of waking up?"

Kerim shook her head. "His breathing and pulse seem all right, and that bump on his head doesn't look really bad, but he hasn't moved at all. Can you think of anything else we might do for him, Gefty?"

"Not at the moment," Gefty said. "He hasn't broken any bones. We'll see how he feels when he comes out of it." He was wondering about Mr. Maulbow and the fact that this charter had showed some unusual features from the beginning.

Kerim was a friendly sort of girl; they'd got to calling each other by their first names within a day or two after the trip started. But after that, she seemed to be avoiding him; and Gefty guessed that Maulbow had spoken to her, probably to make sure that Kerim didn't let any of her employer's secrets slip out.

Maulbow himself was as aloof and taciturn a client as Rammer Spacelines ever had picked up. A lean, blond character of indeterminate age, with pale eyes, hard mouth. Why he had selected a bulky semifreighter like the *Queen* for a mineralogical survey jaunt to a lifeless little sun system far beyond the outposts of civilization was a point he didn't discuss. Gefty, needing the charter money, had restrained his curiosity. If Maulbow wanted only a pilot and preferred to do all the rest of the work himself, that was certainly Maulbow's affair. And if he happened to be up to something illegal–though it was difficult to imagine what–Customs would nail him when they got back to the Hub.

But those facts looked a little different now.

*   *   *   *   *

Gefty scratched his chin, inquired, "Do you happen to know where Mr. Maulbow keeps the keys to the storage vault?"

Kerim looked startled. "Why, no! I couldn't permit you to take the keys anyway while he ... while he's unconscious! You know that."

Gefty grunted. "Any idea of what he has locked up in the vault?"

"You shouldn't ask me–" Her eyes widened. "Why, that couldn't possibly have anything to do with what's happened!"

He might, Gefty thought, have reassured her a little too much. He said, "I wouldn't know. But I don't want to just sit here and wonder about it until Maulbow wakes up. Until we're back in normspace, we'd better not miss any bets. Because one thing's sure–if this has happened to anybody else, they didn't turn up again to report it. You see?"

Kerim apparently did. She went pale, then said hesitantly, "Well ... the sealed cases Mr. Maulbow brought out from the Hub with him had some very expensive instruments in them. That's all I know. He's always trusted me not to pry into his business any more than my secretarial duties required, and of course I haven't."

"You don't know then what it was he brought up from that moon a few hours ago–those two big cases he stowed away in the vault?"

"No, I don't, Gefty. You see, he hasn't told me what the purpose of this trip is. I only know that it's a matter of great importance to him."

Kerim paused, added, "From the careful manner Mr. Maulbow handled the cases with the cranes, I had the impression that whatever was inside them must be quite heavy."

"I noticed that," Gefty said. It wasn't much help. "Well, I'll tell *you* something now," he went on. "I let your boss keep both sets of keys to the storage vault because he insisted on it when he signed the charter. What I didn't tell him was that I could make up a duplicate set any time in around half an hour."

"Oh! Have you–?"

"Not yet. But I intend to take a look at what Mr. Maulbow's got in that vault now, with or without his consent. You'd better run along and get dressed while I take him up to the instrument room."

"Why move him?" Kerim asked.

"The instrument room's got an overall safety field. I've turned it on now, and if something starts banging us around again, the room will be the safest place on the ship. I'll bring his personal luggage up too, and you can start looking through it for the keys. You may find them before I get a new set made. Or he may wake up and tell us where they are."

Kerim Ruse gave her employer a dubious glance, then nodded, said, "I imagine you're right, Gefty," and pattered hurriedly out of the stateroom. A few minutes later, she arrived, fully dressed, in the instrument room. Gefty looked around from the table-shelf where he had laid out his tools, and said, "He hasn't stirred. His suitcases are over there. I've unlocked them."

Kerim gazed at what showed in the screens about the control console and shivered slightly. She said, "I was thinking, Gefty ... isn't there something they call Space Three?"

"Sure. Pseudospace. But that isn't where we are. There're some special-built Navy tubs that can operate in that stuff if they don't stay too long. A ship like the *Queen* ... well, you and I and everything else in here would be frozen solid by now if we'd got sucked somehow into Space Three."

"I see," Kerim said uncomfortably. Gefty heard her move over to the suitcases. After a moment, she asked, "What do the vault keys look like?"

"You can't miss them if he's just thrown them in there. They're over six inches long. What kind of a guy is this Maulbow? A scientist?"

"I couldn't say, Gefty. He's never referred to himself as a scientist. I've had this job a year and a half. Mr. Maulbow is a very considerate employer ... one of the nicest men I've known, really. But it was simply understood that I should ask no questions about the business beyond what I actually needed to know for my work."

"What's the business called?"

"Maulbow Engineering."

"Big help," Gefty observed, somewhat sourly. "Those instruments he brought along ... he build those himself?"

"No, but I think he designed some of them—probably most of them. The companies he had doing the actual work appeared to have a terrible time getting everything exactly the way Mr. Maulbow wanted it—There's nothing that looks like a set of keys in those first two suitcases, Gefty."

"Well," Gefty said, "if you don't find them in the others, you might start thumping around to see if he's got secret compartments in his luggage somewhere."

"I do wish," Kerim Ruse said uneasily, "that Mr. Maulbow would regain consciousness. It seems so ... so underhanded to be doing these things behind his back!"

Gefty grunted noncommittally. He wasn't at all certain by now that he wanted his secretive client to wake up before he'd checked on the contents of the *Queen's* storage vault.

*   *   *   *   *

Fifteen minutes later, Gefty Rammer was climbing down to the storage deck in the *Queen's* broad stern, the newly fashioned set of vault keys clanking heavily in his coat pocket. Kerim had remained with her employer who was getting back his color but still hadn't opened his eyes. She hadn't found the original keys. Gefty wasn't sure she'd tried too hard, though she seemed to realize the seriousness of the situation now. But her loyalty to Mr. Maulbow could make no further difference, and she probably felt more comfortable for it.

Lights went on automatically in the wide passage leading from the cargo lock to the vault as Gefty turned into it. His steps echoed between the steel bulkheads on either side. He paused a moment before the big circular vault doors, listening to the purr of the *Queen's* idling engines in the next compartment. The familiar sound was somehow reassuring. He inserted the first key, turned it over twice, drew it out again and pressed one of the buttons in the control panel beside the door. The heavy slab of steel moved sideways with a soft, hissing sound, vanished into the wall. Gefty slid the other key into the lock of the inner door. A few seconds later, the vault entrance lay open before him.

He stood still again, wrinkling his nose. The area ahead was only dimly illuminated–the shaking-up the *Queen* had undergone had disturbed the lighting system here. And what was that odor? Rather sharp, unpleasant; it might have been spilled ammonia. Gefty stepped through the door into the wide, short entrance passage beyond it, turned to the right and peered about in the semidarkness of the vault.

Two great steel cases–the ones Maulbow had taken down to an airless moon surface, loaded up with something and brought back to the *Queen*–were jammed awkwardly into a corner, in a manner which suggested they'd slid into it when the ship was being knocked around.

One of them was open and appeared to be empty. Gefty wasn't sure of the other. In the dimness beside them lay the loose coils of some very thick, dark cable–And standing near the center of the floor was a thing that at once riveted his attention on it completely. He sucked his breath in softly, feeling chilled.

He realized he hadn't really believed his own hunch. But, of course, if it hadn't been an unheard-of outside force that plucked the *Queen* out of normspace and threw her into this elsewhere, then it must be something Maulbow had put on board. And that something had to be a machine of some kind–

It was.

About it he could make out a thin gleaming of wires–a jury-rigged safety field. Within the flimsy-looking protective cage was a double bank of instruments, some of them alive with the flicker and glow of lights. Those must be the very expensive and difficult-to-build items Maulbow had brought out from the Hub. Beside them stood the machine, squat and ponderous. In the vague light, it looked misshaped and discolored. A piece of equipment that had taken a bad beating of some kind. But it was functioning. As he stared, intermittent bursts of clicking noises rose from it, like the staccato of irregular gunfire.

For a moment, questions raced in disorder through his mind. What was it? Why had it been on that moon? Part of another ship, wrecked now ... a ship that had been at home *here*? Was it some sort of drive?

Maulbow must know. He'd known enough to design the instruments required to bring the battered monster back to life. On the other hand, he had not foreseen in all detail what could happen once the thing was in operation, because the *Queen's* sudden buck-jumping act had surprised him and knocked him out.

The first step, in any event, was to get Maulbow awake now. To tamper with a device like this, before learning as much as one could about it, would be lunatic foolhardiness. It looked like too good a bet that the next serious mistake made by anybody would finish them all—

Perhaps it was only because Gefty's nerves were on edge that he grew aware at that point in his reflections of two minor signals from his senses. One was that the smell of ammonia, which he had almost stopped noticing, was becoming appreciably stronger. The other was the faintest of sounds—a whispering suggestion of motion somewhere behind him. But here in the storage vault nothing should have moved, and Gefty's muscles were tensing as his head came around. Almost in the same instant, he flung himself wildly to one side, stumbling and regaining his balance as something big and dark slapped heavily down on the floor at the point where he had stood. Then he was darting up through the entrance passage, turning, and knocking down the lock switches on the outside door panel.

It came flowing around the corner of the passage behind him as the vault doors began to slide together. He was aware mainly of swift, smooth, oiling motion like that of a big snake; then, for a fraction of a second, a strip of brighter light from the outside passage showed a long, heavy wedge of a head, a green metal-glint of staring eyes.

The doors closed silently into their frames and locked. The thing was inside. But it was almost a minute then before Gefty could control his shaking legs enough to start moving back towards the main deck. In the half-dark of the vault, it had looked like a big coiled cable lying next to the packing cases. Like Maulbow, it might have been battered around and knocked out during the recent disturbance; and when it recovered, it had found Gefty in the vault with it. But it might also have been awake all the while, waiting cunningly until Gefty's attention seemed fixed elsewhere before launching its attack. It was big enough to have flattened him and smashed every bone in his body if the stroke had landed.

Some kind of guard animal–a snakelike watchdog? What other connection could it have with the mystery machine? Perhaps Maulbow had intended to leave it confined in one of the cases, and it had broken loose–

Too many questions by now, Gefty thought. But Maulbow had the answers.

*   *   *   *   *

He was hurrying up the main deck's central passage when Maulbow's voice addressed him sharply from a door he'd just passed.

"Stop right there, Rammer! Don't dare to move! I–"

The voice ended on a note of surprise. Gefty's reaction had not been too rational, but it was prompt. Maulbow's tone and phrasing implied he was armed. Gefty wasn't, but he kept a gun in the instrument room for emergencies. He'd been through a whole series of unnerving experiences, winding up with being shagged out of his storage vault by something that stank of ammonia and looked like a giant snake. To have one of the *Queen's* passengers order him to stand where he was topped it off. Every other consideration was swept aside by a great urge to get his hands on his gun.

He glanced back, saw Maulbow coming out of the half-opened door, something like a twenty-inch, thin, white rod in one hand. Then Gefty went bounding on along the passage, hunched forward and zigzagging from wall to wall to give Maulbow–if the thing he held was a weapon and he actually intended to use it–as small and erratic a target as possible. Maulbow shouted angrily behind him. Then, as Gefty came up to the next cross-passage, a line of white fire seared through the air across his shoulders and smashed off the passage wall.

With that, he was around the corner, and boiling mad. He had no great liking for gunfire, but it didn't shake him like the silently attacking beast in the dark storage had done. He reached the deserted instrument room not many seconds later, had his gun out and cocked, and was faced back towards the passage by which he had entered. Maulbow, if he had pursued without hesitation, should be arriving by now. But the passage stayed quiet. Gefty couldn't see into it from where he stood. He waited, trying to steady his breathing, wondering where Kerim Ruse was and what had got into Maulbow. After a moment, without taking his eyes from the passage entrance, he reached into the wall closet from which he had taken the gun and fished out another souvenir of his active service days, a thin-bladed knife in a slip-sheath. Gefty worked the fastenings of the sheath over his left wrist and up his forearm under his coat, tested the release to make sure it was functioning, and shook his coat sleeve back into place.

The passage was still quiet. Gefty moved softly over to one of the chairs, took a small cushion from it and pitched it out in front of the entrance.

There was a hiss. The cushion turned in midair into a puff of bright white fire. Gefty aimed his gun high at the far passage wall just beyond the entrance and pulled the trigger. It was a projectile gun. He heard the slug screech off the slick plastic bulkhead and go slamming down the passage. Somebody out there made a startled, incoherent noise. But not the kind of a noise a man makes when he's just been hit.

"If you come in here armed," Gefty called, "I'll blow your head off. Want to stop this nonsense now?"

There was a moment's silence. Then Maulbow's voice replied shakily from the passage. He seemed to be standing about twenty feet back from the room.

"If you'll end your thoughtless attempts at interference, Rammer," he said, "there will be no trouble." He was speaking with the restraint of a man who is in a state of cold fury. "You're endangering us all. You must realize that you have no understanding of what you are doing."

Well, the last could be true enough. "We'll talk about it," Gefty said without friendliness. "I haven't done anything yet, but I'm not just handing the ship over to you. And what have you done with Miss Ruse?"

Maulbow hesitated again. "She's in the map room," he said then. "I ... it was necessary to restrict her movements for a while. But you might as well let her out now. We must reach an agreement without loss of time."

Gefty glanced over his shoulder at the small closed door of the map room. There was no lock on the door, and he had heard no sound from inside; this might be some trick. But it wouldn't take long to find out. He backed up to the wall, pushed the door open and looked inside.

Kerim was there, sitting on a chair in one corner of the tiny room. The reason she hadn't made any noise became clear. She and the chair were covered by a rather closely fitting sack of transparent, glistening fabric. She stared out through it despairingly at Gefty, her lips moving urgently. But no sound came from the sack.

Gefty called angrily, "Maulbow—"

"Don't excite yourself, Rammer." There was a suggestion of what might be contempt in Maulbow's tone now. "The girl hasn't been harmed. She can breathe easily through the restrainer. And you can remove it by pulling at the material from outside."

Gefty's mouth tightened. "I'll keep my gun on the passage while I do it—"

Maulbow didn't answer. Gefty edged back into the map room, tentatively grasped the transparent stuff above Kerim's shoulder. To his surprise, it parted like wet tissue. He pulled sharply, and in a moment Kerim came peeling herself out of it, her face tear-stained, working desperately with hands, elbows and shoulders.

"Gefty," she gasped, "he ... Mr. Maulbow—"

"He's out in the passage there," Gefty said. "He can hear you." His glance shifted for an instant to the wall where a second of the shroudlike transparencies was hanging. And who could that have been intended for, he thought, but Gefty Rammer? He added, "We've had a little trouble."

"Oh!" She looked out of the room towards the passage, then at the gun in Gefty's hand, then up at his face.

"Maulbow," Gefty went on, speaking distinctly enough to make sure Maulbow heard, "has a gun, too. He'll stay there in the passage and we'll stay in the instrument room until we agree on what should be done. He's responsible for what's happened and seems to know where we are."

He looked at Kerim's frightened eyes, dropped his voice to a whisper. "Don't let this worry you too much. I haven't found out just what he's up to, but so far his tricks have pretty much backfired. He was counting on taking us both by surprise, for one thing. That didn't work, so now he'd like us to co-operate."

"Are you going to?"

Gefty shrugged. "Depends on what he has in mind. I'm just interested in getting us out of this alive. Let's hear what Maulbow has to say—"

*　　*　　*　　*　　*

Some minutes later Gefty was trying to decide whether it was taking a worse risk to believe what Maulbow said than to keep things stalled on the chance that he was lying.

Kerim Ruse, perched stiffly erect on the edge of a chair, eyes big and round, face almost colorless, apparently believed Maulbow and was wishing she didn't. There was, of course, some supporting evidence ... primarily the improbable appearance of their surroundings. The pencil-thin fire-spouter and the sleazy-looking "restrainer" had a sufficiently unfamiliar air to go with Maulbow's story; but as far as Gefty knew, either of them could have been manufactured in the Hub.

Then there was the janandra—the big, snakish thing in the storage which Maulbow had brought back up from the moon along with the battered machine. It had been, he said, his shipboard companion on another voyage. It wasn't ordinarily aggressive—Gefty's sudden appearance in the vault must have startled it into making an attack. It was not exactly a pet. There was a psychological relationship between it and Maulbow which Maulbow would not attempt to explain because Gefty and Kerim would be unable to grasp its significance. The janandra was essential, in this unexplained manner, to his well-being.

That item was almost curious enough to seem to substantiate his other statements; but it didn't really prove anything. The only point Gefty didn't question in the least was that they were in a bad spot which might be getting worse rapidly. His gaze shifted back to the screens. What he saw out there, surrounding the ship, was, according to Maulbow, an illusion of space created by the time flow in which they were moving.

Also according to Maulbow, there was a race of the future, human in appearance, with machines to sail the current of time through the universe—to run and tack with the winds of time, dipping in and out of the normspace of distant periods and galaxies as they chose. Maulbow, one of the explorers, had met disaster a million light-years from the home of his kind, centuries behind them, his vehicle wrecked on an airless moon with damaged control unit and shattered instruments. He had made his way to a human civilization to obtain the equipment he needed, and returned at last with the *Silver Queen* to where the time-sailer lay buried.

Gefty's lip curled. No, he wasn't buying all that just yet—but if Maulbow was *not* lying, then the unseen stars were racing past, the mass of the galaxy beginning to slide by, eventually to be lost forever beyond a black distance no space drive could span. The matter simply had to be settled quickly. But Maulbow was also strained and impatient, and if his impatience could be increased a little more, he might start telling the things that really mattered, the things Gefty had to know. Gefty asked slowly, as if hesitant to commit himself, "Why did you bring us along?"

The voice from the passage snapped, "Because my resources were nearly exhausted, Rammer! I couldn't obtain a new ship. Therefore I chartered yours; and you came with it. As for Miss Ruse—in spite of every precaution, my activities may have aroused suspicion and curiosity among your people. When I disappeared, Miss Ruse might have been questioned. I couldn't risk being followed to the wreck of the sailer, so I took her with me. And what does that mean against what I have offered you? The greatest adventure—followed, I give you my solemn word, by a safe return to your own place and time, and the most generous compensations for any inconvenience you may have suffered!"

Kerim, looking up at Gefty, shook her head violently. Gefty said, "We find it difficult to take you on trust now, Maulbow. Why do you want to get into the instrument room?"

Maulbow was silent for some seconds. Then he said, "As I told you, this ship would not have been buffeted about during the moments of transfer if the control unit were operating with complete efficiency. Certain adjustments will have to be made in the unit, and this should be done promptly."

*   *   *   *   *

"Where do the ship instruments come in?" Gefty asked.

"I can determine the nature of the problem from them. When I was ... stranded ... the unit was seriously damaged. My recent repairs were necessarily hasty. I—"

"What caused the crack-up?"

Maulbow said, tone taut with impatience, "Certain sections of the Great Current are infested with dangerous forces. I shall not attempt to describe them ..."

"I wouldn't get it?"

"I don't pretend to understand them very well myself, Rammer. They are not life but show characteristics of life—even of intelligent life. If you can imagine radiant energy being capable of conscious hostility...."

There was a chill at the back of Gefty's neck. "A big, fast-moving light?"

"Yes!" Sharp concern showed suddenly in the voice from the passage. "You ... when did you see that?"

Gefty glanced at the screens. "Twice since you've been talking. And once before—immediately after we got tumbled around."

"Then we can waste no more time, Rammer. Those forces are sensitive to the fluctuations of the control unit. If they were close enough to be seen, they're aware the ship is here. They were attempting to locate it."

"What could they do?"

Maulbow said, "A single attack was enough to put the control unit out of operation in my sailer. The Great Current then rejected us instantly. A ship of this size might afford more protection, which is the reason I chose it. But if the control unit is not adjusted immediately to enable it to take us out of this section, the attacks will continue until the ship—and we—have been destroyed."

Gefty drew a deep breath. "There's another solution to that problem, Maulbow. Miss Ruse and I prefer it. And if you meant what you said—that you'd see to it we got back eventually—you shouldn't object either."

The voice asked sharply, "What do you mean?"

Gefty said, "Shut the control unit off. From what you were saying, that throws us automatically back into normspace, while we're still close enough to the Hub. You'll find plenty of people there who'll stake you to a trip to the future if they can go along and are convinced they'll return. Miss Ruse and I don't happen to be that adventurous."

There was silence from the passage. Gefty added, "Take your time to make up your mind about it, if you want to. I don't like the idea of those lights hitting us, but neither do you. And I think I can wait this out as well as you can...."

The silence stretched out. Presently Gefty said, "If you do accept, slide that fire-shooting device of yours into the room before you show up. We don't want accidents."

He paused again. Kerim was chewing her lips, hands clenched into small fists in her lap. Then Maulbow answered, voice flat and expressionless now.

"The worst thing we can do at present," he said, "is to prolong a dispute about possible courses of action. If I disarm, will you lay aside your gun?"

"Yes."

"Then I accept your conditions, disappointing as they are."

He was silent. After a moment, Gefty heard the white rod clatter lightly along the floor of the passage. It struck the passage wall, spun off it, and rolled into the instrument room, coming to rest a few feet away from him. Gefty hesitated, picked it up and laid it on the wall table. He placed his own gun beside it, moved a dozen steps away. Kerim's eyes followed him anxiously.

"Gefty," she whispered, "he might ..."

Gefty looked at her, formed the words "It's all right" with his mouth and called, "Guns have been put aside, Maulbow. Come on in, and let's keep it peaceable."

He waited, arms hanging loosely at his side, heart beating heavily, as quick footsteps came up the passage. Maulbow appeared in the entrance, glanced at Gefty and Kerim, then about the room. His gaze rested for a moment on the wall table, shifted back to Gefty. Maulbow came on into the room, turning towards Gefty, mouth twisting.

He said softly, "It is not our practice, Rammer, to share the secrets of the Great Current with other races. I hadn't foreseen that you might become a dangerous nuisance. But now–"

His right hand began to lift, half closed about some small golden instrument. Gefty's left arm moved back and quickly forwards.

The service knife slid out of its sheath and up from his palm as an arrow of smoky blackness burst from the thing in Maulbow's hand. The blackness came racing with a thin, snarling noise across the floor towards Gefty's feet. The knife flashed above it, turning, and stood hilt-deep in Maulbow's chest.

*   *   *   *   *

Gefty returned a few minutes later from the forward cabin which served as the *Queen's* sick bay, and said to Kerim, "He's still alive, though I don't know why. He may even recover. He's full of anesthetic, and that should keep him quiet till we're back in normspace. Then I'll see what we can do for him."

Kerim had lost some of her white, shocked look while he was gone. "You knew he would try to kill you?" she asked shakily.

"Suspected he had it in mind—he gave in too quick. But I thought I'd have a chance to take any gadget he was hiding away from him first. I was wrong about that. Now we'd better move fast ..."

He switched the emergency check panel back on, glanced over the familiar patterns of lights and numbers. A few minor damage spots were indicated, but the ship was still fully operational. One minor damage spot which did not appear on the panel was now to be found in the instrument room itself, in the corner on which the door of the map room opened. The door, the adjoining bulkheads and section of flooring were scarred, blackened, and as assortedly malodorous as burned things tend to become. That was where Gefty had stood when Maulbow entered the room, and if he had remained there an instant after letting go of the knife, he would have been in very much worse condition than the essentially fireproof furnishings.

Both Maulbow's weapons–the white rod lying innocently on the wall table and the round, golden device which had dropped from his hand spitting darts of smoking blackness–had blasted unnervingly away into that area for almost thirty seconds after Maulbow was down and twisting about on the floor. Then he went limp and the firing instantly stopped. Apparently, Maulbow's control of them had ended as he lost consciousness.

It seemed fortunate that the sick bay cabin's emergency treatment accessories, gentle as their action was, might have been designed for the specific purpose of keeping the most violent of prisoners immobilized–let alone one with a terrible knife wound in him. At the angle along which the knife had driven in and up below the ribs, an ordinary man would have been dead in seconds. But it was very evident now that Maulbow was no ordinary man, and even after the eerie weapons had been pitched out of the ship through the instrument room's disposal tube, Gefty couldn't rid himself of an uncomfortable suspicion that he wasn't done with Maulbow yet–wouldn't be done with him, in fact, until one or the other of them was dead.

He said to Kerim, "I thought the machine Maulbow set up in the storage vault would turn out to be some drive engine, but apparently it has an entirely different function. He connected it with the instruments he had made in the Hub, and together they form what he calls a control unit. The emergency panel would show if the unit were drawing juice from the ship. It isn't, and I don't know what powers it. But we do know now that the control unit is holding us in the time current, and it will go on holding us there as long as it's in operation.

"If we could shut it off, the *Queen* would be 'rejected' by the current, like Maulbow's sailer was. In other words, we'd get knocked back into normspace–which is what we want. And we want it to happen as soon as possible because, if Maulbow was telling the truth on that point, every minute that passes here is taking us farther away from the Hub, and farther from our own time towards his."

Kerim nodded, eyes intent on his face.

"Now I can't just go down there and start slapping switches around on the thing," Gefty went on. "He said it wasn't working right, and even if it were, I couldn't tell what would happen. But it doesn't seem to connect up with any ship systems—it just seems to be holding us in a field of its own. So I should be able to move the whole unit into the cargo lock and eject it from there. If we shift the *Queen* outside its field, that should have the same effect as shutting the control unit off. It should throw us back into normspace."

Kerim nodded again. "What about Mr. Maulbow's janandra animal?"

Gefty shrugged. "Depends on the mood I find it in. He said it wasn't usually aggressive. Maybe it isn't. I'll get into a spacesuit for protection and break out some of the mining equipment to move it along with. If I can maneuver it into an empty compartment where it will be out of the ..."

*   *   *   *   *

He broke off, expression changing, eyes fastened on the emergency panel. Then he turned hurriedly, reached across the side of the console for the intership airseal controls. Kerim asked apprehensively, "What's the matter, Gefty?"

"Wish I knew ... exactly." Gefty indicated the emergency panel. "Little red light there, on the storage deck section—it wasn't showing a minute ago. It means that the vault doors have been opened since then."

He saw the same half-superstitious fear appear in her face that had touched him. "You think *he* did it?"

"I don't know." Maulbow's control of the guns had seemed uncanny enough. But that was a different matter. The guns were a product of his own time and science. But the vault door mechanisms? There might have been sufficient opportunity for Maulbow to study them and alter them, for some purpose of his own, since he'd come aboard....

"I've got the ship compartments and decks sealed off from each other now," Gefty said slowly. "The only connecting points from one to the other are personnel hatches–they're small air locks. So the janandra's confined to the storage deck. If it's come out of the vault, it might be a nuisance until I can get equipment to handle it. But that isn't too serious. The spacesuits are on the second deck, and I'll get into one before I go on to the storage. You wait here a moment, I'll look in on Maulbow again before I start."

If Maulbow wasn't still unconscious, he was doing a good job of feigning it. Gefty looked at the pale, lax face, the half-shut eyes, shook his head and left the cabin, locking it behind him. It mightn't be Maulbow's doing, but having the big snake loose in the storage could, in fact, make things extremely awkward now. He didn't think his gun would make much impression on anything of that size, and while several of the ship's mining tools could be employed as very effective close-range weapons, they happened, unfortunately, to be stored away on the same deck.

He found Kerim standing in the center of the instrument room, waiting for him.

"Gefty," she said, "do you notice anything? An odd sort of smell...."

Then the odor was in Gefty's nostrils, too, and the back of his neck turned to ice as he recognized it. He glanced up at the ventilation outlet, looked back at Kerim.

He took her arm, said softly, "Come this way. Keep very quiet! I don't know how it happened, but the janandra's on the main deck now. That's what it smells like. The smell's coming through the ventilation system, so the thing's moving around in the port section. We'll go the other way."

Kerim whispered, "What will we do?"

"Get ourselves into spacesuits first, and then get Maulbow's control unit out of the ship. The janandra may be looking around for him. If it is, it won't bother us."

*   *   *   *   *

He hadn't wanted to remind Kerim that, from what Maulbow said, there might be more than one reason for getting rid of the control unit as quickly as possible. But it had been constantly in the back of his mind; and twice, in the few minutes that passed after Maulbow's strange weapons were silenced, he had seen a momentary pale glare appear in the unquiet flow of darkness reflecting in the viewscreens. Gefty had said nothing, because if it was true that hostile forces were alert and searching for them here, it added to their immediate danger but not at all to the absolute need to free themselves from the inexorable rush of the Great Current before they were carried beyond hope of return to their civilization.

But those brief glimpses did add to the sense of urgency throbbing in Gefty's nerves, while events, and the equally hard necessity to avoid a fatally mistaken move in this welter of unknown factors, kept blocking him. Now the mysterious manner in which Maulbow's unpleasant traveling companion had appeared on the main deck made it impossible to do anything but keep Kerim at his side. If Maulbow was still capable of taking a hand in matters, there was no reasonably safe place to leave her aboard the *Queen.*

And Maulbow might be capable of it. Twice as they hurried up the narrow, angled passages along the *Queen's* curving hull towards an airseal leading to the next compartment, Gefty caught a trace of the ammonia-like animal odor coming over the ventilating system. They reached the lock without incident; but then, as they came along the second deck hall to the ship's magazine, there was a sharp click in the stillness behind them. Its meaning was disconcertingly apparent. Gefty hesitated, turned Kerim into a side passage, guided her along it.

She looked up at his face. "It's following us?"

"Seems to be." No time for the spacesuits in the magazine now—something had just emerged from the air lock through which they had entered the second deck not many moments before. He helped the girl quickly down a section of ladderlike stairs to the airseal connecting the second deck with the storage, punched a wall button there. As the lock door opened, there was another noise from the passage they had just left, as if something had thudded briefly and heavily against one of the bulkheads. Kerim uttered a little gasp. Then they were in the lock, and Gefty slapped down two other buttons, stood watching the door behind them snap shut and, a few seconds later, the one on the far side open on the dark storage deck.

They scrambled down another twelve feet of ladder to the floor of a side passage, hearing the lock snap shut behind them. As it closed, they were in complete darkness. Gefty seized Kerim's arm, ran with her up the passage to the left, guiding himself with his fingertips on the left bulkhead. When they came to a corner, he turned her to the left again. A few seconds later, he pulled open a small door, bundled the girl through, came in himself, and shut the door to a narrow slit behind them.

Kerim whispered shakily, "What will we do now, Gefty?"

"Stay here for the moment. It'll look for us in the vault first."

And it should go to the storage vault first where it had been guarding Maulbow's machine, to hunt for them there. But it might not. Gefty eased the gun from his pocket on the far side of Kerim. Across the dark compartment was another door. They could retreat a little farther here if it became necessary—but not very much farther.

They waited in a silence that was complete except for their unsteady breathing and the distant, deep pulse of the *Queen's* throttled-down drives. He felt Kerim trembling against him. How did Maulbow's creature move through the airseal locks? The operating mechanisms were simple—a dog might have been taught to use them. But a dog had paws....

There came the soft hiss of the opening lock, the faintest shimmer of light to the right of the passage mouth he was watching through the door. A heavy thump on the floor below the locks followed, then a hard click as the lock closed and complete darkness returned.

The silence resumed. Seconds dragged on. Gefty's imagination pictured the thing waiting, its great, wedge-shaped head raised as its senses probed the dark about it for a sign of the two human beings. Then a vague rushing noise began, growing louder as it approached the passage mouth, crossing it, receding rapidly again to the left.

Gefty let his breath out slowly, eased the door open and stood listening again. Abruptly, there was reflected light in the lock passage, coming now from the left. He said in a whisper, "It's moving around in the main hall, Kerim. We can go on the other way now, but we'll have to be fast and keep quiet. I've thought of how we can get rid of that thing."

*   *   *   *   *

The cargo lock on the storage deck had two inner doors. The one which opened into the side of the vault hall was built to allow passage of the largest chunks of freight the *Queen* was likely to be burdened with; it was almost thirty feet wide and twenty high. The second door was just large enough to let a man in a spacesuit climb in and out of the side of the lock without using the freight door. It opened on a tiny control cubicle from which the lock's mechanisms were operated during loading processes.

Gefty let Kerim and himself into the cubicle from one of the passages, steered the girl through the pitch blackness of the little room to the chair before the control panel and told her to sit down. He groped for a moment at the side of the panel, found a knob and twisted it. There was a faint click. A scattering of pale lights appeared suddenly on the panel, a dark viewscreen, set at a tilt above them, reflecting their gleam.

Gefty explained in a low voice, "Left side of that screen covers the lock. Right one covers the big hall outside. No lights in either at the moment, so you don't see anything. Only way the cargo door to the hall can be opened or closed is with these switches right here. What I want to do is get the janandra into the lock, slam the door on it and lock down the control switches. Then we've got it trapped."

"But how are you going to get it to go in there?"

"No real problem—I'll be three jumps ahead of it. Then I duck back up into this cubicle, and lock both doors. And it'll be inside the lock. You have the picture now?"

Kerim said unsteadily, "I do. But it sounds awfully risky, Gefty."

"Well, I don't like it either," Gefty admitted. "So I'll start right now before I lose my nerve. As soon as I move out into the vault hall, the lighting will go on. That's automatic. You watch the right side of the screen. If you see the janandra coming before I do, yell as loud as you can."

He shifted the two inner door switches to the right. A red spark appeared in the dark viewscreen, high up near the center. A second red light showed on the cubicle bulkhead beside Gefty. Beneath it an oblong section of the bulkhead turned silently away on heavy hinges, became a door two feet in thickness, which stood jutting out at a right angle into the darkness of the cargo lock. A wave of cold air moved through it into the control cubicle.

On the screen, another red spark appeared beside the first one.

"Both doors are open now," Gefty murmured to the girl. "The janandra isn't in the vault hall or the lighting would have turned on, but it may have heard the door open and be on its way. So keep watching the screen."

"I certainly will!" she whispered shakily.

Gefty took an oversized wrench from the wall, climbed quickly and quietly down the three ladder steps to the floor of the lock, and walked across it to the sill of the giant freight door, which now had swung out and down into the vault hall, fitting itself into a depression of the flooring. He hesitated an instant on the sill, then stepped out into the big dark hall. Light filled it immediately in both directions.

He stood quiet, intent on the storage vault entrance far up the hall to his left. He could see the vault was open. The janandra might still be inside it. But the seconds passed, and the dark entrance remained silent and there was no suggestion of motion beyond it. Gefty glanced to the right, moved a dozen steps farther out into the hall, hefted the wrench and spun it through the air towards the ventilator frame on the opposite bulkhead.

The heavy tool clanged loudly against the frame, bounced off and thudded to the floor. Gefty started slowly over to it, heart pounding, with the vault entrance still at the edge of his vision.

Kerim's voice screamed, "*Gefty, it's—*"

He spun around, sprinted back to the cargo lock. The janandra had come silently out of the nearest side passage behind him, was approaching with the remembered oiling swiftness of motion, its great head lifted a yard from the floor. Gefty plunged through the lock, jumped for the top of the cubicle door steps, came stumbling into the cubicle. Kerim was on her feet, staring. He swung the cubicle door switch to the left, slapping it flat to the panel. The door snapped back into the wall behind him with a force that shook the floor.

On the screen, the janandra's thick, dark worm-shape was swinging around in the dim lock to regain the open hall. It had seen the trap. But the freight door switch went flat beside the other, and the freight door rose with massive swiftness. The heavy body smashed against it, went sliding back to the floor as the door slammed shut and the screen section showing the cargo lock turned dark.

"Got it—got it—got it!" Gefty heard himself whispering exultantly. He switched on the lock's interior lights.

Then he swore softly, and, beside him, Kerim sucked in her breath.

*   *   *   *   *

The screen showed the janandra in violent but apparently purposeful motion inside the lock ... and it was also apparent now that it was a more complexly constructed creature than the long worm-body and heavy head had indicated. The skin, to a distance of some eight feet back of the head, had spread out into a wide, flexible frill. From beneath the frill extended half a dozen jointed, bone-white arms, along with waving, ribbonlike appendages less easy to define. The thing was reared half up along the hall door, inspecting its surface with these members; then suddenly it flung itself around and flashed over to the outer lock door. Three arms shot out; wiry fingers caught the three spin-locks simultaneously, began to whirl them.

Gefty said, staring, "Kerim, it's going to ..."

The janandra didn't. The motion checked suddenly, was reversed. The locks drew tight again. The janandra swung back from the door, lifting half its length upwards, big head weaving about as it inspected the tool racks overhead. An arm reached suddenly, snatched something from one of the racks. Then the thing turned again; and in the next instant its head filled the viewscreen. Kerim made a choked sound of fright, jerking back against

Gefty. The bulging, metal-green eyes seemed to stare directly at him. And the screen went black.

Kerim whispered, "Wha ... what happened, Gefty?"

Gefty swallowed, said, "It smashed the view pickup. Must have guessed we were watching and didn't like it...." He added, "I was beginning to think Maulbow must be some kind of superman. But it wasn't any remote-control magic of his that let the janandra out of the vault, and opened the intership locks when it came up to the main deck and followed us down again. It was doing all that for itself. It's Maulbow's partner, not his pet. And it's probably got at least as good a brain as anyone else on board behind that ugly face."

Kerim moistened her lips. "Can it ... could it get out again?"

"Into the ship?" Gefty shook his head decidedly. "Uh-uh. It could dump itself out on the other side—and it almost did before it realized where it was and what it was about to do. But the inner lock doors won't open until someone opens them right on this panel. No, the thing's safely trapped. On the other hand ..."

On the other hand, Gefty realized that he wouldn't now be able to bring himself to eject the janandra out of the cargo lock and into the Great Current. Its intentions obviously hadn't been friendly, but its level of intelligence was as good as his own, and perhaps somewhat better; and at present it was helpless. To dispose of it as he'd had in mind would therefore be the cold-blooded murder of an equal. But so long as that ugly and formidable shipmate of Maulbow's stayed in the cargo lock, the lock couldn't be used to get rid of the control unit in the vault.

A new solution presented itself while Gefty was making a rapid and rather desperate mental review of various heavy-duty tools which might be employed as weapons to force the janandra into submission and haul it off for confinement elsewhere in the ship. Not impossible, but a highly precarious and time-consuming operation at best. Then another thought occurred: the storage vault lay directly against the hull of the *Queen*—

How long to cut through the hull? The ship's mining equipment was on board, and the tools were self-powered. Climb into a spacesuit, empty the air from the entire storage deck, leaving the janandra imprisoned in the cargo lock ... with Maulbow incapacitated in sick bay, and Kerim back in the control compartment and also in a suit, for additional protection. Then cut ship's power to this deck to avoid complications with the *Queen's* involved circuitry and work under space conditions—half an hour if he hurried.

*   *   *   *   *

"Shouldn't take more than another ten minutes," he informed Kerim presently over the suit's intercom.

"I'm very glad to hear it, Gefty." She sounded shaky.

"Anything going on in the screens?" he asked.

She hesitated a little, said, "No. Not at the moment."

Gefty grunted, blinked sweat from his eyes, and took hold of the handgrips of the heavy mining cutter again, turning it nose down towards the vault floor. The guide light found the point he was working on, and the slice beam stabbed out, began nibbling delicately away to extend the curving line it had eaten through the *Queen's* thick skin. He had drawn a twenty-five foot circle around Maulbow's battered control unit and the instruments attached to it, well outside the fragile-looking safety field. The circle was broken at four points where he would plant explosives. The explosives, going off together, should shatter the connecting links with the hull and throw the machine clear. If that didn't release them immediately from its influence, he would see what putting the *Queen's* drives into action would do.

"Gefty?" Kerim's voice asked.

"Uh-huh?"

He could hear her swallow over the intercom. "Those lights are back now."

"How many?"

"Two," Kerim said. "I *think* they're only two. They keep crossing back and forth in front of us." She laughed nervously. "It's idiotic, of course, but I do get the feeling they're looking at us."

Gefty said hesitantly, "Everything's set but I need another minute or two to get this last connection whittled down a little more. If I blow the charge too soon, it mightn't take the gadget clean out of the ship."

Kerim said, "I know. I'll just watch ... they just disappeared again." Her voice changed. "Now there's something else."

"What's that?"

"You know you said to watch the cargo lock lights on the emergency panel."

"Yes."

"The outer lock door has just been opened."

"What!"

"It must have been. The light started blinking red just now as I was looking at it."

Gefty was silent a moment, his mind racing. Why would the janandra open the lock? From what Maulbow had said, it could live for a while without air, but it still could gain nothing but eventual death from leaving the ship–

Unless, Gefty thought, the janandra had become aware in some way that he was about to blow their machine out of the *Queen*. There were grappling lines in the cargo lock, and if four or five of those lines were slapped to the circular section of the hull he'd loosened ...

"Kerim," he said.

"Yes?"

"I'm going to blow the deal right now. Got your suit snapped to the wall braces like I showed you?"

"Yes, Gefty." Her voice was faint but clear.

He turned the cutter away from the line it had dug, sent it rolling off towards the far wall. He hurried around the circle, checking the four charges, lumbered over to the vault passage, stopped just around the corner. He took the firing box from his suit.

"Ready, Kerim?" He opened the box.

"Ready...."

"Here goes!" Gefty reached into the box, twisted the firing handle. Light flared in the vault. The deck shook below him. He came stumbling out from behind the wall.

Maulbow's machine and its stand of instruments had vanished. Where it had stood was a dark circular hole. Nothing else seemed to have happened. Gefty clumped hurriedly over to the mining cutter, swung it around, started more cautiously back towards the hole. He didn't have the faintest idea what would come next, but a definite possibility was that he would see the janandra's dark form flowing up over the rim of the hole. Letting it run into the cutter beam might be the best way to discourage it from re-entering the *Queen*.

Instead, a dazzling brilliance suddenly blotted out everything. The cutter was plucked from Gefty's grasp; then he was picked up, suit and all, and slammed up towards the vault ceiling. He had a feeling that inaudible thunders were shaking the ship. He seemed to be rolling over and over along the ceiling. At last, the suit crashed into something which showed a total disinclination to yield, and Gefty blacked out.

*   *   *   *   *

The left side of his face felt pushed out of shape; his left eye wasn't functioning too well, and there was a severe pulsing ache throughout the top of his head. But Gefty felt happy.

There were a few qualifying considerations.

"Of course," he pointed out to Kerim, "all we can really say immediately is that we're back in normspace and somewhere in the galaxy."

She smiled shakily. "Isn't that saying quite a lot, Gefty?"

"It's something." Gefty glanced around the instrument room. He had placed an emergency light on the console, but except for that, the control compartment was in darkness. The renewed battering the *Queen* had absorbed had knocked out the power in the forward section. The viewscreens were black, every instrument dead. But he'd seen the stars of normspace through the torn vault floor. It was something....

"We might have the light that slugged us to thank for that," he said. "I'm not sure just what did happen there, but it could have been Maulbow's control unit it was attacking rather than the ship. Maulbow said the lights were sensitive to the unit. At any rate, we're here, and we're rid of the gadget–and of the janandra." He hesitated. "I just don't feel you should get your hopes too high. We may find out we're a very long way from the Hub."

Kerim's large eyes showed a degree of confidence which made him almost uncomfortable. "If we are," she said serenely, "you'll get us back somehow."

Gefty cleared his throat. "Well, we'll see. If the power shutoff is something the *Queen's* repair scanners can handle, the instruments will come back on any minute. Give the scanners ten minutes. If they haven't done it by that time, they can't do it and I'll have to play repairman. Then, with the instruments working, we can determine exactly where we are."

Unless, he told himself silently, they'd wound up in a distant cluster never penetrated by the Federation's mapping teams. And there was the other little question of where they now were in time. But Kerim looked rosy with relief, and those details could wait.

He took up another emergency light, switched it on and said, "I'll see how Maulbow is doing while we're waiting for power. If the first aid treatment has pulled him through so far, the autosurgeon probably can fix him up."

Kerim's face suddenly took on a guilty expression. "I forgot all about Mr. Maulbow!" She hesitated. "Should I come along?"

Gefty shook his head. "I won't need help. And if it's a case for the surgeon, you wouldn't like it. Those things work painlessly, but it gets to be a mess for a while."

He shut off the light again when he reached the sick bay which was running on its independent power system. As he opened the cabin door from the dispensary, carrying the autosurgeon, it became evident that Maulbow was still alive but that he might be in delirium. Gefty placed the surgeon on the table, went over to the bed and looked at Maulbow.

To the extent that the emergency treatment instruments' cautious restraints permitted, Maulbow was twisting slowly about on the bed. He was speaking in a low, rapid voice, his face distorted by emotion. The words were not slurred, but they were in a language Gefty didn't know. It seemed clear that Maulbow had reverted mentally to his own time, and for some seconds he remained unaware that Gefty had entered the room. Then, surprisingly, the slitted blue eyes opened wider and focused on Gefty's face. And Maulbow screamed with rage.

Gefty felt somewhat disconcerted. For the reason alone that he was under anesthetic, Maulbow should not have been conscious. But he was. The words were now ones Gefty could understand, and Maulbow was telling him things which would have been interesting enough under different circumstances. Gefty broke in as soon as he could.

"Look," he said quietly, "I'm trying to help you. I ..."

Maulbow interrupted him in turn, not at all quietly. Gefty listened a moment longer, then shrugged. So Maulbow didn't like him. He couldn't say honestly that he'd ever liked Maulbow much, and what he was hearing made him like Maulbow considerably less. But he would keep the man from the future alive if he could.

He positioned the autosurgeon behind the head of the bed to allow the device to begin its analysis, stood back at its controls where he could both follow the progress it made and watch Maulbow without exciting him further by remaining within his range of vision. After a moment, the surgeon shut off the first-aid instruments and made unobtrusive use of a heavy tranquilizing drug. Then it waited.

Maulbow should have lapsed into passive somnolence thirty seconds afterwards. But the drug seemed to produce no more effect on him mentally than the preceding anesthetic. He raged and screeched on. Gefty watched him uneasily, knowing now that he was looking at insanity. There was nothing more he could do at the moment–the autosurgeon's decisions were safer than any nonprofessional's guesswork. And the surgeon continued to wait.

Then, abruptly, Maulbow died. The taut body slumped against the bed and the contorted features relaxed. The eyes remained half open; and when Gefty came around to the side of the bed, they still seemed to be looking up at him, but they no longer moved. A thin trickle of blood started from the side of the slack mouth and stopped again.

*   *   *   *   *

The control compartment was still darkened and without power when Gefty returned to it. He told Kerim briefly what had happened, added, "I'm not at all sure now he was even human. I'd rather believe he wasn't."

"Why that, Gefty?" She was studying his expression soberly.

Gefty hesitated, said, "I thought at first he was furious because we'd upset his plans. But they weren't his plans ... they were the janandra's. He wasn't exactly its servant. I suppose you'd have to say he was something like a pet animal."

Kerim said incredulously, "But that isn't possible! Think of how intelligently Mr. Maulbow ..."

"He was following instructions," Gefty said. "The janandra let him know whatever it wanted done. He was following instructions again when he tried to kill me after I'd got away from the thing in the vault. The real brain around here was the janandra ... and it was a real brain. With a little luck it would have had the ship."

Kerim smiled briefly. "You handled that big brain rather well, I think."

"I was the one who got lucky," Gefty said. "Anyway, where Maulbow came from, it's the janandra's kind that gives the orders. And the thing is, Maulbow liked it that way. He didn't want it to be different. When the light hit us, it killed the janandra on the outside of the ship. Maulbow felt it happen and it cracked him up. He wanted to kill us for it. But since he was helpless, he killed himself. He didn't want to be healed—not by us. At least, that's what it looks like."

He shrugged, checked his watch, climbed out of the chair. "Well," he said, "the ten minutes I gave the *Queen* to turn the power back on are up. Looks like the old girl couldn't do it. So I'll—"

The indirect lighting system in the instrument room went on silently. The emergency light flickered and went out. Gefty's head came around.

Kerim was staring past him at the screens, her face radiant.

"Oh, Gefty!" she cried softly. "Oh, Gefty! Our stars!"

* * * * *

"Green dot here is us," Gefty explained, somewhat hoarsely. He cleared his throat, went on, "Our true ship position, that is—" He stopped, realizing he was talking too much, almost babbling, in an attempt to take some of the tension out of the moment. The next few seconds might not tell them where they were, but it would show whether they had been carried beyond the regions of space charted by Federation instruments. Which would mean the difference between having a chance—whether a good chance or a bad one—of getting home eventually, and the alternative of being hopelessly lost.

There had been nothing recognizably familiar about the brilliantly dense star patterns in the viewscreens, but he gave no further thought to that. Unless the ship's exact position was known or one was on an established route, it was a waste of time looking for landmarks in a sizable cluster.

He turned on the basic star chart. Within the locator plate the green pinpoint of light reappeared, red-ringed and suspended now against the three-dimensional immensities of the Milky Way. It stayed still a moment, began a smooth drift towards Galactic East. Gefty let his breath out carefully. He sensed Kerim's eyes on him but kept his gaze fixed on the locator plate.

The green dot slowed, came to a stop. Gefty's finger tapped the same button four times. The big chart flicked out of existence, and in the plate three regional star maps appeared and vanished in quick succession behind it. The fourth map stayed. For a few seconds, the red-circled green spark was not visible here. Then it showed at the eastern margin of the map, came gliding forwards and to the left, slowed again and held steady. Now the star map began to glide through the locator plate, carrying the fixed green dot with it. It brought the dot up to dead center point in the locator plate and stopped.

Gefty slumped a little. He rubbed his hands slowly down his face and muttered a few words. Then he shook his head.

"Gefty," Kerim whispered, "what is it? Where are we?"

Gefty looked at her.

"After we got hauled into that time current," he said hoarsely, "I tried to find out which way in space we were headed. The direction indicators over there seemed to show we were trying to go everywhere at once. You remember Maulbow's control unit wasn't working right, needed adjustments. Well, all those little impulses must have pretty well canceled out because we weren't taken really far. In the last hour and a half we've covered roughly the distance the *Queen* could have gone on her own in, say, thirty days."

"Then where ..."

"Home," Gefty said simply. "It's ridiculous! Other side of the Hub from where we started." He nodded at the plate. "Eastern Hub Quadrant. Section Six Eight. The G2 behind the green dot–that's the Evalee system. We could be putting down at Evalee Interstellar three hours from now if we wanted to."

Kerim was laughing and crying together. "Oh, Gefty! I knew you would ..."

"A fat lot I had to do with it!" Gefty leaned forward suddenly, switched on the transmitter. "And now let's pick up a live newscast. There's something else I ..."

His voice trailed off. The transmitter screen lit up with a blurred jumble of print, colors, a muttering of voices, music and noises. Gefty twisted a dial. The screen cleared, showed a newscast headline sheet. Gefty blinked at it, glanced sideways at Kerim, grimaced.

"The something else," he said, his voice a little strained, "was something I was also worried about. Looks like I was more or less right."

"Why, what's wrong?"

"Nothing really bad," Gefty assured her. He added, "I think. But take a look at the Federation dateline."

Kerim peered at the screen, frowned. "But ..."

"Uh-huh."

"Why, that ... that's almost ..."

"That," Gefty said, "or rather *this* is the day after we started out from the Hub, headed roughly Galactic west. Three weeks ago. We'd be just past Miam." He knuckled his chin. "Interesting thought, isn't it?"

Kerim was silent for long seconds. "Then they ... or we ..."

"Oh, they're us, all right," Gefty said. "They'd have to be, wouldn't they?"

"I suppose so. It seems a little confusing. But I was thinking. If you send them a transmitter call ..."

Gefty shook his head. "The *Queen's* transmitter isn't too hot, but it might push a call as far as Evalee. Then we could arrange for a Com-Web link-up there, and in another ten minutes or so ... but I don't think we'd better."

"Why not?" Kerim demanded.

"Because we got through it all safely, so we're going to get through it safely. But if we receive that message now and never go on to Maulbow's moon ... you see? There's no way of knowing just what would happen."

Kerim looked hesitant, frowned. "I suppose you're right," she agreed reluctantly at last. "So Mr. Maulbow will have to stay dead now. And that janandra." After a moment she added pensively, "Of course, they weren't really very nice–"

Gefty shivered. One of the things he'd learned from Maulbow's ravings was the real reason he and Kerim had been taken along on the trip. He didn't feel like telling Kerim about it just yet, but it had been solely because of Maulbow's concern for his master's creature comforts. The janandra could go for a long time without food, but after fasting for several years on the moon, a couple of snacks on the homeward run would have been highly welcome.

And the janandra was a gourmet. It much preferred, as Maulbow well knew, to have its snacks still wriggling-fresh as it started them down its gullet.

"No," Gefty said, "I couldn't call either of them really nice."

Ham Sandwich

Originally Published In *Analog Science Fact & Fiction*, June 1963

*It gets difficult to handle the problem of a
man who has a real talent that you need badly
—and he cannot use it if he knows it's honest!*

HAM SANDWICH

There was no one standing or sitting around the tastefully furnished entry hall of the Institute of Insight when Wallace Cavender walked into it. He was almost half an hour late for the regular Sunday night meeting of advanced students; and even Mavis Greenfield, Dr. Ormond's secretary, who always stayed for a while at her desk in the hall to sign in the stragglers, had disappeared. However, she had left the attendance book lying open on the desk with a pen placed invitingly beside it.

Wallace Cavender dutifully entered his name in the book. The distant deep voice of Dr. Aloys Ormond was dimly audible, coming from the direction of the lecture room, and Cavender followed its faint reverberations down a narrow corridor until he reached a closed door. He eased the door open and slipped unobtrusively into the back of the lecture room.

As usual, most of the thirty-odd advanced students present had seated themselves on the right side of the room where they were somewhat closer to the speaker. Cavender started towards the almost vacant rows of chairs on the left, smiling apologetically at Dr. Ormond who, as the door opened, had glanced up without interrupting his talk. Three other faces turned towards Cavender from across the room. Reuben Jeffries, a heavyset man with a thin fringe of black hair circling an otherwise bald scalp, nodded soberly and looked away again. Mavis Greenfield, a few rows further up, produced a smile and a reproachful little headshake; during the coffee break she would carefully explain to Cavender once more that students too tardy to take in Dr. Al's introductory lecture missed the most valuable part of these meetings.

From old Mrs. Folsom, in the front row on the right, Cavender's belated arrival drew a more definite rebuke. She stared at him for half a dozen seconds with a coldly severe frown, mouth puckered in disapproval, before returning her attention to Dr. Ormond.

Cavender sat down in the first chair he came to and let himself go comfortably limp. He was dead-tired, had even hesitated over coming to the Institute of Insight tonight. But it wouldn't do to skip the meeting. A number of his fellow students, notably Mrs. Folsom, already regarded him as a black sheep; and if enough of them complained to Dr. Ormond that Cavender's laxness threatened to retard the overall advance of the group towards the goal of Total Insight, Ormond might decide to exclude him from further study. At a guess, Cavender thought cynically, it would have happened by now if the confidential report the Institute had obtained on his financial status had been less impressive. A healthy bank balance wasn't an absolute requirement for membership, but it helped ... it helped! All but a handful of the advanced students were in the upper income brackets.

Cavender let his gaze shift unobtrusively about the group while some almost automatic part of his mind began to pick up the thread of Dr. Al's discourse. After a dozen or so sentences, he realized that the evening's theme was the relationship between subjective and objective reality, as understood in the light of Total Insight. It was a well-worn subject; Dr. Al repeated himself a great deal. Most of the audience nevertheless was following his words with intent interest, many taking notes and frowning in concentration. As Mavis Greenfield liked to express it, quoting the doctor himself, the idea you didn't pick up when it was first presented might come clear to you the fifth or sixth time around. Cavender suspected, however, that as far as he was concerned much of the theory of Total Insight was doomed to remain forever obscure.

He settled his attention on the only two students on this side of the room with him. Dexter Jones and Perrie Rochelle were sitting side by side in front-row chairs–the same chairs they usually occupied during these meetings. They were exceptions to the general run of the group in a number of ways. Younger, for one thing; Dexter was twenty-nine and Perrie twenty-three while the group averaged out at around forty-five which happened to be Cavender's age. Neither was blessed with worldly riches; in fact, it was questionable whether the Rochelle girl, who described herself as a commercial artist, even had a bank account. Dexter Jones, a grade-school teacher, did have one but was able to keep it barely high enough to cover his rent and car payment checks. Their value to the Institute was of a different kind. Both possessed esoteric mental talents, rather modest ones, to be sure, but still very interesting, so that on occasion they could state accurately what was contained in a sealed envelope, or give a recognizable description of the photograph of a loved one hidden in another student's wallet. This provided the group with encouraging evidence that such abilities were, indeed, no fable and somewhere along the difficult road to Total Insight might be attained by all.

In addition, Perrie and Dexter were volunteers for what Dr. Aloys Ormond referred to cryptically as "very advanced experimentation." The group at large had not been told the exact nature of these experiments, but the implication was that they were mental exercises of such power that Dr. Al did not wish other advanced students to try them, until the brave pioneer work being done by Perrie and Dexter was concluded and he had evaluated the results....

*   *   *   *   *

"Headaches, Dr. Al," said Perrie Rochelle. "Sometimes quite bad headaches–" She hesitated. She was a thin, pale girl with untidy arranged brown hair who vacillated between periods of vivacious alertness and activity and somewhat shorter periods of blank-faced withdrawal. "And then," she went on, "there are times during the day when I get to feeling sort of confused and not quite sure whether I'm asleep or awake ... you know?"

Dr. Ormond nodded, gazing at her reflectively from the little lectern on which he leaned. His composed smile indicated that he was not in the least surprised or disturbed by her report on the results of the week's experiments–that they were, in fact, precisely the results he had expected. "I'll speak to you about it later, Perrie," he told her gently. "Dexter ... what experiences have you had?"

Dexter Jones cleared his throat. He was a serious young man who appeared at meetings conservatively and neatly dressed and shaved to the quick, and rarely spoke unless spoken to.

"Well, nothing very dramatic, Dr. Al," he said diffidently. "I did have a few nightmares during the week. But I'm not sure there's any connection between them and, uh, what you were having us do."

Dr. Ormond stroked his chin and regarded Dexter with benevolence. "A connection seems quite possible, Dexter. Let's assume it exists. What can you tell us about those nightmares?"

Dexter said he was afraid he couldn't actually tell them anything. By the time he was fully awake he'd had only a very vague impression of what the nightmares were about, and the only part he could remember clearly now was that they had been quite alarming.

Old Mrs. Folsom, who was more than a little jealous of the special attention enjoyed by Dexter and Perrie, broke in eagerly at that point to tell about a nightmare *she'd* had during the week and which *she* could remember fully; and Cavender's attention drifted away from the talk. Mrs. Folsom was an old bore at best, but a very wealthy old bore, which was why Dr. Ormond usually let her ramble on a while before steering the conversation back to the business of the meeting. But Cavender didn't have to pretend to listen.

From his vantage point behind most of the group, he let his gaze and thoughts wander from one to the other of them again. For the majority of the advanced students, he reflected, the Institute of Insight wasn't really too healthy a place. But it offered compensations. Middle-aged or past it on the average, financially secure, vaguely disappointed in life, they'd found in Dr. Al a friendly and eloquent guide to lead them into the fascinating worlds of their own minds. And Dr. Al was good at it. He had borrowed as heavily from yoga and western mysticism as from various orthodox and unorthodox psychological disciplines, and composed his own system, almost his own cosmology. His exercises would have made conservative psychiatrists shudder, but he was clever enough to avoid getting his flock into too serious mental difficulties. If some of them suffered a bit now and then, it made the quest of Total Insight and the thought that they were progressing towards that goal more real and convincing. And meeting after meeting Dr. Al came up with some intriguing new twist or device, some fresh experience to keep their interest level high.

"Always bear in mind," he was saying earnestly at the moment, "that an advance made by any member of the group benefits the group as a whole. Thus, because of the work done by our young pioneers this week I see indications tonight that the group is ready to attempt a new experiment ... an experiment at a level I frankly admit I hadn't anticipated you would achieve for at least another two months."

Dr. Ormond paused significantly, the pause underlining his words. There was an expectant stirring among the students.

"But I must caution you!" he went on. "We cannot, of course, be certain that the experiment will succeed ... in fact, it would be a very remarkable thing if it did succeed at a first attempt. But if it should, you will have had a rather startling experience! You will have seen a thing generally considered to be impossible!"

He smile reassuringly, stepping down from the lectern. "Naturally, there will be no danger. You know me well enough to realize that I never permit the group or individuals to attempt what lies beyond their capability."

*   *   *   *   *

Cavender stifled a yawn, blinked water from his eyes, watching Ormond walk over to a small polished table on the left side of the room in front of the rows of chairs. On it Mavis Greenfield had placed a number of enigmatic articles, some of which would be employed as props in one manner or another during the evening's work. The most prominent item was a small suitcase in red alligator hide. Dr. Ormond, however, passed up the suitcase, took a small flat wooden plate from the table and returned to the center of the room.

"On this," he said, holding up the plate, "there rests at this moment the air of this planet and nothing else. But in a minute or two—for each of you, in his or her world of subjective reality—something else *will* appear on it."

The students nodded comprehendingly. So far, the experiment was on familiar ground. Dr. Ormond gave them all a good-humored wink.

"To emphasize," he went on, "that we deal here with practical, down-to-earth, *real* matters ... not some mystical nonsense ... to emphasize that, let us say that the object each of you will visualize on this plate will be—a ham sandwich!"

There were appreciative chuckles. But Cavender felt a twinge of annoyance. At the moment, when along with fighting off fatigue he'd been trying to forget that he hadn't eaten since noon, Dr. Al's choice looked like an unfortunate one. Cavender happened to be very fond of ham.

"Now here," Ormond continued, putting the plate down, "is where this experiment begins to differ from anything we have done before. For all of us will try to imagine—to visualize as being on this plate—*the same ham sandwich.* And so there will be no conflict in our projections, let's decide first on just what ingredients we want to put on it." He smiled. "We'll make this the finest ham sandwich our collective imagination can produce!"

There were more chuckles. Cavender cursed under his breath, his mouth beginning to water. Suggestions came promptly.

"Mustard?" Dr. Ormond said, "Of course—Not too sharp though, Eleanor?" He smiled at Mrs. Folsom. "I agree! A light touch of delicate salad mustard. Crisp lettuce ... finely chopped gherkins. Very well!"

"Put it all on rye," Cavender said helplessly. "Toasted rye."

"Toasted rye?" Ormond smiled at him, looked around. "Any objections? No? Toasted rye it shall be, Wally. And I believe that completes our selection."

He paused, his face turning serious. "Now as to that word of caution I gave you. For three minutes each of you will visualize the object we have chosen on the plate I will be holding up before me. You will do this with your eyes open, and to each of you, in your own subjective reality, the object will become, as you know, more or less clearly discernible.

"But let me tell you this. Do not be too surprised if at the end of that time, when the exercise is over, the object *remains visible to* you ... does not disappear!"

There was silence for a moment. Then renewed chuckles, but slightly nervous ones, and not too many.

Dr. Ormond said sternly, "I am serious about that! The possibility, though it may be small tonight, is there. You have learned that, by the laws of Insight, any image of subjective reality, if it can be endowed with *all* the attributes of objective reality by its human creator, *must* spontaneously become an image in objective reality!

"In this case, our collective ham sandwich, if it were perfectly visualized, could not only be seen by you but felt, its weight and the texture of each of its ingredients perceived, their appetizing fragrance savored"–Cavender groaned mentally–"and more: if one of you were to eat this sandwich, he would find it exactly as nourishing as any produced by the more ordinary methods of objective reality.

"There are people in the world today," Dr. Ormond concluded, speaking very earnestly now, "who can do this! There always have been people who could do this. And you are following in their footsteps, being trained in even more advanced skills. I am aware to a greater extent than any of you of the latent power that is developing–has developed–in this group. Tonight, for the first time, that power will be focused, drawn down to a pinpoint, to accomplish one task.

"Again, I do not say that at the end of our exercise a ham sandwich will lie on this plate. Frankly, I don't expect it. But I suggest very strongly that you don't let it surprise or startle you too much if we find it here!"

There was dead stillness when he finished speaking. Cavender had a sense that the lecture room had come alive with eerie little chills. Dr. Ormond lifted the plate solemnly up before him, holding it between the fingertips of both hands.

"Now, if you will direct your attention here ... no, Eleanor, with your eyes open!

"Let us begin...."

*   *   *   *   *

Cavender sighed, straightened up in his chair, eyes fixed obediently on the wooden plate, and banned ham sandwiches and every other kind of food firmly from his thoughts. There was no point in working his appetite up any further when he couldn't satisfy it, and he would have to be on guard a little against simply falling asleep during the next three minutes. The cloudiness of complete fatigue wasn't too far away. At the edge of his vision, he was aware of his fellow students across the room, arranged in suddenly motionless rows like staring zombies. His eyelids began to feel leaden.

The three minutes dragged on, came to an end. Ormond slowly lowered his hands. Cavender drew a long breath of relief. The wooden plate, he noted, with no surprise, was still empty.

"You may stop visualizing," Ormond announced.

There was a concerted sighing, a creaking of chairs. The students came out of their semitrances, blinked, smiled, settled into more comfortable positions, waiting for Dr. Al's comments.

"No miracles this time!" Ormond began briskly. He smiled.

Mrs. Folsom said, "Dr. Al–"

He looked over at her. "Yes, Eleanor?"

Eleanor Folsom hesitated, shook her head. "No," she said. "Go on. I'm sorry I interrupted."

"That's all right." Dr. Al gave her a warm smile. It had been, he continued, a successful exercise, a very promising first attempt, in spite of the lack of an immediate materialization, which, of course, had been only a remote possibility to start with. He had no fault to find with the quality of the group's effort. He had sensed it ... as they, too, presently would be able to sense it ... as a smooth flow of directed energy. With a little more practice ... one of these days ...

Cavender stifled one yawn, concealed another which didn't allow itself to be stifled behind a casually raised hand. He watched Ormond move over to the prop table, put the wooden plate down beside the red suitcase without interrupting his encouraging summary of the exercise, hesitate, then pick up something else, something

which looked like a flexible copper trident, and start back
to the center of the room with it.

Mrs. Folsom's voice said shrilly, *"Dr. Al–!"*

"Yes, Eleanor? What is it?"

"Just now," Mrs. Folsom said, her voice still holding
the shrill note, "just a moment ago, on the plate over
there, I'm certain ... I'm almost certain I saw the ham
sandwich!"

She added breathlessly, "And that's what I was going
to say before, Dr. Al! Right after you told us to stop
visualizing I thought I saw the sandwich on the plate!
But it was only for a moment and I wasn't sure. But now
I'm sure, almost sure, that I saw it again on the plate on
the table!"

The old woman was pointing a trembling finger
towards the table. Her cheeks showed spots of hectic red.
In the rows behind her, the students looked at one
another, shook their heads in resignation, some obviously
suppressing amusement. Others looked annoyed. They
were all familiar with Eleanor Folsom's tendency to
produce such little sensations during the meetings. If the
evening didn't promise to bring enough excitement,
Eleanor always could be counted on to take a hand in
events.

Cavender felt less certain about it. This time, Mrs.
Folsom sounded genuinely excited. And if she actually
believed she'd seen something materialize, she might be
fairly close to getting one of those little heart attacks she
kept everyone informed about.

*   *   *   *   *

Dr. Al could have had the same thought. He glanced
back at the prop table, asked gravely, "You don't see it
there now, do you, Eleanor?"

Mrs. Folsom shook her head. "No. No, of course not! It
disappeared again. It was only there for a second. But I'm
sure I saw it!"

"Now this is very interesting," Ormond said seriously. "Has anyone else observed anything at all unusual during the last few minutes?"

There was a murmured chorus of dissent, but Cavender noticed that the expressions of amusement and annoyance had vanished. Dr. Al had changed the tune, and the students were listening intently. He turned back to Mrs. Folsom.

"Let us consider the possibilities here, Eleanor," he said. "For one thing, you should be congratulated in any case, because your experience shows that your visualization was clear and true throughout our exercise. If it hadn't been, nothing like this could have occurred.

"But precisely what was the experience? There we are, as of this moment, on uncertain ground. You saw something. That no one else saw the same thing might mean simply that no one else happened to be looking at the plate at those particular instances in time. I, for example, certainly gave it no further attention after the exercise was over. You *may* then have observed a genuine materialization!"

Mrs. Folsom nodded vigorously. "Yes, I–"

"But," Ormond went on, "under the circumstances, the scientific attitude we maintain at this Institute demands that we leave the question open. For now. Because you might also, you understand, have projected–for yourself only–a vivid momentary impression of the image you had created during our exercise and were still holding in your mind."

Mrs. Folsom looked doubtful. The flush of excitement began to leave her face.

"Why ... well, yes, I suppose so," she acknowledged unwillingly.

"Of course," Ormond said. "So tonight we shall leave it at that. The next time we engage in a similar exercise ... well, who knows?" He gave her a reassuring smile. "I must say, Eleanor, that this is a very encouraging indication of the progress you have made!" He glanced over the group, gathering their attention, and raised the trident-like device he had taken from the table.

"And now for our second experiment this evening–"

Looking disappointed and somewhat confused, Eleanor Folsom settled back in her chair. Cavender also settled back, his gaze shifting sleepily to the remaining items on the prop table. He was frowning a little. It wasn't his business, but if the old woman had started to hypnotize herself into having hallucinations, Dr. Al had better turn to a different type of meeting exercises. And that probably was exactly what Ormond would do; he seemed very much aware of danger signals. Cavender wondered vaguely what the red suitcase on the table contained.

There was a blurry shimmer on the wooden plate beside the suitcase. Then something thickened there suddenly as if drawing itself together out of the air. Perrie Rochelle, sitting only ten feet back from the table, uttered a yelp–somewhere between surprise and alarm. Dexter Jones, beside her, abruptly pushed back his chair, made a loud, incoherent exclamation of some kind.

Cavender had started upright, heart hammering. The thing that had appeared on the wooden plate vanished again.

But it had remained visible there for a two full seconds. And there was no question at all of what it had been.

For several minutes, something resembling pandemonium swirled about the walls of the lecture room of the Institute of Insight. The red suitcase had concealed the wooden plate on the prop table from the eyes of most of the students sitting on the right side of the room, but a number of those who could see it felt they had caught a glimpse of something. Of just what they weren't sure at first, or perhaps they preferred not to say.

Perrie and Dexter, however, after getting over their first shock, had no such doubts. Perrie, voice vibrant with excitement, answered the questions flung at her from across the room, giving a detailed description of the ham sandwich which had appeared out of nowhere on the polished little table and stayed there for an incredible instant before it vanished. Dexter Jones, his usually impassive face glowing and animated, laughing, confirmed the description on every point.

On the opposite side of the room, Eleanor Folsom, surrounded by her own group of questioners, was also having her hour of triumph, in the warmth of which a trace of bitterness that her first report of the phenomenon had been shrugged off by everyone—even, in a way, by Dr. Al—gradually dissolved.

Dr. Al himself, Cavender thought, remained remarkably quiet at first, though in the excitement this wasn't generally noticed. He might even have turned a little pale. However, before things began to slow down he had himself well in hand again. Calling the group to a semblance of order, he began smilingly to ask specific questions. The witnesses on the right side of the room seemed somewhat more certain now of what they had observed.

Dr. Ormond looked over at Cavender.

"And you, Wally?" he asked. "You were sitting rather far back, to be sure—"

Cavender smiled and shrugged.

"Sorry, Dr. Al. I just wasn't looking in that direction at the moment. The first suggestion I had that anything unusual was going on was when Perrie let out that wild squawk."

There was general laughter. Perrie grinned and flushed.

"Well, I'd have liked to hear *your* squawk," she told Cavender, "if you'd seen a miracle happen right before your nose!"

"Not a miracle, Perrie," Ormond said gently. "We must remember that. We are working here with natural forces which produce natural phenomena. Insufficiently understood phenomena, perhaps, but never miraculous ones. Now, how closely did this materialization appear to conform to the subjective group image we had decided on for our exercise?"

"Well, I could only see it, of course, Dr. Al. But as far as I saw it, it was exactly what we'd ... no, wait!" Perrie frowned, wrinkling her nose. "There was something added!" She giggled. "At least, I don't remember anyone saying we should imagine the sandwich wrapped in a paper napkin!"

Across the room, a woman's voice said breathlessly, "Oh! A *green* paper napkin, Perrie?"

Perrie looked around, surprised. "Yes, it was, Mavis."

Mavis Greenfield hesitated, said with a nervous little laugh, "I suppose I did that. I added a green napkin after we started the exercise." Her voice quavered for an instant. "I thought the image looked neater that way." She looked appealingly at the students around her. "This is really incredible, isn't it."

They gave her vague smiles. They were plainly still floating on a cloud of collective achievement–if they hadn't created that sandwich, there could have been nothing to see!

It seemed to Cavender that Dr. Ormond's face showed a flicker of strain when he heard Mavis' explanation. But he couldn't be sure because the expression–if it had been there–was smoothed away at once. Ormond cleared his throat, said firmly and somewhat chidingly. "No, not incredible, Mavis! Although–"

He turned on his smile. "My friends, I must admit that you *have* surprised me! Very pleasantly, of course. But what happened here is something I considered to be only a very remote possibility tonight. You are truly more advanced than I'd realized.

"For note this. If even one of you had been lagging behind the others, if there had been any unevenness in the concentration each gave to the exercise tonight, this materialization simply could not have occurred! And that fact forces me now to a very important decision."

He went over to the prop table, took the suitcase from it. "Mavis," he said gravely, "you may put away these other devices. We will have no further need for them in this group! Dexter, move the table to the center of the room for me, please."

He waited while his instructions were hastily carried out, then laid the suitcase on the table, drew up a chair and sat down. The buzz of excited conversation among the students hushed. They stared at him in anticipatory silence. It appeared that the evening's surprises were not yet over—and they were ready for *anything* now!

*   *   *   *   *

"There is a point," Dr. Ormond began in a solemn voice, riveting their eager attention on him, "a point in the orderly advance towards Total Insight at which further progress becomes greatly simplified and accelerated, because the student has now developed the capability to augment his personal efforts by the use of certain instruments."

Cavender thoughtfully reached inside his coat, brought out a cigarette case, opened it and slowly put a cigarette to his lips. About to flick on a lighter, he saw Ruben Jeffries watching him with an expression of disapproval from across the aisle. Jeffries shook his head, indicated the NO SMOKING sign on the wall. Cavender nodded, smiling a rueful apology for his absent-mindedness, and returned the cigarette to its case. He shoved his hands into his trousers pockets, slouched back in the chair.

"I have told you," Ormond was saying, "that the contributions many of you so generously made to the Institute were needed for and being absorbed by vital research. Tonight I had intended to give you a first inkling of what that research was accomplishing." He tapped the suitcase on the table before him. "In there is an instrument of the kind I have mentioned. The beneficial forces of the Cosmos are harnessed by it, flow through it. And I believe I can say that my efforts in recent months have produces the most effective such device ever seen...."

"Dr. Al," Mrs. Folsom interrupted firmly, "I think you should let them know how the instrument cured my heart condition."

Faces shifted toward her, then back to Dr. Al. The middle-aged majority of the students pricked their ears. For each of them, conscious of the years of increasingly uncertain health to come, Mrs. Folsom's words contained a personal implication, one that hit home. But in spite of the vindication of her claim to have seen a materialized ham sandwich, they weren't quite ready to trust her about this.

Dr. Ormond's face was grave.

"Eleanor," he said reprovingly, "that was letting the cat out of the bag, wasn't it? I hadn't intended to discuss that part of the matter just yet."

He hesitated, frowning, tapping the table top lightly with his knuckles. Mrs. Folsom looked unabashed. She had produced another sensation and knew it.

"Since it was mentioned," Ormond said with deliberation at last, "it would be unfair not to tell you, at least in brief, the facts to which Eleanor was alluding. Very well then—Eleanor has served during the past several weeks as the subject of certain experiments connected with this instrument. She reports that after her first use of it, her periodically recurring heart problem ceased to trouble her."

Mrs. Folsom smiled, nodded vigorously. "I have not," she announced, "had one single touch of pain or dizziness in all this time!"

"But one should, of course," Dr. Ormond added objectively, "hesitate to use the word 'cure' under such circumstances."

In the front row someone asked, "Dr. Al, will the instrument heal ... well, other physical conditions?"

Ormond looked at the speaker with dignity. "John, the instrument does, and is supposed to do, one thing. Providing, as I've said, that the student working with it has attained a certain minimum level of Insight, it greatly accelerates his progress towards Total Insight. Very greatly!

"Now, as I have implied before: as one approaches the goal of Total Insight, the ailments and diseases which commonly afflict humanity simply disappear. Unfortunately, I am not yet free to show you proof for this, although I have the proof and believe it will not be long before it can be revealed at least to the members of this group. For this reason, I have preferred not to say too much on the point.... Yes, Reuben? You have a question?"

"Two questions, Dr. Al," Reuben Jeffries said. "First, is it your opinion that our group has now reached the minimum level of Insight that makes it possible to work with those instruments?"

Ormond nodded emphatically. "Yes, it has. After tonight's occurrence there is no further question about that."

"Then," Jeffries said, "my second question is simply—*when do we start?*"

There was laughter, a scattering of applause. Ormond smiled, said, "An excellent question, Reuben! The answer is that a number of you will start immediately.

"A limited quantity of the instruments—fifteen, I believe—are available now on the premises, stored in my office. Within a few weeks I will have enough on hand to supply as many of you as wish to speed up their progress by this method. Since the group's contributions paid my research expenses, I cannot in justice ask more from you individually now than the actual cost in material and labor for each instrument. The figure ... I have it somewhere ... oh, yes!" Ormond pulled a notebook from his pocket, consulted it, looked up and said, mildly, "Twelve hundred dollars will be adequate, I think."

Cavender's lips twitched sardonically. Three or four of the group might have flinched inwardly at the price tag, but on the whole they were simply too well heeled to give such a detail another thought. Checkbooks were coming hurriedly into sight all around the lecture room. Reuben Jeffries, unfolding his, announced, "Dr. Al, I'm taking one of the fifteen."

Half the students turned indignantly to stare at him. "Now wait a minute, Reuben!" someone said. "That isn't fair! It's obvious there aren't enough to go around."

Jeffries smiled at him. "That's why I spoke up, Warren!" He appealed to Ormond. "How about it, Dr. Al?"

Ormond observed judiciously, "It seems fair enough to me. Eleanor, of course, is retaining the instrument with which she has been working. As for the rest of you–first come, first served, you know! If others would like to have Mavis put down their names...."

*   *   *   *   *

There was a brief hubbub as this suggestion was acted on. Mavis, Dexter Jones and Perrie Rochelle then went to the office to get the instruments, while Dr. Ormond consoled the students who had found themselves left out. It would be merely a matter of days before the new instruments began to come in ... and yes, they could leave their checks in advance. When he suggested tactfully that financial arrangements could be made if necessary, the less affluent also brightened up.

Fifteen identical red alligator-hide suitcases appeared and were lined up beside Ormond's table. He announced that a preliminary demonstration with the instrument would be made as soon as those on hand had been distributed. Mavis Greenfield, standing beside him, began to read off the names she had taken down.

Reuben Jeffries was the fifth to come up to the table, hand Ormond his check and receive a suitcase from the secretary. Then Cavender got unhurriedly to his feet.

"Dr. Ormond," he said, loudly enough to center the attention of everyone in the room on him, "may I have the floor for a moment?"

Ormond appeared surprised, then startled. His glance went up to Reuben Jeffries, still standing stolidly beside him, and his face slowly whitened.

"Why ... well, yes, Wally." His voice seemed unsteady. "What's on your mind?"

Cavender faced the right side of the room and the questioning faces turned towards him.

"My name, as you know," he told the advanced students, "is Wallace Cavender. What you haven't known so far is that I am a police detective, rank of lieutenant, currently attached to the police force of this city and in temporary charge of its bunco squad."

He shifted his gaze towards the front of the room. Ormond's eyes met his for a moment, then dropped.

"Dr. Ormond," Cavender said, "you're under arrest. The immediate charge, let's say, is practicing medicine without a license. Don't worry about whether we can make it stick or not. We'll have three or four others worked up by the time we get you downtown."

For a moment, there was a shocked, frozen stillness in the lecture room. Dr. Ormond's hand began to move out quietly towards the checks lying on the table before him. Reuben Jeffries' big hand got there first.

"I'll take care of these for now, Dr. Al," Jeffries said with a friendly smile. "The lieutenant thinks he wants them."

*   *   *   *   *

Not much more than thirty minutes later, Cavender unlocked the door to Dr. Ormond's private office, went inside, leaving the door open behind him, and sat down at Ormond's desk. He rubbed his aching eyes, yawned, lit a cigarette, looked about in vain for an ashtray, finally emptied a small dish of paper clips on the desk and placed the dish conveniently close to him.

There had been an indignant uproar about Dr. Al's arrest for a while, but it ended abruptly when uniformed policemen appeared in the two exit doors and the sobering thought struck the students that any publicity given the matter could make them look personally ridiculous and do damage to their business and social standing.

Cavender had calmed their fears. It was conceivable, he said, that the district attorney's office would wish to confer with some of them privately, in connection with charges to be brought against William Fitzgerald Grady— which, so far as the police had been able to establish, was Dr. Ormond's real name. However, their association with the Institute of Insight would not be made public, and any proceedings would be carried out with the discretion that could be fully expected by blameless citizens of their status in the community.

They were fortunate, Cavender went on, in another respect. Probably none of them had been aware of just how much Grady had milked from the group chiefly through quiet private contributions and donations during the two years he was running the Institute. The sum came to better than two hundred thousand dollars. Grady naturally had wasted none of this in "research" and he was not a spendthrift in other ways. Cavender was, therefore, happy to say that around two thirds of this money was known to be still intact in various bank accounts, and that it would be restored eventually to the generous but misled donors.

Dr. Al's ex-students were beginning to look both chastened and very much relieved. Cavender briefly covered a few more points to eliminate remaining doubts. He touched on Grady's early record as a confidence man and blackmailer, mentioned the two terms he had spent in prison and the fact that for the last eighteen years he had confined himself to operations like the Institute of

Insight where risks were less. The profits, if anything, had been higher because Grady had learned that it paid off, in the long run, to deal exclusively with wealthy citizens and he was endowed with the kind of personality needed to overcome the caution natural to that class. As for the unusual experiences about which some of them might be now thinking, these, Cavender concluded, should be considered in the light of the fact that Grady had made his living at one time as a stage magician and hypnotist, working effectively both with and without trained accomplices.

The lecture had gone over very well, as he'd known it would. The ex-students left for their homes, a subdued and shaken group, grateful for having been rescued from an evil man's toils. Even Mrs. Folsom, who had announced at one point that she believed she had a heart attack coming on, recovered sufficiently to thank Cavender and assure him that in future she would take her problems only to a reliable physician.

*   *   *   *   *

Footsteps were coming down the short hall from the back of the building. Then Reuben Jeffries' voice said, "Go into the office. The lieutenant's waiting for you there."

Cavender stubbed out his cigarette as Dexter Jones, Perrie Rochelle and Mavis Greenfield filed into the office. Jeffries closed the door behind them from the hall and went off.

"Sit down," Cavender said, lighting a fresh cigarette.

They selected chairs and settled down stiffly, facing him. All three looked anxious and pale; and Perrie's face was tear-stained.

Cavender said, "I suppose you've been wondering why I had Sergeant Jeffries tell you three to stay behind."

Perrie began, her eyes and voice rather wild, "Mr. Cavender ... Lieutenant Cavender...."

"Either will do," Cavender said.

"Mr. Cavender, I swear you're wrong! We didn't have anything to do with Dr. Al's ... Mr. Grady's cheating those people! At least, I didn't. I swear it!"

"I didn't say you had anything to do with it, Perrie," Cavender remarked. "Personally I think none of you had anything to do with it. Not voluntarily, at any rate."

He could almost feel them go limp with relief. He waited. After a second or two, Perrie's eyes got the wild look back. "But...."

"Yes?" Cavender asked.

Perrie glanced at Dexter Jones, at Mavis.

"But then what *did* happen?" she asked bewilderedly, of the other two as much as of Cavender. "Mr. Cavender, I saw something appear on that plate! I know it did. It was a sandwich. It looked perfectly natural. I don't think it could have possibly been something Mr. Grady did with mirrors. And how could it have had the paper napkin Mavis had just been thinking about wrapped around it, unless...."

"Unless it actually was a materialization of a mental image you'd created between you?" Cavender said. "Now settle back and relax, Perrie. There's a more reasonable explanation for what happened tonight than that."

He waited a moment, went on. "Grady's one real interest is money and since none of you have any to speak of, his interest in you was that you could help him get it. Perrie and Dexter showed some genuine talent to start with, in the line of guessing what card somebody was thinking about and the like. It's not too unusual an ability, and in itself it wasn't too useful to Grady.

"But he worked on your interest in the subject. All the other students, the paying students, had to lose was a sizable amount of cash ... with the exception of Mrs. Folsom who's been the next thing to a flip for years anyway. She was in danger. And you three stood a good chance of letting Grady wreck your lives. I said he's a competent hypnotist. He is. Also a completely ruthless one."

He looked at Mavis. "As far as I know, Mavis, you haven't ever demonstrated that you have any interesting extrasensory talents like Dexter's and Perrie's. Rather the contrary. Right?"

She nodded, her eyes huge.

"I've always tested negative. Way down negative. That's why I was really rather shocked when that.... Of course, I've always been fascinated by such things. And he insisted it would show up in me sometime."

"And," Cavender said, "several times a week you had special little training sessions with him, just as his two star pupils here did, to help it show up. You were another perfect stooge, from Grady's point of view. Well, what it amounts to is that Grady was preparing to make his big final killing off this group before he disappeared from the city. He would have collected close to thirty thousand dollars tonight, and probably twice as much again within the next month or so before any of the students began to suspect seriously that Dr. Al's instruments could be the meaningless contraptions they are.

"You three have been hypnotically conditioned to a fare-you-well in those little private sessions you've had with him. During the past week you were set up for the role you were to play tonight. When you got your cue—at a guess it was Mrs. Folsom's claim that she'd seen the ham sandwich materialize—you started seeing, saying, acting, and thinking exactly as you'd been told to see, say, act, and think. There's no more mystery about it than that. And in my opinion you're three extremely fortunate young people in that we were ready to move in on Grady when we were."

*   *   *   *   *

There was silence for a moment. Then Perrie Rochelle said hesitantly, "Then Mrs. Folsom...."

"Mrs. Folsom," Cavender said, "has also enjoyed the benefits of many private sessions with Grady. She, of course, was additionally paying very handsomely for them. Tonight, she reported seeing what she'd been told to report seeing, to set off the hypnotic chain reaction."

"But," Perrie said, "she said her heart attacks stopped after she started using the instrument. I really don't see how that could have been just her imagination?"

"Very easily," Cavender said. "I've talked with her physician. Mrs. Folsom belongs to a not uncommon type of people whose tickers are as sound as yours or mine, but who are convinced they have a serious heart ailment and can dish up symptoms impressive enough to fool anyone but an informed professional. They can stop dishing them up just as readily if they think they've been cured." He smiled faintly. "You look as if you might be finally convinced, Perrie."

She nodded. "I ... yes, I guess so. I guess I am."

"All right," Cavender said. He stood up. "You three can run along then. You won't be officially involved in this matter, and no one's going to bother you. If you want to go on playing around with E.S.P. and so forth, that's your business. But I trust that in future you'll have the good sense to keep away from characters like Grady. Periods of confusion, chronic nightmares—even chronic headaches—are a good sign you're asking for bad trouble in that area."

They thanked him, started out of the office in obvious relief. At the door, Perrie Rochelle hesitated, looked back.

"Mr. Cavender...."

"Yes?"

"You don't think I ... I need...."

"Psychiatric help? No. But I understand," Cavender said, "that you have a sister in Maine who's been wanting you to spend the summer with her. I think that's a fine idea! A month or two of sun and salt water is exactly what you can use to drive the last of this nonsense out of your mind again. So good night to the three of you, and good luck!"

*   *   *   *   *

Cavender snapped the top of the squat little thermos flask back in place and restored it to the glove compartment of Jeffries' car. He brushed a few crumbs from the knees of his trousers and settled back in the seat, discovering he no longer felt nearly as tired and washed out as he had been an hour ago in the lecture room. A few cups of coffee and a little nourishment could do wonders for a man, even at the tail end of a week of hard work.

The last light in the Institute building across the street went out and Cavender heard the click of the front door. The bulky figure of Detective Sergeant Reuben Jeffries stood silhouetted for a moment in the street lights on the entrance steps. Then Jeffries came down the steps and crossed the street to the car.

"All done?" Cavender asked.

"All done," Jeffries said through the window. He opened the door, eased himself in behind the wheel and closed the door.

"They took Grady away by the back entrance," he told Cavender. "The records in his files ... he wasn't keeping much, of course ... and the stuff in the safe and those instruments went along with him. He was very co-operative. He's had a real scare."

Cavender grunted. "He'll get over it."

Jeffries hesitated, said, "I'm something of a Johnny-come-lately in this line of work, you know. I'd be interested in hearing how it's handled from here on."

"In this case it will be pretty well standard procedure," Cavender said. "Tomorrow around noon I'll have Grady brought in to see me. I'll be in a curt and bitter mood–the frustrated honest cop. I'll tell him he's in luck. The D. A.'s office has informed me that because of the important names involved in this fraud case, and because all but around forty thousand dollars of the money he collected in this town have been recovered, they've decided not to prosecute. He'll have till midnight to clear out. If he ever shows up again, he gets the book."

"Why leave him the forty thousand?" Jeffries asked. "I understood they know darn well where it's stashed."

Cavender shrugged. "The man's put in two years of work, Reuben. If we clean him, he might get discouraged enough to get out of the racket and try something else. As it is, he'll have something like the Institute of Insight going again in another city three months from now. In an area that hasn't been cropped over recently. He's good in that line ... one of the best, in fact."

Jeffries thoughtfully started the car, pulled out from the curb. Halfway down the block, he remarked, "You gave me the go-ahead sign with the cigarette right after the Greenfield girl claimed she'd put the paper napkin into that image. Does that mean you finally came to a decision about her?"

"Uh-huh."

Jeffries glanced over at him, asked, "Is there any secret about how you're able to spot them?"

"No ... except that I don't know. If I could describe to anyone how to go about it, we might have our work cut in half. But I can't, and neither can any other spotter. It's simply a long, tedious process of staying in contact with people you have some reason to suspect of being the genuine article. If they are, you know it eventually. But if it weren't that men with Grady's type of personality attract them somehow from ten miles around, we'd have no practical means at present of screening prospects out of the general population. You can't distinguish one of them from anyone else if he's just walking past you on the street."

Jeffries brought the car to a halt at a stop light.

"That's about the way I'd heard it," he acknowledged. "What about negative spotting? Is there a chance there might be an undiscovered latent left among our recent fellow students?"

"No chance at all," Cavender said. "The process works both ways. If they aren't, you also know it eventually–and I was sure of everyone but Greenfield over three weeks ago. She's got as tough a set of obscuring defenses as I've ever worked against. But after the jolt she got tonight, she came through clear immediately."

The light changed and the car started up. Jeffries asked, "You feel both of them can be rehabilitated?"

"Definitely," Cavender said. "Another three months of Grady's pseudoyoga might have ruined them for good. But give them around a year to settle out and they'll be all right. Then they'll get the call. It's been worth the trouble. Jones is good medium grade–and that Greenfield! She'll be a powerhouse before she's half developed. Easily the most promising prospect I've come across in six years."

"You're just as certain about Perrie Rochelle?"

"Uh-huh. Protopsi–fairly typical. She's developed as far as she ever will. It would be a complete waste of time to call her. You can't train something that just isn't there."

Jeffries grunted. "Never make a mistake, eh?"

Cavender yawned, smiled. "Never have yet, Reuben! Not in that area."

"How did you explain the sandwich to them–and Greenfield's napkin? They couldn't have bought your stage magic idea."

"No. Told them those were Dr. Al's posthypnotic suggestions. It's the other standard rationalization."

*   *   *   *   *

They drove on in silence for a while. Then Jeffries cleared his throat.

"Incidentally," he said. "I should apologize for the slip with the sandwich, even though it turned out to our advantage. I can't quite explain it. I was thinking of other matters at the moment, and I suppose I...."

Cavender, who had been gazing drowsily through the windshield, shook his head.

"As you say, it turned out very well, Reuben. Aside from putting the first crack in Mavis Greenfield's defenses, it shook up Dr. Al to the point where he decided to collect as much as he could tonight, cash the checks, and clear out. So he set himself up for the pinch. We probably gained as much as three or four weeks on both counts."

Jeffries nodded. "I realize that. But...."

"Well, you'd have no reason to blame yourself for the slip in any case," Cavender went on. "The fact is I'd been so confoundedly busy all afternoon and evening, I forgot to take time out for dinner. When that sandwich was being described in those mouth-watering terms, I realized I was really ravenous. At the same time I was fighting off sleep. Between the two, I went completely off guard for a moment, and it simply happened!"

He grinned. "As described, by the way, it was a terrific sandwich. That group had real imagination!" He hesitated, then put out his hand, palm up, before him. "As a matter of fact, just talking about it again seems to be putting me in a mood for seconds...."

Something shimmered for an instant in the dim air wrapped in its green tissue napkin, a second ham sandwich appeared.

Gone Fishing

Originally Published In *Analog Science Fact & Fiction*,
May 1961

There is no predictable correlation between intelligence and ethics, nor is ruthlessness necessarily an evil thing. And there is nothing like enforced, uninterrupted contemplation to learn to distinguish one from another....

GONE FISHING

Barney Chard, thirty-seven—financier, entrepreneur, occasional blackmailer, occasional con man, and very competent in all these activities—stood on a rickety wooden lake dock, squinting against the late afternoon sun, and waiting for his current business prospect to give up the pretense of being interested in trying to catch fish.

The prospect, who stood a few yards farther up the dock, rod in one hand, was named Dr. Oliver B. McAllen. He was a retired physicist, though less retired than was generally assumed. A dozen years ago he had rated as one of the country's top men in his line. And, while dressed like an aging tramp in what he had referred to as fishing togs, he was at the moment potentially the country's wealthiest citizen. There was a clandestine invention he'd fathered which he called the McAllen Tube. The Tube was the reason Barney Chard had come to see McAllen.

Gently raising and lowering the fishing rod, and blinking out over the quiet water, Dr. McAllen looked preoccupied with disturbing speculations not connected with his sport. The man had a secrecy bug. The invention, Barney thought, had turned out to be bigger than the inventor. McAllen was afraid of the Tube, and in the forefront of his reflections must be the inescapable fact that the secret of the McAllen Tube could no longer be kept without Barney Chard's co-operation. Barney had evidence of its existence, and didn't really need the evidence. A few hints dropped here and there would have made McAllen's twelve years of elaborate precaution quite meaningless.

Ergo, McAllen must be pondering now, how could one persuade Mr. Chard to remain silent?

But there was a second consideration Barney had planted in the old scientist's mind. Mr. Chard, that knowledgeable man of the world, exuded not at all by chance the impression of great quantities of available cash. His manner, the conservatively tailored business suit, the priceless chip of a platinum watch ... and McAllen needed cash badly. He'd been fairly wealthy himself at one time; but since he had refrained from exploiting the Tube's commercial possibilities, his continuing work with it was exhausting his capital. At least that could be assumed to be the reason for McAllen's impoverishment, which was a matter Barney had established. In months the old man would be living on beans.

Ergo again, McAllen's thoughts must be running, how might one not merely coax Mr. Chard into silence, but actually get him to come through with some much-needed financial support? What inducement, aside from the Tube, could be offered someone in his position?

Barney grinned inwardly as he snapped the end of his cigarette out on the amber-tinted water. The mark always sells himself, and McAllen was well along in the process. Polite silence was all that was necessary at the moment. He lit a fresh cigarette, feeling a mild curiosity about the little lake's location. Wisconsin, Minnesota, Michigan seemed equally probable guesses. What mattered was that half an hour ago McAllen's Tube had brought them both here in a wink of time from his home in California.

*   *   *   *   *

Dr. McAllen thoughtfully cleared his throat.

"Ever do any fishing, Mr. Chard?" he asked. After getting over his first shock at Barney's revelations, he'd begun speaking again in the brisk, abrupt manner Barney remembered from the last times he'd heard McAllen's voice.

"No," Barney admitted smiling. "Never quite got around to it."

"Always been too busy, eh?"

"With this and that," Barney agreed.

McAllen cleared his throat again. He was a roly-poly little man; over seventy now but still healthy-looking, with an apple-cheeked, sunburned face. Over a pair of steel-rimmed glasses his faded blue eyes peered musingly at Barney. "Around thirty-five, aren't you?"

"Thirty-seven."

"Married?"

"Divorced."

"Any particular hobbies?"

Barney laughed. "I play a little golf. Not very seriously."

McAllen clicked his tongue. "Well, what do you do for fun?"

"Oh ... I'd say I enjoy almost anything I get involved in." Barney, still smiling, felt a touch of wariness. He'd been expecting questions from McAllen, but not quite this kind.

"Mainly making money, eh? Well," McAllen conceded, "that's not a bad hobby. Practical, too. I ... whup! Just a moment."

The tip of the slender rod in his left hand dipped slightly, and sixty feet out beyond the end of the old dock a green and white bobber began twitching about. Then the bobber suddenly disappeared. McAllen lifted the rod tip a foot or two with a smooth, swift motion, and paused.

"Hooked!" he announced, looking almost childishly pleased.

The fish on the far end of the line didn't seem to put up much of a struggle, but the old man reeled it in slowly and carefully, giving out line from time to time, then taking it back. He seemed completely absorbed. Not until the fish had been worked close to the dock was there a brief minor commotion near the surface. Then McAllen was down on one knee, holding the rod high with one hand, reaching out for his catch with the other. Barney had a glimpse of an unimpressive green and silver disk, reddish froggy eyes. "*Very* nice crappie!" McAllen informed him with a broad smile. "Now–" He placed the rod on the dock, reached down with his other hand. The fish's tail slapped the water; it turned sideways, was gone.

"Lost it!" Barney commented, surprised.

"Huh?" McAllen looked around. "Well, no, young man–I *turned* him loose. He wasn't hooked bad. Crappies have delicate lips, but I use a barbless hook. Gives them better than a fighting chance." He stood up with the rod, dusting the knees of his baggy slacks. "Get all the eating fish I want anyway," he added.

"You really enjoy that sport, don't you?" Barney said curiously.

*　　*　　*　　*　　*

McAllen advised him with the seriousness of the true devotee to try it some time. "It gets to you. It can get to be a way of living. I've been fishing since I was knee-high. Three years ago I figured I'd become good enough to write a book on the subject. I got more arguments over that book–sounder arguments too, I'd say–than about any paper I've published in physics." He looked at Barney a moment, still seriously, and went on. "I told you wetting a line would calm me down after that upset you gave me. Well, it has–fishing is as good a form of therapy as I know about. Now I've been doing some thinking. I'd be interested ... well, I'd like to talk some more about the Tube with you, Mr. Chard. And perhaps about other things too."

"Very gratifying to hear that, doctor," Barney said gravely. "I did regret having to upset you, you know."

McAllen shrugged. "No harm done. It's given me some ideas. We'll talk right here." He indicated the weather-beaten little cabin on the bank behind Barney. "I'm not entirely sure about the California place. That's one reason I suggested this trip."

"You feel your houseman there mightn't be entirely reliable?"

"Fredericks unreliable? Heavens no! He knows about the Tube, of course, but Fredericks *expects* me to invent things. It wouldn't occur to him to talk to an outsider. He's been with me for almost forty years."

"He was," remarked Barney, "listening in on the early part of our conversation today."

"Well, he'll do that," McAllen agreed. "He's very curious about anyone who comes to see me. But otherwise ... no, it's just that in these days of sophisticated listening devices one shouldn't ever feel too sure of not being overheard."

"True enough." Barney glanced up at the cabin. "What makes you so sure of it here, doctor?"

"No reason why anyone would go to the trouble," McAllen said. "The property isn't in my name. And the nearest neighbor lives across the lake. I never come here except by the Tube so I don't attract any attention."

He led the way along the dock. Barney Chard followed, eyes reflectively on the back of McAllen's sunburned neck and the wisps of unclipped white hair sticking out beneath his beaked fishing cap. Barney had learned to estimate accurately the capacity for physical violence in people he dealt with. He would have offered long odds that neither Dr. McAllen nor Fredericks, the elderly colored man of all work, had the capacity. But Barney's right hand, slid idly into the pocket of his well-tailored coat, was resting on a twenty-five caliber revolver. This was, after all, a very unusual situation. The human factors in themselves were predictable.

Human factors were Barney's specialty. But here they were involved with something unknown—the McAllen Tube.

When it was a question of his personal safety, Barney Chard preferred to take no chances at all.

From the top of the worn wooden steps leading up to the cabin, he glanced back at the lake. It occurred to him there should have been at least a suggestion of unreality about that placid body of water, and the sun low and red in the west beyond it. Not that he felt anything of the kind. But less than an hour ago they had been sitting in McAllen's home in Southern California, and beyond the olive-green window shades it had been bright daylight.

"But I can't ... I really can't imagine," Dr. McAllen had just finished bumbling, his round face a study of controlled dismay on the other side of the desk, "whatever could have brought you to these ... these extraordinary conclusions, young man."

Barney had smiled reassuringly, leaning back in his chair. "Well, indirectly, sir, as the pictures indicate, we might say it was your interest in fishing. You see, I happened to notice you on Mallorca last month...."

*   *   *   *   *

By itself, the chance encounter on the island had seemed only moderately interesting. Barney was sitting behind the wheel of an ancient automobile, near a private home in which a business negotiation of some consequence was being conducted. The business under discussion happened to be Barney's, but it would have been inexpedient for him to attend the meeting in person. Waiting for his associates to wind up the matter, he was passing time by studying an old man who was fishing from a small boat offshore, a hundred yards or so below the road. After a while the old fellow brought the boat in, appeared a few minutes later along the empty lane carrying his tackle and an apparently empty gunny sack, and trudged unheedingly past the automobile and its occupant. As he went by, Barney had a sudden sense of recognition. Then, in a flash, his mind jumped back twelve years.

Dr. Oliver B. McAllen. Twelve years ago the name had been an important one in McAllen's field; then it was not so much forgotten as deliberately buried. Working under government contract at one of the big universities, McAllen had been suddenly and quietly retired. Barney, who had a financial interest in one of the contracts, had made inquiries; he was likely to be out of money if McAllen had been taken from the job. Eventually he was informed, in strict confidence, that Dr. McAllen had flipped. Under the delusion of having made a discovery of tremendous importance, he had persuaded the authorities to arrange a demonstration. When the demonstration ended in complete failure, McAllen angrily accused some of his most eminent colleagues of having sabotaged his invention, and withdrew from the university. To protect a once great scientist's name, the matter was being hushed up.

So Mallorca was where the addled old physicist had elected to end his days—not a bad choice either, Barney had thought, gazing after the retreating figure. Pleasant island in a beautiful sea—he remembered having heard about McAllen's passion for angling.

A day later, the Mallorca business profitably concluded, Barney flew back to Los Angeles. That evening he entertained a pair of tanned and shapely ladies whose idea of high fun was to drink all night and go deep-sea fishing at dawn. Barney shuddered inwardly at the latter notion, but promised to see the sporting characters to the Sweetwater Beach Municipal Pier in time to catch a party boat, and did so. One of the girls, he noticed not without satisfaction—he had become a little tired of the two before morning—appeared to turn a delicate green as she settled herself into the gently swaying half-day boat beside the wharf. Barney waved them an amiable farewell and was about to go when he noticed a plump old man sitting in the stern of the boat among other anglers, rigging up his tackle. Barney checked sharply, and blinked. He was looking at Oliver B. McAllen again.

It was almost a minute before he felt sure of it this time. Not that it was impossible for McAllen to be sitting in that boat, but it did seem extremely unlikely. McAllen didn't look in the least like a man who could afford nowadays to commute by air between the Mediterranean and California. And Barney felt something else trouble him obscurely as he stared down at the old scientist; a notion of some kind was stirring about in the back corridors of his mind, but refused to be drawn to view just then.

*   *   *   *   *

He grew aware of what it was while he watched the party boat head out to sea a few minutes later, smiled at what seemed an impossibly fanciful concoction of his unconscious, and started towards the pier's parking lot. But when he had reached his car, climbed in, turned on the ignition, and lit a cigarette, the notion was still with him and Barney was no longer smiling. Fanciful it was, extremely so. Impossible, in the strict sense, it was not. The longer he played it around, the more he began to wonder whether his notion mightn't hold water after all. If there was anything to it, he had run into one of the biggest deals in history.

Later Barney realized he would still have let the matter drop there if it hadn't been for other things, having nothing to do with Dr. McAllen. He was between operations at present. His time wasn't occupied. Furthermore he'd been aware lately that ordinary operations had begun to feel flat. The kick of putting over a deal, even on some other hard, bright character of his own class, unaccountably was fading. Barney Chard was somewhat frightened because the operator game was the only one he'd ever found interesting; the other role of well-heeled playboy wasn't much more than a manner of killing time. At thirty-seven he was realizing he was bored with life. He didn't like the prospect.

Now here was something which might again provide him with some genuine excitement. It could be simply his imagination working overtime, but it wasn't going to do any harm to find out. Mind humming with pleased though still highly skeptical speculations, Barney went back to the boat station and inquired when the party boat was due to return.

He was waiting for it, well out of sight, as it came chugging up to the wharf some hours later. He had never had anything to do directly with Dr. McAllen, so the old man wouldn't recognize him. But he didn't want to be spotted by his two amazons who might feel refreshed enough by now to be ready for another tour of the town.

He needn't have worried. The ladies barely made it to the top of the stairs; they phoned for a cab and were presently whisked away. Dr. McAllen meanwhile also had made a telephone call, and settled down not far from Barney to wait. A small gray car, five or six years old but of polished and well-tended appearance, trundled presently up the pier, came into the turnaround at the boat station, and stopped. A thin old Negro, with hair as white as the doctor's, held the door open for McAllen. The car moved unhurriedly off with them.

The automobile's license number produced Dr. McAllen's California address for Barney a short while later. The physicist lived in Sweetwater Beach, fifteen minutes' drive from the pier, in an old Spanish-type house back in the hills. The chauffeur's name was John Emanuel Fredericks; he had been working for McAllen for an unknown length of time. No one else lived there.

Barney didn't bother with further details about the Sweetwater Beach establishment at the moment. The agencies he usually employed to dig up background information were reasonably trustworthy, but he wanted to attract no more attention than was necessary to his interest in Dr. McAllen.

That evening he took a plane to New York.

*   *   *   *   *

Physicist Frank Elby was a few years older than Barney, an acquaintance since their university days. Elby was ambitious, capable, slightly dishonest; on occasion he provided Barney with contraband information for which he was generously paid.

Over lunch Barney broached a business matter which would be financially rewarding to both of them, and should not burden Elby's conscience unduly. Elby reflected, and agreed. The talk became more general. Presently Barney remarked, "Ran into an old acquaintance of ours the other day. Remember Dr. McAllen?"

"Oliver B. McAllen? Naturally. Haven't heard about him in years. What's he doing?"

Barney said he had only seen the old man, hadn't spoken to him. But he was sure it was McAllen.

"Where was this?" Elby asked.

"Sweetwater Beach. Small town down the Coast."

Elby nodded. "It must have been McAllen. That's where he had his home."

"He was looking hale and hearty. They didn't actually institutionalize him at the time of his retirement, did they?"

"Oh, no. No reason for it. Except on the one subject of that cockeyed invention of his, he behaved perfectly normally. Besides he would have hired a lawyer and fought any such move. He had plenty of money. And nobody wanted publicity. McAllen was a pretty likable old boy."

"The university never considered taking him back?"

Elby laughed. "Well, hardly! After all, man—a matter transmitter!"

Barney felt an almost electric thrill of pleasure. Right on the nose, Brother Chard! Right on the nose.

He smiled. "Was that what it was supposed to be? I never was told all the details."

Elby said that for the few who were informed of the details it had been a seven-day circus. McAllen's reputation was such that more people, particularly on his staff, had been ready to believe him that were ready to admit it later. "When he'd left–you know, he never even bothered to take that 'transmitter' along–the thing was taken apart and checked over as carefully as if somebody thought it might still suddenly start working. But it was an absolute Goldberg, of course. The old man had simply gone off his rocker."

"Hadn't there been any indication of it before?"

"Not that I know of. Except that he'd been dropping hints about his gadget for several months before he showed it to anyone," Elby said indifferently. The talk turned to other things.

*   *   *   *   *

The rest was routine, not difficult to carry out. A small cottage on Mallorca, near the waterfront, was found to be in McAllen's name. McAllen's liquid assets were established to have dwindled to something less than those of John Emanuel Fredericks, who patronized the same local bank as his employer. There had been frequent withdrawals of large, irregular sums throughout the past years. The withdrawals were not explained by McAllen's frugal personal habits; even his fishing excursions showed an obvious concern for expense. The retention of the Mediterranean retreat, modest though it was, must have a reason beyond simple self-indulgence.

Barney arranged for the rental of a bungalow in the outskirts of Sweetwater beach, which lay uphill from the old house in which McAllen and Fredericks lived, and provided a good view of the residence and its street entry.

He didn't go near the place himself. Operatives of a Los Angeles detective agency went on constant watch in the bungalow, with orders to photograph the two old men in the other house and any visitors at every appearance, and to record the exact times the pictures were taken. At the end of each day the photographs were delivered to an address from where they promptly reached Barney's hands.

A European agency was independently covering the Mallorca cottage in the same manner.

Nearly four weeks passed before Barney obtained the exact results he wanted. He called off the watch at both points, and next day came up the walk to McAllen's home and rang the doorbell. John Fredericks appeared, studied Barney's card and Barney with an air of mild disapproval, and informed him that Dr. McAllen did not receive visitors.

"So I've been told," Barney acknowledged pleasantly. "Please be so good as to give the doctor this."

Fredericks' white eyebrows lifted by the barest trifle as he looked at the sealed envelope Barney was holding out. After a moment's hesitation he took it, instructed Barney to wait, and closed the door firmly.

Listening to Fredericks' footsteps receding into the house, Barney lit a cigarette, and was pleased to find that his hands were as steady as if he had been on the most ordinary of calls. The envelope contained two sets of photographs, dated and indicating the time of day. The date was the same for both sets; the recorded time showed the pictures had been taken within fifteen minutes of one another. The central subject in each case was Dr. McAllen, sometimes accompanied by Fredericks. One set of photographs had been obtained on Mallorca, the other in Sweetwater Beach at McAllen's house.

Barring rocket assists, the two old men had been documented as the fastest moving human beings in all history.

Several minutes passed before Fredericks reappeared. With a face which was now completely without expression, he invited Barney to enter, and conducted him to McAllen's study. The scientist had the photographs spread out on a desk before him. He gestured at them.

"Just what–if anything–is this supposed to mean, sir?" he demanded in an unsteady voice.

Barney hesitated aware that Fredericks had remained in the hall just beyond the study. But Fredericks obviously was in McAllen's confidence. His eavesdropping could do no harm.

"It means this, doctor–" Barney began, amiably enough; and he proceeded to tell McAllen precisely what the photographs meant. McAllen broke in protestingly two or three times, then let Barney conclude his account of the steps he had taken to verify his farfetched hunch on the pier without further comment. After a few minutes Barney heard Fredericks' steps moving away, and then a door closing softly somewhere, and he shifted his position a trifle so that his right side was now toward the hall door. The little revolver was in the right-hand coat pocket. Even then Barney had no real concern that McAllen or Fredericks would attempt to resort to violence, but when people are acutely disturbed–and McAllen at least was–almost anything can happen.

* * * * *

When Barney finished, McAllen stared down at the photographs again, shook his head, and looked over at Barney.

"If you don't mind," he said, blinking behind his glasses, "I should like to think about this for a minute or two."

"Of course, doctor," Barney said politely. McAllen settled back in the chair, removed his glasses and half closed his eyes. Barney let his gaze rove. The furnishings of the house were what he had expected—well-tended, old, declining here and there to the downright shabby. The only reasonably new piece in the study was a radio-phonograph. The walls of the study and of the section of a living room he could see through a small archway were lined with crammed bookshelves. At the far end of the living room was a curious collection of clocks in various types and sizes, mainly antiques, but also some odd metallic pieces with modernistic faces. Vacancies in the rows indicated Fredericks might have begun to dispose discreetly of the more valuable items on his employer's behalf.

McAllen cleared his throat finally, opened his eyes, and settled the spectacles back on his nose.

"Mr. Chard," he inquired, "have you had scientific training?"

"No."

"Then," said McAllen, "the question remains of what your interest in the matter is. Perhaps you'd like to explain just why you put yourself to such considerable expense to intrude on my personal affairs—"

Barney hesitated perceptibly. "Doctor," he said, "there is something tantalizing about an enigma. I'm fortunate in having the financial means to gratify my curiosity when it's excited to the extent it was here."

McAllen nodded. "I can understand curiosity. Was that your only motive?"

Barney gave him his most disarming grin. "Frankly no. I've mentioned I'm a businessman—"

"Ah!" McAllen said, frowning.

"Don't misunderstand me. One of my first thoughts admittedly was that here were millions waiting to be picked up. But the investigation soon made a number of things clear to me."

"What were they?"

"Essentially, that you had so sound a reason for keeping your invention a secret that to do it you were willing to ruin yourself financially, and to efface yourself as a human being and as a scientist."

"I don't feel," McAllen observed mildly, "that I really have effaced myself, either as a human being or as a scientist."

"No, but as far as the public was concerned you did both."

McAllen smiled briefly. "That strategem was very effective—until now. Very well, Mr. Chard. You understand clearly that under no circumstances would I agree to the commercialization of ... well, of my matter transmitter?"

Barney nodded. "Of course."

"And you're still interested?"

"Very much so."

McAllen was silent for a few seconds, biting reflectively at his lower lip. "Very well," he said again. "You were speaking of my predilection for fishing. Perhaps you'd care to accompany me on a brief fishing trip?"

"Now?" Barney asked.

"Yes, now. I believe you understand what I mean ... I see you do. Then, if you'll excuse me for a few minutes—"

*   *   *   *   *

Barney couldn't have said exactly what he expected to be shown. His imaginings had run in the direction of a camouflaged vault beneath McAllen's house—some massively-walled place with machinery that powered the matter transmitter purring along the walls ... and perhaps something in the style of a plastic diving bell as the specific instrument of transportation.

The actual experience was quite different. McAllen returned shortly, having changed into the familiar outdoor clothing—apparently he had been literal about going on a fishing trip. Barney accompanied the old physicist into the living room, and watched him open a small but very sturdy wall safe. Immediately behind the safe door, an instrument panel had been built in the opening.

Peering over the spectacles, McAllen made careful adjustments on two sets of small dials, and closed and locked the safe again.

"Now, if you'll follow me, Mr. Chard–" He crossed the room to a door, opened it, and went out. Barney followed him into a small room with rustic furnishings and painted wooden walls. There was a single, heavily curtained window; the room was rather dim.

"Well," McAllen announced, "here we are."

It took a moment for that to sink in. Then, his scalp prickling eerily, Barney realized he was standing farther from the wall than he had thought. He looked around, and discovered there was no door behind him now, either open or closed.

He managed a shaky grin. "So that's how your matter transmitter works!"

"Well," McAllen said thoughtfully, "of course it isn't really a matter transmitter. I call it the McAllen Tube. Even an educated layman must realize that one can't simply disassemble a living body at one point, reassemble it at another, and expect life to resume. And there are other considerations–"

"Where are we?" Barney asked. "On Mallorca?"

"No. We haven't left the continent–just the state. Look out the window and see for yourself."

McAllen turned to a built-in closet, and Barney drew back the window hangings. Outside was a grassy slope, uncut and yellowed by the summer sun. The slope dropped sharply to a quiet lakefront framed by dark pines. There was no one in sight, but a small wooden dock ran out into the lake. At the far end of the dock an old rowboat lay tethered. And–quite obviously–it was no longer the middle of a bright afternoon; the air was beginning to dim, to shift towards evening.

Barney turned to find McAllen's mild, speculative eyes on him, and saw the old man had put a tackle box and fishing rod on the table.

"Your disclosures disturbed me more than you may have realized," McAllen remarked by way of explanation. His lips twitched in the shadow of a smile. "At such times I find nothing quite so soothing as to drop a line into water for a while. I've got some thinking to do, too. So let's get down to the dock. There ought to be a little bait left in the minnow pail."

*   *   *   *   *

When they returned to the cabin some time later, McAllen was in a pensive mood. He started a pot of coffee in the small kitchen, then quickly cleaned the tackle and put it away. Barney sat at the table, smoking and watching him, but made no attempt at conversation.

McAllen poured the coffee, produced sugar and powdered milk, and settled down opposite Barney. He said abruptly, "Have you had any suspicions about the reason for the secretive mumbo jumbo?"

"Yes," Barney said, "I've had suspicions. But it wasn't until *that* happened"—he waved his hand at the wall out of which they appeared to have stepped—"that I came to a definite conclusion."

"Eh?" McAllen's eyes narrowed suddenly. "What was the conclusion?"

"That you've invented something that's really a little too good."

"Too good?" said McAllen. "Hm-m-m. Go on."

"It doesn't take much power to operate the thing, does it?"

"Not," said McAllen dryly, "if you're talking about the kind of power one pays for."

"I am. Can the McAllen Tube be extended to any point on Earth?"

"I should think so."

"And you financed the building of this model yourself. Not very expensive. If the secret leaked out, I'd never know who was going to materialize in my home at any time, would I? Or with what intentions."

"That," McAllen nodded, "is about the size of it."

Barney crushed out his cigarette, lit a fresh one, blew out a thin streamer of smoke. "Under the circumstances," he remarked, "it's unfortunate you can't get the thing shut off again, isn't it?"

McAllen was silent for some seconds. "So you've guessed that, too," he said finally. "What mistake did I make?"

"None that I know of," Barney said. "But you're doing everything you can to keep the world from learning about the McAllen Tube. At the same time you've kept it in operation—which made it just a question of time before somebody else noticed something was going on, as I did. Your plans for the thing appear to have gone wrong."

McAllen was nodding glumly. "They have," he said. "They have, Mr. Chard. Not irreparably wrong, but still—" He paused. "The first time I activated the apparatus," he said, "I directed it only at two points. Both of them within structures which were and are my property. It was fortunate I did so."

"That was this cabin and the place on Mallorca?"

"Yes. The main operational sections of the Tube are concealed about my California home. But certain controls have to be installed at any exit point to make it possible to return. It wouldn't be easy to keep those hidden in any public place.

"It wasn't until I compared the actual performance of the Tube with my theoretical calculations that I discovered there was an unforeseen factor involved. To make it short, I could not—to use your phrasing—shut the Tube off again. But that would certainly involve some extremely disastrous phenomena at three different points of our globe."

"Explosions?" Barney asked.

"Weee-ll," McAllen said judiciously, "implosions might come a little closer to describing the effect. The exact term isn't contained in our vocabulary, and I'd prefer it *not* to show up there, at least in my lifetime. But you see my dilemma, don't you? If I asked for help, I revealed the existence of the Tube. Once its existence was known, the research that produced it could be duplicated. As you concluded, it isn't really too difficult a device to construct. And even with the present problem solved, the McAllen Tube is just a little too dangerous a thing to be at large in our world today."

"You feel the problem can be solved?"

"Oh, yes." McAllen took off his glasses and rubbed his eyes. "That part of it's only a matter of time. At first I thought I'd have everything worked out within three or four years. Unfortunately I badly underestimated the expense of some of the required experimentation. That's what's delayed everything."

"I see. I had been wondering," Barney admitted, "why a man with something like this on his mind would be putting in *quite* so much time fishing."

McAllen grinned. "Enforced idleness. It's been very irritating really, Mr. Chard. I've been obliged to proceed in the most inexpensive manner possible, and that meant–very slowly."

Barney said, "If it weren't for that question of funds, how long would it take to wind up the operation?"

"A year–perhaps two years." McAllen shrugged. "It's difficult to be too exact, but it certainly wouldn't be longer than two."

"And what would be the financial tab?"

McAllen hesitated. "A million is the bottom figure, I'm afraid. It should run closer to a million and a half."

"Doctor," Barney said, "let me make you a proposition."

*   *   *   *   *

McAllen looked at him. "Are you thinking of financing the experiments, Mr. Chard?"

"In return," Barney said, "for a consideration."

"What's that?" McAllen's expression grew wary.

"When you retired," Barney told him, "I dropped a nice piece of money as a consequence. It was the first beating I'd taken, and it hurt. I'd like to pick that money up again. All right. We're agreed it can't be done on the McAllen Tube. The Tube wouldn't help make the world a safer place for Barney Chard. But the Tube isn't any more remarkable than the mind that created it. Now I know a company which could be top of the heap in electronics precision work–one-shot specialties is what they go in for–if it had your mind as technical advisor. I can buy a controlling interest in that company tomorrow, doctor. And you can have the million and a half paid off in not much more time than you expect to take to get your monster back under control and shut down. Three years of your technical assistance, and we're clear."

McAllen's face reddened slowly. "I've considered hiring out, of course," he said. "Many times. I need the money very badly. But aren't you overlooking something?"

"What?"

"I went to considerable pains," said McAllen, "to establish myself as a lunatic. It was distasteful, but it seemed necessary to discourage anyone from making too close an investigation of some of my more recent lines of research. If it became known now that I was again in charge of a responsible project–"

Barney shook his head. "No problem, doctor. We'd be drawing on outside talent for help in specific matters– very easy to cover up any leads to you personally. I've handled that general sort of thing before."

McAllen frowned thoughtfully. "I see. But I'd have– There wouldn't be so much work that–"

"No," Barney said. "I guarantee that you'll have all the time you want for your own problem." He smiled.

"Considering what you told me, I'd like to hear that one's been solved myself!"

McAllen grinned briefly. "I can imagine. Very well. Ah ... when can you let me have the money, Mr. Chard?"

$$* \quad * \quad * \quad * \quad *$$

The sun was setting beyond the little lake as Barney drew the shades over the cabin window again. Dr. McAllen was half inside the built-in closet at the moment, fitting a pair of toggle switches to the concealed return device in there.

"Here we go," he said suddenly.

Three feet from the wall of the room the shadowy suggestion of another wall, and of an open door, became visible.

Barney said dubiously, "We came out of *that?*"

McAllen looked at him, sad, "The appearance is different on the exit side. But the Tube's open now—Here, I'll show you."

He went up to the apparition of a door, abruptly seemed to melt into it. Barney held his breath, and followed. Again there was no sensory reaction to passing through the Tube. As his foot came down on something solid in the shadowiness into which he stepped, the living room in Sweetwater Beach sprang into sudden existence about him.

"Seems a little odd from that end, the first time through, doesn't it?" McAllen remarked.

Barney let out his breath.

"If I'd been the one who invented the Tube," he said honestly, "I'd never have had the nerve to try it."

McAllen grinned. "Tell you the truth, I did need a drink or two the first time. But it's dead-safe if you know just what you're doing."

Which was not, Barney felt, too reassuring. He looked back. The door through which they had come was the one by which they had left. But beyond it now lay a section of the entrance hall of the Sweetwater Beach house.

"Don't let that fool you," said McAllen, following his gaze. "If you tried to go out into the hall at the moment, you'd find yourself right back in the cabin. Light rays passing through the Tube can be shunted off and on." He went over to the door, closed and locked it, dropping the key in his pocket. "I keep it locked. I don't often have visitors, but if I had one while the door was open it could be embarrassing."

"What about the other end?" Barney asked. "The door appeared in the cabin when you turned those switches. What happens now? Suppose someone breaks into the cabin and starts prowling around–is the door still there?"

McAllen shook his head. "Not unless that someone happened to break in within the next half-minute." He considered. "Let's put it this way. The Tube's permanently centered on its two exit points, but the effect ordinarily is dissipated over half a mile of the neighborhood at the other end. For practical purposes there is no useful effect. When I'm going to go through, I bring the exit end down to a focus point ... does that make sense? Very well. It remains focused for around sixty or ninety seconds, depending on how I set it; then it expands again." He nodded at the locked door. "In the cabin, that's disappeared by now. Walk through the space where it's been, and you'll notice nothing unusual. Clear?"

Barney hesitated. "And if that door were still open here, and somebody attempted to step through after the exit end had expanded–"

"Well," McAllen said, moving over to a wall buzzer and pressing it, "that's what I meant when I said it could be embarrassing. He'd get expanded too–disastrously. Could you use a drink, Mr. Chard? I know I want one."

*   *   *   *   *

The drinks, served by Fredericks, were based on a rather rough grade of bourbon, but Barney welcomed them. There was an almost sick fascination in what was a certainty now: he was going to get the Tube. That tremendous device was his for the taking. He was well inside McAllen's guard; only carelessness could arouse the old man's suspicions again, and Barney was not going to be careless. No need to hurry anything. He would play the reserved role he had selected for himself, leave developments up to the fact that McAllen had carried the burden of his secret for twelve years, with no more satisfactory confidant than Fredericks to trust with it. Having told Barney so much, McAllen wanted to tell more. He would have needed very little encouragement to go on talking about it now.

Barney offered no encouragement. Instead, he gave McAllen a cautiously worded reminder that it was not inconceivable they had an audience here, at which McAllen reluctantly subsided. There was, however, one fairly important question Barney still wanted answered today. The nature of the answer would tell him the manner in which McAllen should now be handled.

He waited until he was on his feet and ready to leave before presenting it. McAllen's plump cheeks were flushed from the two highballs he had put away; in somewhat awkward phrases he had been expressing his gratitude for Barney's generous help, and his relief that because of it the work on the Tube now could be brought to an end.

"Just one thing about that still bothers me a little, doctor," Barney said candidly.

McAllen looked concerned. "What's that, Mr. Chard?"

"Well ... you're in good health, I'd say." Barney smiled. "But suppose something did happen to you before you succeeded in shutting the McAllen Tube down." He inclined his head toward the locked door.

"That thing would still be around waiting for somebody to open it and step through...."

McAllen's expression of concern vanished. He dug a forefinger cheerfully into Barney's ribs. "Young man, you needn't worry. I've been aware of the possibility, of course, and believe me I'm keeping *very* careful notes and instructions. Safe deposit boxes ... we'll talk about that tomorrow, eh? Somewhere else? Had a man in mind, as a matter of fact, but we can make better arrangements now. You see, it's really so ridiculously *easy* at this stage."

Barney cleared his throat. "Some other physicist–?"

"*Any* capable physicist," McAllen said decidedly. "Just a matter, you see of how reliable he is." He winked at Barney. "Talk about that tomorrow too–or one of these days."

Barney stood looking down, with a kind of detached surprise, at a man who had just pronounced sentence of death casually on himself, and on an old friend. For the first time in Barney's career, the question of deliberate murder not only entered an operation, but had become in an instant an unavoidable part of it. Frank Elby, ambitious and money-hungry, could take over where McAllen left off. Elby was highly capable, and Elby could be controlled. McAllen could not. He could only be tricked; and, if necessary, killed.

It was necessary, of course. If McAllen lived until he knew how to shut the Tube down safely, he simply would shut it down, destroy the device and his notes on it. A man who had gone to such extreme lengths to safeguard the secret was not going to be talked out of his conviction that the McAllen Tube was a menace to the world. Fredericks, the morose eavesdropper, had to be silenced with his employer to assure Barney of his undisputed possession of the Tube.

Could he still let the thing go, let McAllen live? He couldn't, Barney decided. He'd dealt himself a hand in a new game, and a big one–a fantastic, staggering game when one considered the possibilities in the Tube. It meant new interest, it meant life for him. It wasn't in his nature to pull out. The part about McAllen was cold necessity. A very ugly necessity, but McAllen–pleasantly burbling something as they walked down the short hall to the front door–already seemed a little unreal, a roly-poly, muttering, fading small ghost.

In the doorway Barney exchanged a few words–he couldn't have repeated them an instant later–with the ghost, became briefly aware of a remarkably firm hand clasp, and started down the cement walk to the street. Evening had come to California at last; a few houses across the street made dim silhouettes against the hills, some of the windows lit. He felt, Barney realized, curiously tired and depressed. A few steps behind him, he heard McAllen quietly closing the door to his home.

The walk, the garden, the street, the houses and hills beyond, vanished in a soundlessly violent explosion of white light around Barney Chard.

*   *   *   *   *

His eyes might have been open for several seconds before he became entirely aware of the fact. He was on his back looking up at the low raftered ceiling of a room. The light was artificial, subdued; it gave the impression of nighttime outdoors.

Memory suddenly blazed up. "Tricked!" came the first thought. Outsmarted. Outfoxed. And by–Then that went lost in a brief, intense burst of relief at the realization he was still alive, apparently unhurt. Barney turned sharply over on his side–bed underneath, he discovered–and stared around.

The room was low, wide. Something undefinably odd– He catalogued it quickly. Redwood walls, Navaho rugs on the floor, bookcases, unlit fireplace, chairs, table, desk with a typewriter and reading lamp. Across the room a tall dark grandfather clock with a bright metal disk instead of a clock-face stood against the wall. From it came a soft, low thudding as deliberate as the heart-beat of some big animal. It was the twin of one of the clocks he had seen in McAllen's living room.

The room was McAllen's, of course. Almost luxurious by comparison with his home, but wholly typical of the man. And now Barney became aware of its unusual feature; there were no windows. There was one door, so far to his right he had to twist his head around to see it. It stood half open; beyond it a few feet of a narrow passage lay within his range of vision, lighted in the same soft manner as the room. No sound came from there.

Had he been left alone? And what had happened? He wasn't in McAllen's home or in that fishing shack at the lake. The Tube might have picked him up—somehow—in front of McAllen's house, transported him to the Mallorca place. Or he might be in a locked hideaway McAllen had built beneath the Sweetwater Beach house.

Two things were unpleasantly obvious. His investigations hadn't revealed all of McAllen's secrets. And the old man hadn't really been fooled by Barney Chard's smooth approach. Not, at any rate, to the extent of deciding to trust him.

Hot chagrin at the manner in which McAllen had handed the role of dupe back to him flooded Barney for a moment. He swung his legs over the side of the bed and stood up. His coat had been hung neatly over the back of a chair a few feet away; his shoes stood next to the bed. Otherwise he was fully clothed. Nothing in the pockets of the coat appeared to have been touched; billfold, cigarette case, lighter, even the gun, were in place; the gun, almost startingly, was still loaded. Barney thrust the revolver thoughtfully into his trousers pocket. His wrist watch seemed to be the only item missing.

He glanced about the room again, then at the half-open door and the stretch of narrow hallway beyond. McAllen must have noticed the gun. The fact that he hadn't bothered to take it away, of at least to unload it, might have been reassuring under different circumstances. Here, it could have a very disagreeable meaning. Barney went quietly to the door, stood listening a few seconds, became convinced there was no one within hearing range, and moved on down the hall.

In less than two minutes he returned to the room, with the first slow welling of panic inside him. He had found a bathroom, a small kitchen and pantry, a storage room twice as wide and long as the rest of the place combined, crammed with packaged and crated articles, and with an attached freezer. If it was mainly stored food, as Barney thought, and if there was adequate ventilation and independent power, as seemed to be the case, then McAllen had constructed a superbly self-sufficient hideout. A man might live comfortably enough for years without emerging from it.

There was only one thing wrong with the setup from Barney's point of view. The thing he'd been afraid of. Nowhere was there an indication of a window or of an exit door.

The McAllen Tube, of course, might make such ordinary conveniences unnecessary. And if the Tube was the only way in or out, then McAllen incidentally had provided himself with an escape-proof jail for anyone he preferred to keep confined. The place might very well have been built several hundred feet underground. A rather expensive proposition but, aside from that, quite feasible.

Barney felt his breath begin to quicken, and told himself to relax. Wherever he was, he shouldn't be here long. McAllen presently would be getting in contact with him. And then–

His glance touched the desk across the room, and now he noticed his missing wrist watch on it. He went over, picked it up, and discovered that the long white envelope on which the watch had been placed was addressed to him.

For a moment he stared at the envelope. Then, his fingers shaking a little, he tore open the envelope and pulled out the typewritten sheets within.

*   *   *   *   *

The letterhead, he saw without surprise, was OLIVER
B. MCALLEN.

The letter read:

Dear Mr. Chard:

*An unfortunate series of circumstances, combined
with certain character traits in yourself, make it necessary
to inconvenience you in a rather serious manner.*

*To explain: The information I gave you regarding
the McAllen Tube and my own position was not entirely
correct. It is not the intractable instrument I presented it
as being–it can be "shut off" again quite readily and
without any attendant difficulties. Further, the decision to
conceal its existence was not reached by myself alone. For
years we–that is, Mr. Fredericks, who holds a degree in
engineering and was largely responsible for the actual
construction of the Tube–and I, have been members of an
association of which I cannot tell you too much. But I may
say that it acts, among other things, as the present
custodian of some of the more dangerous products of
human science, and will continue to do so until a more
stable period permits their safe release. To keep
developments such as the McAllen Tube out of
irresponsible hands is no easy task these days, but a
variety of effective devices are employed to that end. In
this instance, you happened upon a "rigged" situation,
which had been designed to draw action from another
man, an intelligent and unscrupulous individual who
lately had indicated a disturbing interest in events
connected with the semipublic fiasco of my "matter
transmitter" some years ago. The chances of another
person becoming aware of the temporal incongruities
which were being brought to this man's attention were
regarded as so remote that they need be given no practical
consideration. Nevertheless, the unexpected happened: you
became interested. The promptness with which you acted
on your chance observations shows a bold and*

imaginative manner of thinking on which you may be genuinely congratulated.

However, a perhaps less commendable motivation was also indicated. While I appeared to stall on coming to decisions you may have regarded as inevitable, your background was being investigated by the association. The investigation confirmed that you fall within a personality category of which we have the greatest reason to be wary. Considering the extent of what you had surmised and learned, falsified though the picture was, this presented a serious problem. It was made more acute by the fact that the association is embarking on a "five-year-plan" of some importance. Publicity during this period would be more than ordinarily undesirable. It will therefore be necessary to see to it that you have no opportunity to tell what you know before the plan is concluded. I am sure you can see it would be most unwise to accept your simple word on the matter. Your freedom of movement and of communication must remain drastically restricted until this five-year period is over. Within the next two weeks, as shown by the clock in your quarters, it will have become impossible for me or for any member of the association to contact you again before the day of your release. I tell you this so that you will not nourish vain hopes of changing the situation in your favor, but will adjust as rapidly as you can to the fact that you must spend the next five years by yourself. What ameliorations of this basic condition appeared possible have been provided. It is likely that you will already have tried to find a way out of the cabin in which you were left. The manner of doing this will become apparent to you exactly twenty-four hours after I conclude and seal this letter. It seemed best to advise you of some details of your confinement before letting you discover that you have been given as much limited freedom as circumstances allowed.

Sincerely yours,
OLIVER B. MCALLEN

Barney dropped the letter on the desk, stared down at it, his mouth open. His face had flushed red. "Why, he's crazy!" he said aloud at last. "He's crazier than–" He straightened, looked uneasily about the room again.

Whether a maniac McAllen made a more desirable jailer than a secret association engaged in keeping dangerous scientific developments under cover could be considered an open question. The most hopeful thought was that Dr. McAllen was indulging an unsuspected and nasty sense of humor.

Unfortunately, there wasn't the slightest reason to believe it. McAllen was wise to him. The situation was no gag–and neither was it necessarily what McAllen wanted him to think. Unless his watch had been reset, he had been knocked out by whatever hit him for roughly five hours–or seventeen, he amended. But he would have been hungry if it had been the longer period; and he wasn't.

Five hours then. Five hours wouldn't have given them time to prepare the "cabin" as it was prepared: for someone's indefinite stay. At a guess, McAllen had constructed it as a secure personal retreat in the event of something like a nuclear holocaust. But, in that case, why vacate it now for Barney Chard?

Too many questions, he thought. Better just keep looking around.

*   *   *   *   *

The blank metal face on the grandfather clock swung back to reveal a group of four dials, each graduated in a different manner, only one of them immediately familiar. Barney studied the other three for some seconds, then their meaning suddenly came clear. The big clock had just finished softly talking away the fourth hour of the first day of the first month of Year One. There were five figures on the Year Dial.

He stared at it. A five-year period of–something seemed to be the key to the entire setup.

Barney shook his head. Key it might be, but not one he could read without additional data. He snapped the cover disk shut on the unpleasantly suggestive dials, and began to go mentally over McAllen's letter.

The business that in twenty-four hours–twenty now– the manner of leaving the cabin would become "apparent" to him–that seemed to dispose of the possibility of being buried underground here. McAllen would hardly have provided him with a personal model of the Tube; he must be speaking of an ordinary door opening on the immediate environment, equipped with a time lock.

In that case, where was the door?

Barney made a second, far more careful search. Three hours later, he concluded it. He'd still found no trace of an exit. But the paneling in any of the rooms might slide aside to reveal one at the indicated time, or a section of the floor might swing back above a trap door. There was no point in attempting to press the search any further. After all, he only had to wait.

On the side, he'd made other discoveries. After opening a number of crates in the storage room, and checking contents of the freezer, he could assume that there was in fact more than enough food here to sustain one man for five years. Assuming the water supply held out–there was no way of checking on it; the source of the water like that of the power and the ventilation lay outside the area which was accessible to him–but if the water could be depended on, he wouldn't go hungry or thirsty. Even tobacco and liquor were present in comparably liberal quantities. The liquor he'd seen was all good; almost at random he had selected a bottle of cognac and brought it and a glass to the main room with him. The thought of food wasn't attractive at the moment. But he could use a drink.

He half filled the glass, emptied it with a few swallows, refilled it and took it over to one of the armchairs. He began to feel more relaxed almost at once. But the truth was, he acknowledged, settling back in the chair, that the situation was threatening to unnerve him completely. Everything he'd seen implied McAllen's letter came close to stating the facts; what wasn't said became more alarming by a suggestion of deliberate vagueness. Until that melodramatically camouflaged door was disclosed–seventeen hours from now–he'd be better off if he didn't try to ponder the thing out. And the best way to do that might be to take a solid load on rapidly, and then sleep away as much of the intervening time as possible. He wasn't ordinarily a hard drinker, but he'd started on the second bottle before the cabin began to blur on him. Afterwards, he didn't remember making it over to the bed.

*   *   *   *   *

Barney woke up ravenous and without a trace of hangover. Making a mental adjustment to his surroundings took no more time than opening his eyes; he'd been dreaming Dr. McAllen had dropped him into a snake pit and was sadistically dangling a rope twelve feet above his head, inviting him to climb out. To find himself still in the softly lit cabin was–for a few seconds, at any rate–a relief.

The relief faded as he sat up and looked at his watch. Still over an hour to go before McAllen's idiotic door became "apparent." Barney swore and headed for the bathroom to freshen up.

There was an electric shaver there, the end of its cord vanishing into the wall. Barney used it as meticulously as if he were embarking on a day of normal activities, prepared a breakfast in the kitchen and took it to the main room. He ate unhurriedly, absorbed in his thoughts, now and then glancing about the room. After a few minutes he uneasily pushed back the plate and stood up. If McAllen's twenty-four hours began with the moment the big clock in the room had been started, the door should be in evidence by now.

Another tour of the place revealed nothing and left him nervous enough to start biting his nails. He moved about the room, looking over things he'd already investigated. A music cabinet–he'd thought it was a radio at first, but it was only an elaborate hi-fi record player; two enclosed racks of records went with it–mainly classical stuff apparently. And a narrow built-in closet with three polished fishing rods and related gear, which would have allowed for speculation on the nature of the cabin's surroundings, except that McAllen might feel compelled to have a sampling of his toys around him wherever he was. Barney closed the closet door morosely, stood regarding the two crowded bookcases next to it. Plenty of books–reflecting the McAllen taste again. Technical tomes. Great Literature. Dickens, Melville, the Life of Gandhi.

Barney grunted, and was turning away when another title caught his eye. He glanced back at it, hauled out the book:

"Fresh Water Game Fish; Tested Methods of Their Pursuit." The author: O. B. McAllen.

Barney was opening the book when the cabin's door also opened.

* * * * *

Bright light–daylight–filled the room with so sudden a gush that Barney's breath caught in his throat. The book seemed to leap out of his hands. With the same glance he saw then the low, wide picture window which abruptly had appeared in the opposite wall, occupying almost half its space–and, in the other wall on the far left, a big door which was still swinging slowly open into the room. Daylight poured in through window and door. And beyond them–

For seconds he stared at the scene outside, barely aware of what he was looking at, while his mind raced on. He had searched every inch of the walls. And those thick wooden panels hadn't simply slid aside; the surfaces of doorframe and window were flush with the adjoining wall sections. So the McAllen Tube was involved in these changes in the room—and he might have guessed, Barney thought, that McAllen would have found more than one manner of putting the space-twisting properties of his device to use. And then finally he realized what he was seeing through the window and beyond the door. He walked slowly up to the window, still breathing unevenly.

The scene was unfamiliar but not at all extraordinary. The cabin appeared to be part way up one side of a heavily forested, rather narrow valley. It couldn't be more than half a mile to the valley's far slope which rose very steeply, almost like a great cresting green wave, filling the entire window. Coming closer Barney saw the skyline above it, hazy, summery, brilliantly luminous. This cabin of McAllen's might be in one of the wilder sections of the Canadian Rockies.

Or—and this was a considerably less happy thought—it probably could have been set up just as well in some area like the Himalayas.

But a more immediate question was whether the cabin actually *was* in the valley or only appearing to be there. The use of the Tube made it possible that this room and its seeming surroundings were very far apart in fact. And just what would happen to him then if he decided to step outside?

There were scattered sounds beyond the open door: bird chirpings and whistles, and the continuous burring calls of what Barney decided would be a wild pigeon. Then a swirl of wind stirred the nearer branches. He could feel the wash of the breeze in the room.

It looked and sounded—and felt—all right.

Barney scowled undecidedly, clearing his throat, then discovered that a third item had appeared in the room along with the door and the window. In the wall just this side of the door at shoulder-height was a small ivory plate with two black switches on it. Presumably the controls for door and window....

Barney went over, gingerly touched the one on the right, watching the window; then flicked up the switch. Instantly, the window had vanished, the wood paneling again covered the wall. Barney turned the switch down. The window was back.

The door refused to disappear until he pushed it shut. Then it obeyed its switch with the same promptness.

He went back across the room, returned with one of McAllen's fishing poles, and edged its tip tentatively out through the door. He wouldn't have been surprised if the tip had disintegrated in that instant. But nothing at all occurred. He dug about with the pole in the loose earth beyond the doorsill, then drew it back. The breeze was flowing freely past him; a few grains of soil blew over the sill and into the room. The door seemed to be concealing no grisly tricks and looked to be safe enough.

Barney stepped out on the sill, moved on a few hesitant steps, stood looking about. He had a better view of the valley here—and the better view told him immediately that he was not in the Canadian Rockies. At least, Canada, to his knowledge, had no desert. And, on the left, this valley came to an end perhaps a little more than a mile away from the cabin, its wooded slopes flowing steeply down to a landscape which was dull rust-red—flat sand stretches alternating with worn rock escarpments, until the desert's rim rose toward and touched the hazy white sky. Not so very different from—

Barney's eyes widened suddenly. Could he be in the Sierras—perhaps not more than three or four hours' drive from Los Angeles?

Three or four hours' drive if he'd had a car, or course. But even so—

He stared around, puzzled. There were no signs of a human being, of human habitation. But somebody else must be here. Somebody to keep guard on him. Otherwise there was nothing to stop him from walking away from this place—though it might very well be a long, uncomfortable hike to any civilized spot.

Even if this did turn out to be the Himalayas, or some equally remote area, there must be hill tribes about if one went far enough—there should even be an occasional airplane passing overhead.

Barney stood just outside the door, frowning, pondering the situation again, searching for the catch in it. McAllen and his friends, whatever else they might be, weren't stupid. There was something involved here that he hadn't become aware of yet.

Almost without thought then, he turned up his head, squinting at the bright hazy sky above him—

And saw IT.

His breath sucked in and burst from his lungs in a half-strangled, terrified squawk as he staggered backward into the cabin, slammed the door shut, then spun around and began slapping frantically at the switches on the wall-plate until door and window were gone, and only the cabin's soft illumination was around him again. Then he crouched on the floor, his back against the wall, shaking with a terror he could hardly have imagined before.

He knew what the catch was now. He had understood it completely in the instant of glancing up and seeing that tiny brilliant blue-white point of light glare down at him through the incandescent cloud layers above. Like a blazing, incredibly horrible insect eye....

This world's sun.

THE END OF YEAR ONE

Barney Chard came up out of an uneasy sleep to the sudden sharp awareness that something was wrong. For some seconds he lay staring about the unlit cabin, mouth dry, heart hammering with apprehension. Then he discovered it was only that he had left the exit door open and the window switched on.... Only? This was the first time since they had left him here that he had gone to sleep without sealing the cabin first—even when blind drunk, really embalmed.

He thought of climbing out of bed and taking care of it now, but decided to let the thing ride. After all he knew there was nothing in the valley—nothing, in fact, on this world—of which he had a realistic reason to be afraid. And he felt dead tired. Weak and sick. Feeling like that no longer alarmed him as it had done at first; it was a simple physical fact. The sheet under him was wet with sweat, though it was no more than comfortably warm in the room. The cabin never became more than comfortably warm. Barney lay back again, trying to figure out how it had happened he had forgotten about the window and the door.

It had been night for quite a while when he went to sleep, but regardless of how long he'd slept, it was going to go on being night a good deal longer. The last time he had bothered to check—which, Barney decided on reflection, might be several months ago now—the sunless period had continued for better than fifty-six hours. Not long before dropping on the bed, he was standing in front of the big clock while the minute hand on the hour dial slid up to the point which marked the end of the first year in Earth time he had spent in the cabin. Watching it happen, he was suddenly overwhelmed again by the enormity of his solitude, and it looked as if it were going to turn into another of those periods when he sat with the gun in his hand, sobbing and swearing in a violent muddle of self-pity and helpless fury. He decided to knock off the lamenting and get good and drunk instead. And he would make it a drunk to top all drunks on this happy anniversary night.

But he hadn't done that either. He had everything set up, downright festively—glasses, crushed ice, a formidable little squad of fresh bottles. But when he looked at the array, he suddenly felt sick in advance. Then there was a wave of leaden heaviness, of complete fatigue. He hadn't had time to think of sealing the cabin. He had simply fallen into the bed then and there, and for all practical purposes passed out on the spot.

Barney Chard lay wondering about that. It had been, one might say, a rough year. Through the long days in particular, he had been doing his level best to obliterate his surroundings behind sustained fogs of alcoholism. The thought of the hellishly brilliant far-off star around which this world circled, the awareness that only the roof and walls of the cabin were between himself and that blazing alien watcher, seemed entirely unbearable. The nights, after a while, were easier to take. They had their strangeness too, but the difference wasn't so great. He grew accustomed to the big green moon, and developed almost an affection for a smaller one, which was butter-yellow and on an orbit that made it a comparatively infrequent visitor in the sky over the valley. By night he began to leave the view window in operation and finally even the door open for hours at a time. But he had never done it before when he wanted to go to sleep.

Alcoholism, Barney decided, stirring uneasily on the sweat-soiled, wrinkled sheet, hadn't been much of a success. His body, or perhaps some resistant factor in his mind, let him go so far and no farther. When he exceeded the limit, he became suddenly and violently ill. And remembering the drunk periods wasn't pleasant. Barney Chard, that steel-tough lad, breaking up, going to pieces, did not make a pretty picture. It was when he couldn't keep that picture from his mind that he most frequently had sat there with the gun, turning it slowly around in his hand. It had been a rather close thing at times.

Perhaps he simply hated McAllen and the association too much to use the gun. Drunk or sober, he brooded endlessly over methods of destroying them. He had to be alive when they came back. Some while ago there had been a space of several days when he was hallucinating the event, when McAllen and the association seemed to be present, and he was arguing with them, threatening them, even pleading with them. He came out of that period deeply frightened by what he was doing. Since then he hadn't been drinking as heavily.

But this was the first time he'd gone to sleep without drinking at all.

*   *   *   *   *

He sat up on the edge of the bed, found himself shaking a little again after that minor effort, but climbed to his feet anyway, and walked unsteadily over to the door. He stood there looking out. The cloud layers always faded away during the night, gathered again at dawn. By now the sky was almost clear. A green glow over the desert to the left meant the larger moon was just below the horizon. The little yellow moon rode high in the sky above it. If they came up together, this would be the very bright part of the night during which the birds and other animal life in the valley went about their pursuits as if it were daytime. He could hear bird-chirpings now against the restless mutter of the little stream which came down the center of the valley, starting at the lake at the right end and running out into stagnant and drying pools a short distance after it entered the desert.

He discovered suddenly he had brought the gun along from the bed with him and was holding it without having been in the least aware of the fact. Grinning twistedly at the old and pointless precaution, he shoved the gun into his trousers pocket, brought out matches, a crumpled pack of cigarettes, and began to smoke. Very considerate of them to see to it he wouldn't run out of minor conveniences ... like leaving him liquor enough to drink himself to death on any time he felt like it during these five years.

Like leaving him the gun–

From the association's standpoint those things were up to him, of course, Barney thought bitterly. In either unfortunate event, he wouldn't be on *their* consciences.

He felt a momentary spasm of the old hate, but a feeble one, hardly more than a brief wash of the early torrents of rage. Something had burned out of him these months; an increasing dullness was moving into its place—

And just what, he thought, startled, was he doing outside the cabin door now? He hadn't consciously decided to go that far; it must have been months, actually, since he had walked beyond the doorway at all. During the first few weeks he had made half a dozen attempts to explore his surroundings by night, and learned quickly that he was confined to as much of the valley as he could see from the cabin. Beyond the ridges lay naked desert and naked mountain ranges, silent and terrifying in the moonlight.

Barney glanced up and down the valley, undecided but not knowing quite what he was undecided about. He didn't feel like going back into the cabin, and to just stand here was boring.

"Well," he said aloud, sardonically, "it's a nice night for a walk, Brother Chard."

Well, why not? It was bright enough to see by now if he kept away from the thickest growths of trees, and getting steadily brighter as the big moon moved up behind the distant desert rim. He'd walk till he got tired, then rest. By the time he got back to the cabin he'd be ready to lie down and sleep off the curious mood that had taken hold of him.

Barney started off up the valley, stepping carefully and uncertainly along the sloping, uneven ground.

*   *   *   *   *

During the early weeks he had found a thick loose-leaf binder in the back of one of the desk drawers. He thought it might have been left there intentionally. Its heading was NOTES ON THE TERRESTRIAL ECOLOGICAL BASE OF THE EIGHTEENTH SYSTEM, VOLUME III.

After leafing through them once, it had been a while before Barney could bring himself to study the notes in more detail. He didn't, at that time, want to know too much about the situation he was in. He was still numbed by it.

But eventually he went over the binder carefully. The various reports were unsigned, but appeared to have been compiled by at least four or five persons—McAllen among them; his writing style was not difficult to recognize. Leaving out much that was incomprehensible or nearly so, Barney could still construe a fairly specific picture of the association project of which he was now an unscheduled and unwilling part. Selected plants and animals had been moved from Earth through the McAllen Tube to a world consisting of sand, rock and water, without detected traces of indigenous life in any form. At present the Ecological Base was only in its ninth year, which meant that the larger trees in the valley had been nearly full-grown when brought here with the soil that was to nourish them. From any viewpoint, the planting of an oasis of life on the barren world had been a gigantic undertaking, but there were numerous indications that the McAllen Tube was only one of the array of improbable devices the association had at its disposal for such tasks. A few cryptic paragraphs expressed the writer's satisfaction with the undetailed methods by which the Base's localized climatic conditions were maintained.

So far even the equipment which kept the cabin in uninterrupted operation had eluded Barney's search. It and the other required machinery might be buried somewhere in the valley. Or it might, he thought, have been set up just as easily some distance away, in the desert or among the remotely towering mountain ranges. One thing he had learned from the binder was that McAllen had told the truth in saying no one could contact him from Earth before the full period of his exile was over. The reason had seemed appalling enough in itself. This world had moved to a point in its orbit where the radiance of its distant sun was thickening between it and Earth, growing too intense to be penetrated by the forces of the McAllen Tube. Another four years would pass before the planet and the valley emerged gradually from behind that barrier again.

*   *   *   *   *

He walked, rested, walked again. Now and then he was troubled by a burst of violent sweating, followed by shivering fits until his clothes began to dry again. The big moon edged presently over the ridge above him, and in the first flood of its light the opposite slope of the valley took on the appearance of a fanciful sub-oceanic reef. The activity of the animal life about Barney increased promptly. It was no darker now than an evening hour on Earth, and his fellow occupants of the Ecological Base seemed well-adjusted to the strange shifts of day and night to which they had been consigned.

He pushed through a final thicket of shrubbery, and found himself at the edge of the lake. Beyond the almost circular body of water, a towering wall of cliffs sealed the upper end of the valley. He had come almost a mile, and while a mile—a city mile, at least—wouldn't have meant much to Barney Chard at one time, he felt quite exhausted now. He sat down at the edge of the water, and, after a minute or two, bent forward and drank from it. It had the same cold, clear flavor as the water in the cabin.

The surface of the water was unquiet. Soft-flying large insects of some kind were swarming about, stippling the nearby stretch of the lake with their touch, and there were frequent swift swirls as fish rose from beneath to take down the flyers. Presently one of them broke clear into the air—a big fish, thick-bodied and shining, looking as long as Barney's arm in the moonlight—and dropped back with a splash. Barney grinned twistedly. The NOTES indicated Dr. McAllen had taken some part in stocking the valley, and one could trust McAllen to see to it that the presence of his beloved game fish wasn't overlooked even in so outlandish a project.

He shifted position, became aware of the revolver in his pocket and brought it out. A wave of dull anger surged slowly through him again. What they did with trees and animals was their own business. But what they had done to a human being....

He scrambled suddenly to his feet, drew his arm back, and sent the gun flying far out over the lake. It spun through the moonlight, dipped, struck the surface with less of a splash than the fish had made, and was gone.

Now why, Barney asked himself in amazement, did I do that? He considered it a moment, and then, for the first time in over a year, felt a brief touch of something not far from elation.

He wasn't going to die here. No matter how politely the various invitations to do himself in had been extended by McAllen or the association, he was going to embarrass them by being alive and healthy when they came back to the valley four years from now. They wouldn't kill him then; they'd already shown they didn't have the guts to commit murder directly. They would have to take him back to Earth.

And once he was there, it was going to be too bad for them. It didn't matter how closely they watched him; in the end he would find or make the opportunity to expose them, pull down the whole lousy, conceited crew, see them buried under the shambles an outraged world would make of the secret association....

THE END OF YEAR TWO

The end of Year Two on the Ecological Base in the Eighteenth System arrived and went by without Barney's being immediately aware of the fact. Some two hours later, he glanced at his wrist watch, pushed back the chair, got up from the desk and went over to the big grandfather clock to confirm his surmise.

"Well, well, Brother Chard," he said aloud. "Another anniversary ... and three of them to go. We're almost at the halfway mark—"

He snapped the cover plate back over the multiple clock faces, and turned away. Three more years on the Ecological Base was a gruesome stretch of time when you thought of it as a whole....

Which was precisely why he rarely let himself think of it as a whole nowadays.

This last year, at any rate, Barney conceded to himself, had to be regarded as an improvement on the first. Well, he added irritably, and what wouldn't be? It hadn't been delightful, he'd frequently felt almost stupefied with boredom. But physically, at least, he was fit—considerably fitter, as a matter of fact, than he'd ever been in his life.

Not very surprising. When he got too restless to be able to settle down to anything else, he was walking about the valley, moving along at his best clip regardless of obstacles until he was ready to drop to the ground wherever he was. Exertion ate up restlessness eventually—for a while. Selecting another tree to chop into firewood took the edge off the spasms of rage that tended to come up if he started thinking too long about that association of jerks somewhere beyond the sun. Brother Chard was putting on muscle all over. And after convincing himself at last—after all, the animals weren't getting hurt—that the glaring diamond of fire in the daytime sky couldn't really be harmful, he had also rapidly put on a Palm Beach tan. When his carefully rationed sleep periods eventually came around, he was more than ready for them, and slept like a log.

Otherwise: projects. Projects to beat boredom, and never mind how much sense they made in themselves. None of them did. But after the first month or two he had so much going that there was no question any more of not having something to do. Two hours allotted to work out on the typewriter a critical evaluation of a chapter from one of McAllen's abstruse technical texts. If Barney's mood was sufficiently sour, the evaluation would be unprintable; but it wasn't being printed, and two hours had been disposed of. A day and a half–Earth Standard Time–to construct an operating dam across the stream. He was turning into an experienced landscape architect; the swimming pool in the floor of the valley beneath the cabin might not have been approved by Carstairs of California, but it was the one project out of which he had even drawn some realistic benefit.

Then:

Half an hour to improve his knife-throwing technique.

Fifteen minutes to get the blade of the kitchen knife straightened out afterwards.

Two hours to design a box trap for the capture of one of the fat gray squirrels that always hung about the cabin.

Fifty minutes on a new chess problem. Chess, Barney had discovered, wasn't as hairy as it looked.

Five hours to devise one more completely foolproof method of bringing about the eventual ruin of the association. That made no more practical sense than anything else he was doing–and couldn't, until he knew a great deal more about McAllen's friends than he did now.

But it was considerably more absorbing, say, than even chess.

Brother Chard could beat boredom. He could probably beat another three years of boredom.

He hadn't forgiven anyone for making him do it.

THE END OF YEAR FIVE

For some hours, the association's Altiplano station had been dark and almost deserted. Only the IMT transit lock beneath one of the sprawling ranch houses showed in the vague light spreading out of the big scanning plate in an upper wall section. The plate framed an unimpressive section of the galaxy, a blurred scattering of stars condensing toward the right, and, somewhat left of center, a large misty red globe.

John Emanuel Fredericks, seated by himself in one of the two Tube operator chairs, ignored the plate. He was stooped slightly forwards, peering absorbedly through the eyepieces of the operator scanner before him.

Melvin Simms, Psychologist, strolled in presently through the transit lock's door, stopped behind Fredericks, remarked mildly, "Good evening, doctor."

Fredericks started and looked around. "Never heard you arrive, Mel. Where's Ollie?"

"He and Spalding dropped in at Spalding's place in Vermont. They should be along in a few minutes."

"Spalding?" Fredericks repeated inquiringly. "Our revered president intends to observe the results of Ollie's experiment in person?"

"He'll represent the board here," Simms said. "Whereas I, as you may have guessed, represent the outraged psychology department." He nodded at the plate. "That the place?"

"That's it. ET Base Eighteen."

"Not very sharp in the Tube, is it?"

"No. Still plenty of interfering radiation. But it's thinned out enough for contact. Reading 0.19, as of thirty minutes ago." Fredericks indicated the chair beside him. "Sit down if you want a better look."

"Thanks." The psychologist settled himself in the chair, leaned forward and peered into the scanner. After a few seconds he remarked, "Not the most hospitable-looking place–"

Fredericks grunted. "Any of the ecologists will tell you Eighteen's an unspoiled beauty. No problems there–except the ones we bring along ourselves."

Simms grinned faintly. "Well, we're good at doing that, aren't we? Have you looked around for uh ... for McAllen's subject yet?"

"No. Felt Ollie should be present when we find out what's happened. Incidentally, how did the meeting go?"

"You weren't tuned in?" Simms asked, surprised.

"No. Too busy setting things up for contact."

"Well"–Simms sat back in his chair–"I may say it was a regular bear garden for a while, doctor. Psychology expressed itself as being astounded, indignant, offended. In a word, they were hopping mad. I kept out of it, though I admit I was startled when McAllen informed me privately this morning of the five-year project he's been conducting on the quiet. He was accused of crimes ranging ... oh, from the clandestine to the inhumane. And, of course, Ollie was giving it back as good as he got."

"Of course."

"His arguments," Simms went on, pursing his lips reflectively, "were not without merit. That was recognized. Nobody enjoys the idea of euthanasia as a security device. Many of us feel–I do–that it's still preferable to the degree of brain-washing required to produce significant alterations in a personality type of Chard's class."

"Ollie feels that, too," Fredericks said. "The upshot of the original situation, as he saw it, was that Barney Chard had been a dead man from the moment he got on the association's trail. Or a permanently deformed personality."

Simms shook his head. "Not the last. We wouldn't have considered attempting personality alteration in his case."

"Euthanasia then," Fredericks said. "Chard was too intelligent to be thrown off the track, much too unscrupulous to be trusted under any circumstances. So Ollie reported him dead."

*   *   *   *   *

The psychologist was silent for some seconds. "The point might be this," he said suddenly. "After my talk with McAllen this morning, I ran an extrapolation on the personality pattern defined for Chard five years ago on the basis of his background. Results indicate he went insane and suicided within a year."

"How reliable are those results?" Fredericks inquired absently.

"No more so than any other indication in individual psychology. But they present a reasonable probability ... and not a very pleasant one."

Fredericks said, "Oliver wasn't unaware of that as a possible outcome. One reason he selected Base Eighteen for the experiment was to make sure he couldn't interfere with the process, once it had begun.

"His feeling, after talking with Chard for some hours, was that Chard was an overcondensed man. That is Oliver's own term, you understand. Chard obviously was intelligent, had a very strong survival drive. He had selected a good personal survival line to follow—good but very narrow. Actually, of course, he was a frightened man. He had been running scared all his life. He couldn't stop."

Simms nodded.

"Base Eighteen stopped him. The things he'd been running from simply no longer existed. Ollie believed Chard would go into a panic when he realized it. The question was what he'd do then. Survival now had a very different aspect. The only dangers threatening him were the ones inherent in the rigid personality structure he had maintained throughout his adult existence. Would he be intelligent enough to understand that? And would his survival urge—with every alternative absolutely barred to him for five years—be strong enough to overcome those dangers?"

"And there," Simms said dryly, "we have two rather large questions." He cleared his throat. "The fact remains, however, that Oliver B. McAllen is a good practical psychologist—as he demonstrated at the meeting."

"I expected Ollie would score on the motions," Fredericks said. "How did that part of it come off?"

"Not too badly. The first motion was passed unanimously. A vote of censure against Dr. McAllen."

Fredericks looked thoughtful. "His seventeenth–I believe?"

"Yes. The fact was mentioned. McAllen admitted he could do no less than vote for this one himself. However, the next motion to receive a majority was, in effect, a generalized agreement that men with such ... ah ... highly specialized skills as Barney Chard's and with comparable intelligence actually would be of great value as members of the association, if it turned out that they could be sufficiently relieved of their more flagrant antisocial tendencies. Considering the qualification, the psychology department could hardly avoid backing that motion. The same with the third one–in effect again that Psychology is to make an unprejudiced study of the results of Dr. McAllen's experiment on Base Eighteen, and report on the desirability of similar experiments when the personality of future subjects appears to warrant them."

"Well," Fredericks said, after a pause, "as far as the association goes, Ollie got what he wanted. As usual." He hesitated. "The other matter–"

"We'll know that shortly." Simms turned his head to listen, added in a lowered voice, "They're coming now."

* * * * *

Dr. Stephen Spalding said to Simms and Fredericks: "Dr. McAllen agrees with me that the man we shall be looking for on Base Eighteen may be dead. If this is indicated, we'll attempt to find some evidence of his death before normal ecological operations on Eighteen are resumed.

"Next, we may find him alive but no longer sane. Dr. Simms and I are both equipped with drug-guns which will then be used to render him insensible. The charge is sufficient to insure he will not wake up again. In this circumstance, caution will be required since he was left on the Base with a loaded gun.

"Third, he may be alive and technically sane, but openly or covertly hostile to us." Spalding glanced briefly at each of the others, then went on, "It is because of this particular possibility that our contact group here has been very carefully selected. If such has been the result of Dr. McAllen's experiment, it will be our disagreeable duty to act as Chard's executioners. To add lifelong confinement or further psychological manipulation to the five solitary years Chard already has spent would be inexcusable.

"Dr. McAllen has told us he did not inform Chard of the actual reason he was being marooned—"

"On the very good grounds," McAllen interrupted, "that if Chard had been told at the outset what the purpose was, he would have preferred killing himself to allowing the purpose to be achieved. Any other human being was Chard's antagonist. It would have been impossible for him to comply with another man's announced intentions."

Simms nodded. "I'll go along on that point, doctor."

Spalding resumed, "It might be a rather immaterial point by now. In any event, Chard's information was that an important 'five-year-plan' of the association made it necessary to restrict him for that length of time. We shall observe him closely. If the indications are that he would act against the association whenever he is given the opportunity, our line will be that the five-year-plan has been concluded, and that he is, therefore, now to be released and will receive adequate compensation for his enforced seclusion. As soon as he is asleep, he will, of course, receive euthanasia. But up to that time, everything must be done to reassure him."

He paused again, concluded, "There is the final possibility that Dr. McAllen's action has had the results he was attempting to bring about.... Ollie, you might speak on that yourself."

McAllen shrugged. "I've already presented my views. Essentially, it's a question of whether Barney Chard was capable of learning that he could live without competing destructively with other human beings. If he has grasped that, he should also be aware by now that Base Eighteen is presently one of the most interesting spots in the known universe."

Simms asked: "Do you expect he'll be grateful for what has occurred?"

"We-e-ll," McAllen said judiciously, turning a little pale, "that, of course, depends on whether he *is* still alive and sane: But if he has survived the five years, I do believe that he will not be dissatisfied with what has happened to him. However"–he shrugged again–"let's get ahead with it. Five years has been a long time to find out whether or not I've murdered a man."

In the momentary silence that followed, he setted himself in the chair Fredericks had vacated, and glanced over at Simms. "You stay seated, Mel," he said. "You represent Psychology here. Use your chair scanner. The plate's still showing no indications of clearing, John?"

"No," said Fredericks. "In another two hours we might have a good picture there. Hardly before."

McAllen said, "We won't wait for it. Simms and I can determine through the scanners approximately what has been going on." He was silent a few seconds; then the blurred red globe in the plate expanded swiftly, filled two thirds of the view space, checked for a moment, then grew once more; finally stopped.

McAllen said irritably, "John, I'm afraid you'll have to take over. My hands don't seem steady enough to handle this properly."

*   *   *   *   *

A minute or two passed. The big plate grew increasingly indistinct, all details lost in a muddy wash of orange-brown shades. Green intruded suddenly; then McAllen muttered, "Picking up the cabin now."

There was a moment of silence, then Fredericks cleared his throat. "So far so good, Oliver. We're looking into the cabin. Can't see your man yet–but someone's living here. Eh, Simms?"

"Obviously," the psychologist acknowledged. He hesitated. "And at a guess it's no maniac. The place is in reasonably good order."

"You say Chard isn't in the cabin?" Spalding demanded.

Fredericks said, "Not unless he's deliberately concealing himself. The exit door is open. Hm-m-m. Well, the place isn't entirely deserted, after all."

"What do you mean?" asked Spalding.

"Couple of squirrels sitting in the window," Simms explained.

"In the window? Inside the cabin?"

"Yes," said Fredericks. "Either they strayed in while he was gone, or he's keeping them as pets. Now, should we start looking around outside for Chard?"

"No," Spalding decided. "The Base is too big to attempt to cover at pin-point focus. If he's living in the cabin and has simply gone out, he'll return within a few hours at the most. We'll wait and see what we can deduce from the way he behaves when he shows up." He turned to McAllen. "Ollie," he said, "I think you might allow yourself to relax just a little. This doesn't seem at all bad!"

McAllen grunted. "I don't know," he said. "You're overlooking one thing."

"What's that?"

"I told Chard when to expect us. Unless he's smashed the clock, he knows we're due today. If nothing's wrong– wouldn't he be waiting in the cabin for us?"

Spalding hesitated. "That is a point. He seems to be hiding out. May have prepared an ambush, for that matter. John–"

"Yes?" Fredericks said.

"Step the tubescope down as fine as it will go, and scan that cabin as if you were vacuuming it. There may be some indication–"

"He's already doing that," Simms interrupted.

There was silence again for almost two minutes. Forefinger and thumb of Fredericks' right hand moved with infinite care on a set of dials on the side of the scanner; otherwise neither he nor Simms stirred.

"Oh-hoo-hoo-HAW!" Dr. John Fredericks cried suddenly. "Oh-hoo-hoo-HAW! A message, Ollie! Your Mr. Chard has left you a ... hoo-hoo ... message."

For a moment McAllen couldn't see clearly through the scanner. Fredericks was still laughing; Simms was saying in a rapid voice, "It's quite all right, doctor! Quite all right. Your man's sane, quite sane. In fact you've made, one might guess, a one hundred per cent convert to the McAllen approach to life. Can't you *see* it?"

"No," gasped McAllen. He had a vague impression of the top of the desk in the main room of the cabin, of something white–a white card–taped to it, of blurred printing on the card. "Nothing's getting *that* boy unduly excited any more," Simms' voice went on beside him. "Not even the prospect of seeing visitors from Earth for the first time in five years. But he's letting you know it's perfectly all right to make yourself at home in his cabin until he gets back. Here, let me–"

He reached past McAllen, adjusted the scanner. The printing on the card swam suddenly into focus before McAllen's eyes.

The message was terse, self-explanatory, to the point:
GONE FISHING,
Regards,

B. Chard.

And Now a Message . . .
By Greg Fowlkes

A short Story from the upcoming Book - *Back Road to the Stars*

And Now A Message . . .

For the third time that night Jack Olsen was about to nod off over the copy of *Statistical Information Theory* that he was attempting to read. Giving it up as a bad effort, he shut the book and looked out the window of the control room at the giant bowl of the Arecibo radio telescope. Theoretically he was running the huge instrument, but in reality all the controlling was being done by the computers in the room around him. For six months he had been working eight hour shifts every night, and his job had consisted of the five minutes a shift that it took to enter the coordinates to be examined on the control console. Other than that, he was on hand only for the off chance that the monitoring programs would recognize some pattern in the radio noise, in which case an alarm would sound. So far, in the six months, it hadn't happened.

He walked over to the coffee machine in the hopes that a cup would revive him enough so that he could continue his studies. He never made it, for as if to prove the lie of his earlier thoughts, the alarm sounded. For a moment Jack was frozen, the alarm beating raucously in his ears, then he pulled himself together and flicked off the switch on the bell. With the room returned to the relative quiet of the whoosh of the cooling fans on the equipment, Jack sat down at the console and keyed in an enquiry. Within seconds the computer had replied that it was receiving a strong periodic signal on the 42 centimeter band. Further questioning showed that it was not a program malfunction but a genuine signal.

Jack picked up the phone and dialed his boss's number. It was three in the morning, but his instructions had been clear. If anything was received that could possibly be an intelligent signal, he was supposed to contact his superior immediately.

Despite the long drive through the mountains in the cool Puerto Rican night, Professor Kraft showed up with his eyes still sleepy. Shuffling over to the coffee pot by the window he poured himself a large mug before he said anything. "You'd better have something good to get me up at this hour."

"I think so," Jack said, aware that his boss's irritation was only feigned. "I've been checking with the computer since I called you. It shows a strong periodic signal with a sharp pulse every fifty milliseconds. It runs on like that for about two and a half minutes before the signal fades below the background."

"Any chance that it might be a pulsar?" Kraft asked, referring to the radio signals of rapidly rotating neutron stars. "That's within the range of periods for them. When the first one was discovered, they thought that they had received intelligent signals."

"I thought of that, so I checked the record of the broad band receiver." Jack brought out a long strip of graph paper and pointed to the evenly spaced patterns of peaks on it. "Where the narrow band shows only a single repetitive pulse, the wide band gives us this fine structure. It's far too regular to be a pulsar and much too detailed. It's more like some sort of timing signal or spacer. And in between the pulses there is another signal. It's not as repetitive as the main pulse. That's why the program doesn't bring it out. But there definitely is some sort of transmission in between. It's weaker, but I think that we can write a processing program to pick it out from the noise."

Kraft looked at the trace in his hand thoughtfully. "I hate to make snap judgements. You can be suckered in too easily that way. But it does look like some kind of artificial signal. We'll get the team working on it in the morning. Have you received any additional signals?"

"No. I've kept the dish tracking the source, but all we get on 42 cm. is background noise. It's like there was a moment of freak atmospheric conditions that opened a window, and then it shut again. Just like you get with shortwave sometimes because of the ionosphere."

"Well, we should be grateful for what we've got. I don't think I can sleep anymore tonight, so I'll keep you company. I'd like to be here if we get any more messages from our friends out there," he said, pointing with his cup towards the star filled sky that loomed over the radio telescope's antenna.

"Frustrating, isn't it?" Prof. Kraft remarked to the team of graduate students and post doctoral fellows that were working under him on the interstellar communications project. And frustrating it had been. For six months they had continuously monitored the sky searching for signs of life finally to be rewarded by a two minute snippet of extraterrestrial conversation.

Now, another six months later, they had still made no sense of the signal, nor had they received any further transmissions from that part of the sky, though they had concentrated their efforts in that direction.

"Rumors have leaked out about our discovery, and I've been getting requests for the data. I'd sure hate to have someone else steal our thunder by deciphering the signal, but if we don't make some progress soon, we're going to have to release it." He looked around the table at the young faces of his assistants. At the moment they didn't look nearly as bright and intelligent as he knew they were.

"Why don't I summarize what we've found so far in hopes that it will give us some new ideas?"

"First, we've got this repetitive pattern of pulses every twentieth of a second as regular as clockwork. So regular, in fact, that we can't decide whether they serve as breaks in the message or were just put there to attract our attention. Remember, it was these pulses that were first recognized by the computer."

"But the pulses aren't the real message. That lays in the spaces in between. We've been able to deduce that the messages are digitized and the computer has been able to enhance them so that we have a fairly error free record of them. There is some repetitive structure to them, and they do vary in some sort of progression, but beyond that, we haven't been able to get the least notion of what they mean. Anyone have something to add?"

Bill Warden, one of the post docs, spoke up. "Well, we've tried mathematical analysis on the signals and have gotten zero results. It has already been assumed that any sort of interstellar communications would be based on sort of easily recognizable mathematical progression. Like one, two three. Something like that to show that they were rational. From there you can always build up more complicated concepts."

"With this message we don't have that, which leads us to one of two assumptions. One, we have only a fragment of a broadcast, and from a very advanced lesson at that. If that's the case, I don't see much hope of our being able to decipher the message until we can receive more signals to give us a broader base to work from."

"The other alternative is that they, whoever they are, just don't think like us. Their minds work in some fashion so that this mess we have makes sense to them. If so, I don't see any hope at all. Their minds may just be too foreign for us to hold a dialog with them."

"Thank you for that optimistic note," Prof. Kraft said wryly. "For the first time mankind has received a message from another species and we can't tell whether it is a cure for cancer, a means of achieving universal peace, or a recipe for sauerbraten. Any comments?"

"If it's sauerbraten, where do we go for a tablespoon of powdered bandersnatch egg?" quipped one of the grad students. They all laughed at the joke more than it deserved. Six months of unrewarded work had left them all a little giddy. After the giggles and comments had died down, Jack Olsen coughed, trying to get their attention.

"You've got something useful to say, Jack?" Kraft asked. "You might as well tell us. I don't think anyone else has anything useful to add," he said, pointedly looking at the wisecracker.

"I've been thinking about the signal, and I remember something that I said to you the night it came in. I don't know if you recall, but I called the pulses timing signals. Now there is one type of common transmission that has the same kind of pulses, and that's television. They use the pulses to synchronize the frames. It's possible that the message in between each pulse is a picture, and the whole transmission is meant to be viewed in sequence."

"How long have you been sitting on this while the rest of us were beating our brains out?" Kraft asked.

"It just came to me," Jack said, his face flushed. "I should have thought of it earlier, but like Bill said, we've all been conditioned to look for something like one plus one equals two."

"I think that we should all have seen it," Kraft said. "It makes as much sense as anything else that's been suggested. Do you think that you can get us a picture?"

"If it's there, I should be able to pick it out using the computer," Jack answered.

"Good. Then, since it was your idea, you're in charge. Dragoon anything or anybody that you need to help you."

Five days later they were all gathered around the conference room table again, but this time there was a TV set and a video recorder on a cart at its end. From the nervous stubbing of cigarette butts and fingers drumming on the table, it was obvious that all the members of the team were in a state of anticipation.

"It took some time to figure out exactly how the signal was put together," Jack began. "After all, we didn't know how many lines there were in each frame or how many bits made up each unit of picture. In the end, I had to have the computer run through all the likely possibilities for one of the frames. It took a lot of computer time, but I've finally got some recognizable pictures."

"It turns out that the original broadcast was in color. That threw us for a while, but we finally psyched it out. The aliens must have eyes structurally different from ours; there are only two colors, not three in the signal. Which colors they are is anybody's guess. They might be ultraviolet and infrared for all we can tell. Arbitrarily, I've assigned them red and bluish green, so keep that in mind. Also, because the video recorder uses thirty frames a second instead of the twenty in the transmission, it was necessary to compress the program a bit. This means that everything you'll be seeing has been speeded up about fifty percent.

"I guess you're all more interested in seeing the tape than in listening to me." A snort from Prof. Kraft indicated agreement. Jack flicked off the lights and started the tape. For a minute the screen showed only snow, then a face became recognizable. It was a sickly chartreuse, and there was no nose between the two large, oval eyes, but it was recognizable as a face. The figures movements were quick and jerky like an old silent movie, the result of the difference in frame speed, and the picture left a lot to be desired in clarity, the product of interstellar noise, but it was a picture, the first of an alien race.

As the tape played, a weird, sings song voice came from the speaker sounding something like a Chinese chipmunk. "I forgot to mention that there was also an audio track along with the signal. Again, it's only a reconstruction and may not bear much resemblance to the original, but then, we'll never know," Jack commented. They had determined that the source of the transmission was at least several dozen light years away. It would take twice that number of years to send a message and receive a reply, by which time they would all be dead.

They continued to watch the tape. The camera had drawn back to show the alien from the waist up revealing rounded shoulders and a pair of six fingered hands. Apparently he was standing behind a low lectern or a table of some sort. The fuzzy picture and camera angle made it hard to tell which. As he, or her, or it, spoke, the alien pointed at a chart or poster suspended on the backdrop. A pattern of red and blue that hurt the eye with violent contrasts seemed to be some sort of text. The voice continued as the picture disappeared in a sea of snow and then it broke into static. The transmission had ended.

"You've done a fine job, Jack," Prof. Kraft said after they had played the tape through a half dozen times. "It's actually far better than I thought it would be, and I think we can accept any of the shortcomings that you mentioned."

"So, we've got a face and body of what certainly is a rational creature. He seemed to be giving us a lesson or lecture of some sort, though I for one don't have the faintest idea of what he was talking about. We have an idea of what they look like which I am sure will give the biologists a lot to speculate on, so I guess that we should be thankful for small favors, but I still don't see how we're going to learn any more about them without receiving further signals."

"I wouldn't hold out much hope of that," Jack interjected. "I think that it's clear now that the signal we picked up was not meant for interstellar communication. Any such signal would have been designed with much greater noise immunity. We were able to receive it only because of an accident of atmospheric conditions. It was actually just a local TV broadcast. As we haven't received anything since, those conditions must be rare."

"So," Kraft said, "we have a message of great potential import, that at the very least could provide us with insights on a totally alien culture, and no way to decipher it."

"I've got an idea," Bill said. "We've all been looking at the problem from the point of view of hardware and computer programs. That's natural because of our backgrounds, but now that we have what amounts to an artifact, maybe we should call in a specialist. We need someone who is trained in resurrecting a culture from its fragments. I suggest that we show the tape to some archeologists and get their opinions."

Convincing an archeologist to look at the tape was harder than it had sounded. Most of them were more interested in ancient rather than alien civilizations. Jack suspected that they felt out of their depth with the computers and electronics. With some pressure and pleading, a group finally agreed to view the tape, but after the showing, only one evinced any interest in following up on it.

A visiting lecturer from Norway, she was reputed to have a good background in languages, though Jack lacked the knowledge to judge her qualifications. However, as she was young, blond, and attractive, he was quite willing to spend the time required to familiarize her with the tape and the equipment they had used to come up with it. Together, they spent hours viewing the tape, studying it frame by frame attempting to pick out the slightest piece of information.

The project team had been assembled in the conference room, and this time it was the archeologist's turn to address them. For three weeks Cristina Peterson had been studying the tape almost constantly, and now she was ready to give her opinion. With the exception of Jack, who had been working closely with her, they were all, even Prof. Kraft, eagerly awaiting the report. There had been a great deal of speculation about what her findings would be.

"First," she began, "before I get your hopes up, I want to say that I have not been able to get a word for word translation of the voice on the tape. The sample of speech is just too brief for that to be possible. If the scene had contained more action, I might have been more successful, but we were not that fortunate. I have, however, been able to form a hypothesis based on the spoken word as well as visual clues such as facial expression, setting, and so on."

"An important point to remember is that the aliens, despite certain differences in appearance, are not too dissimilar from ourselves. They are bipedal, intelligent, and possess opposable thumbs. They have binocular vision and a form of color perception as well. Brain size is about the same in relationship to total body size as in humans, and I would be greatly surprised if they were much larger or smaller than ourselves. That much can be guessed on the basis of physiology from the picture and the nature of the signal. From this information, I think that we can draw the conclusion that their planet is, within limits, earthlike."

"Probably more relevant is their state of culture. They obviously have a technology and one that is recognizable in terms of our own. That we can receive their signals is proof of that. Also, they speak, they wear clothing, we can even guess at the purpose of some of the objects visible in the tape. I might add that this is more than we can do for some of the artifacts of primitive human cultures. In some ways we have more in common with the aliens than we do with the Tasadi or Bushman."

"I want you to bear in mind that these beings are not greatly different from ourselves. If we are to properly analyze the contents of the message, we must remember that they are influenced by the same drives and forces as humans." There was an uneasy shifting in their seats on the part of the team members as they took in the meaning of her statement.

"If we accept this premise, and replace the alien with a human, we can make an educated guess as to what we are seen on the tape. I'll run it again for you so that you can make the substitution." Jack tapped the switch, and for the next minute and a half they watched the now familiar scene replay itself.

"Before I give my own opinion, would anyone else like to make a guess?" Cristina asked.

Kraft looked around the room, but it appeared as though no one had the courage to be the first to put his own views forward. To break the silence he said, "It's only a guess, but to start the discussion, I'd say that the alien might be a lecturer. He's obviously standing at some sort of podium or speaker's table."

"He seems a little too impassioned for a lecturer, at least in the physical sciences," one of the grad students remarked. "I've never seen you that excited before a class." Kraft smiled at the reference to his own low keyed classroom delivery.

"Maybe it's a political science class. They get more aroused."

Bill Warden broke in, "Why a class? It looks to me more like he's a politician trying to persuade the voters. He must be up for reelection. The sign in back could be an election poster." That brought a couple of laughs and a few less than serious comments.

"We've all had a crack at it," Prof. Kraft said. "You obviously have your own interpretation, and I think that we've been kept in suspense long enough. From the look on Jack's face, it must be a good one. Let's hear it now. After all, the communication between two species is one of the most important events in human history."

She smiled at the jibe. "All your suggestions are plausible, but I've spent more time analyzing the tape than you have. I'll play it again for you and point out the features that have led me to my interpretation."

"The first thing that caught my attention was the fact that the word 'gratach' was mentioned fourteen times, an unusually high incidence in such a brief speech. Furthermore, at least four of those times the speaker pointed to the symbols on the chart behind him. I think that we can assume that 'gratach' is a name, and the symbols form the written version."

"Now here's something that I want you to see." She froze the picture on the television. "Note the artifacts on the table, a bowl filled with a substance and a box or container. There appears to be some writing on the box, but the resolution of the picture isn't good enough to allow us to make it out. However," she said as the tape began to roll again, "as the alien points to the box and says 'gratach' it is likely that the symbols again spell out the name in the chart behind the alien. Note, too, the expression on his face. Despite the lack of a nose, the face is surprisingly human, and if that expression was on a human face, it would be one of approval or pleasure."

"I think that if you put all the clues together, you can come to only one conclusion. Dr. Warden was not far off when he suggested a political campaign. The speaker is definitely trying to persuade his audience, but it is the package, not himself, that he is trying to sell."

"Oh, god," Kraft sputtered. "You can't mean it. The first communication from another planet and it's only . . ."

"Yes, I'm afraid so," Cristina said. "The first and only signal received from another world is nothing more than a breakfast food commercial."

Special Preview!

THE LAWS OF MAGIC
BY GREG FOWLKES
© 2010

Now available from The Fictional Press
www.TheFictionalPress.com

THE LAWS OF MAGIC
WITHOUT LICENSE

☆   ☆   ☆   ☆   ☆

As Egil Njalsson climbed the steps of the criminal courts building he wondered if it was really worth it. Eighteen months of practicing law on his own and here he was in his only suit, about to attend the preliminary hearing in a petty case for which with luck he would be able to recover his expenses. It wasn't even a paying client. The state would be picking up the tab for this one, and he'd ended up being the lawyer appointed by the court. At the moment it wasn't clear who would benefit most from the charity, the client or the lawyer. He hadn't had a case in three months and he'd just been eking out a living writing briefs for other lawyers. He could do that well enough. His technical background gave him a depth of knowledge most lawyers lacked when it came to cases involving points of science as well as law. If he hadn't had that he'd be starving.

He'd been thinking about that a lot lately; whether he had made the right decision giving up science and going into the law. At the time, with the aerospace industry in a depression in the early seventies, it had seemed like a good idea. Engineers were pumping gas and PhD's in physics were selling insurance. Being a lawyer had seemed like a good way to make money. A stable income, no ups and downs. He'd put in his time at law school and done well. After the grind at CalThaum, law school had been a snap. So here he was a lawyer barely making ends meet and his school mates, the ones who had stuck with science were all making it rich designing personal calculating engines and disk storage units.

He tried to put all these thoughts out of his mind as he passed through the big brass doors of the court house. After all, he did have a client to defend, and a duty to him. It wasn't easy, though. It wasn't, after all, a very important case. Just a charge of fortune telling and practicing the Art without a license. Minor offenses, probably not even any jail time involved. This wouldn't even be a trial today, just a plea and arranging of bail.

It wouldn't even have amounted to that if his client hadn't instisted on pleading not guilty. He'd met him at the county jail, an old man, one Jake Schmidts. He'd tried to talk him out of pleading not guilty, too. A guilty plea, a small fine, and they both could be done with it. His client, though, had turned out to be something of a character. So here he was.

It took an hour and a half before their case came up. The judge looked at him questioningly when he had pleaded not guilty, but thankfully had released his client on his own recognizance when he indicated he had a permanent address. It was over in five minutes.

They got the release papers and the court date from the bailiff. Egil started to head out when he noticed that his client seemed lost and disoriented by it all. "Do you have car fare home?"

"No," Schmidts said. "I didn't have any money on me when they came and arrested me. Not a cent."

"Which way do you live?"

The old man gave an address on Fair Oaks Street. It wasn't far out of his way. Neither one of them lived in the best part of town.

"I can give you a lift," Egil said.

"That's kind of you, Mr. Njalsson," Schmidts said. The mister was ironic. The arrest report hadn't given an age, just "somewhere around seventy." As far as Egil could tell that might have been off by a decade or two.

The address turned out to be a sort of second hand junk store. The operative word was junk. If the pieces in the dirty window were the best of the lot then Egil could see how Schmidts qualified as indigent.

"Thanks for the ride. I've a beer inside if you'd like."

Njalsson looked at his watch. It wasn't too early to start drinking, at least just a beer. The work at the office would wait. He had to talk to Schmidts anyway to prepare a case. Besides, the old man seemed to want to pay him back for the ride.

If anything, the shop was worse on the inside than it looked from the front. Odd bits of bric-a-brac were strewn around everywhere; most of it looking like it hadn't been moved or even dusted in twenty years. Broken down pieces of furniture were covered with moldering sheets.

The old man led him to the back and up some stairs to an apartment above the shop. The kitchen was cleaner, though still hardly spotless. Of course, Egil's own small apartment wasn't the neatest of place, either.

The refrigerator looked as old as Schmidt's, but the beer was cold. Schmidt's took out two and motioned him to a chair at the kitchen table.

"So what happens now, Mr. Njalsson?"

"The trial will be held on the date on the summons. The district attorney will call his witnesses and make his case. Then I'll make my case. The judge will then decide."

"No jury?" Schmidt's asked disappointedly.

"Not unless we've got a very strong case to present. This is a small matter. It's better left to a judge. A jury would be considered a waste of time, I'm afraid, and would probably result in a higher fine. Maybe even jail."

"So you think I'm guilty?"

"I don't think you have much of a case."

"That's different?"

"To a lawyer it is."

Schmidts snorted in disgust.

"I don't want to disillusion you, Mr. Schmidts, but you've got to face the facts. Do you have a license to practice Magic?"

"No."

"Did you tell the fortune of one Mrs. Einar Johnson?"

"Yes, and an ungrateful woman she is, too. Just because I told her the truth about that shifty salesman she thinks is going to marry her. He's just after her late husband's money."

Egil raised an eyebrow.

"It's the truth. I've been reading the cards longer than you've been alive, Mr. Njalsson, and I know what I'm doing. That salesman is the one that got her to swear out a complaint against me."

"It doesn't matter whether what you said was the truth or not. What matters is that you were practicing the Art without a license. Magic is a potentially dangerous business. It's not something that untrained people should be dealing with. That's what the law is about."

"What would you know about the Art, Mr. Lawyer?" Schmidts asked sharply.

"I know more than most, Mr. Schmidts. I studied applied metaphysics at the California Institute of Thaumaturgy for four years before going into the law. I've got a Bachelor's of Science degree. I've also got my practitioner's license from both the state of California and Wisconsin. I may not be the greatest practitioner of the Art, but I am competent enough to know what I am and am not capable of."

"So maybe you did study at a fancy school out west. Those scientists don't know everything. They think that they've discovered magic, but magic goes back. Way back. Back before Helmholtz and Gauss. Before the Egyptians and Babylonians. Magic is old, Mr. Njalsson, and the doctors and professors haven't learned half of it."

"And you have?" Egil asked sarcastically. He was getting annoyed at the old man's pretensions of knowledge. He was surprised, though, that Schmidts knew that the two physicists Helmholtz and Gauss had been instrumental in proving the scientific basis for magic.

"No. I'm no fool. I've been studying the Art all my life. I know what I know and I have a good idea of what I don't. What I do know is more than a youngster like you learns in four years at college, even if it is a fancy one."

"Look, Mr. Schmidts," Egil said. "This isn't working out. Maybe you should get yourself a different lawyer."

The old man looked at him in surprise, then shook his head. "No. I guess you were just telling me the way it is. I may not like it, but I can't fault you for telling the truth."

"Okay. Is there anything I can use in your defense?"

"Guess not."

"Well, where did you learn to tell fortunes, to read the cards?" Egil asked.

"From an old Romany woman," the old man answered.

"Where? Here in the city?"

"No, it was a long time ago. Bohemia, I think it was."

"Bohemia? You mean Czechoslovakia."

"Yes, that's what they call it now I think. Prague. I was a student there."

"A student? At a university? I thought you didn't believe in learning."

"I was younger then. I thought there were things I might learn. I was wrong."

"Did you get a degree, though? That might carry some weight, especially a foreign one."

"Wait a moment. I think I have one someplace. Let me go look." Schmidts went down to his shop. From below Egil could hear noises as if boxes were being moved around. He didn't quite know what to make of the old man's gypsy tale. Bohemia had become part of Czechoslovakia after the First World War in the breakup of the Austrian Empire. It hadn't been a separate country since the Hapsburgs.

There were footsteps on the stairway and Schmidts showed up with a small picture frame carrying a piece of parchment. It was certainly a degree, but not from the University of Prague. The writing had faded with age and Egil had never learned French, but it appeared to be a doctorate granted by the Sorbonne. It was also made out to one Jacques Krieger.

"This isn't your name."

"It was the name I was using then."

"Can you prove that?"

"Not that I can see."

"Oh well. Maybe we can use it. If you can find anymore old papers like this save them for me. We might have some defense if we can prove you had an education, particularly if it was before the current examination system went into effect."

"I'll do that, Mr. Njalsson."

"Well I've got to get going now. Can I take this with me?" the lawyer asked, holding up the sheepskin.

"Yes, if it will help."

Egil let himself out through the shop. He dumped the diploma on the car seat next to him and started the car. While the engine was warming up he glanced down at it. The date was written in Roman numerals. It took him a moment to figure out the year. It was 1847. Either the old man was lying to him or he might find himself defending him in a commitment hearing.

Also From Resurrected Press

Science Fiction Authors Resurrected

Fyfe Resurrected - The Stories of H. B. Fyfe

Stories from the Golden Age of Science Fiction by the author of D-99. dealing with the interaction of humans and aliens on far off worlds in ways that were as creative as they were imaginative.

Bone Resurrected - The Stories of J. F. Bone

More stories from the Golden Age of Science Fiction. Includes "The Issahar Artifact," "Assassin," "To Choke an Ocean" and more.

Nourse Resurrected - The Stories of Alan E. Nourse

Stories from the Golden Age of Science Fiction. Includes "Contamination Crew." "Coffin Cure," "The Link," and more.

Dick Resurrected - The Early Stories of Philip K. Dick

Early stories from the author of the novels that inspired "Blade Runner," "Total Recall," and through a scanner darkly. Science Fiction Authors Resurrected

OTHER CLASSIC SCIENCE FICTION NOVELS BEING RESURRECTED SOON

TALENTS, INCORPORATED - BY MURRAY LEINSTER
When a Mekinese fleet conquers his home planet, Captain Bors turns to Talents, Incorporated for help using their collection of individuals with unusual abilities to defeat the enemy and save the galaxy.

THE PIRATES OF ERSATZ - BY MURRAY LEINSTER
Bran Hodden just wanted to be an electronic engineer and marry a delightful girl. But when he's framed by the powers on Walden he's forced to turn back to his family's trade, piracy. Also published as The Pirates of Zan.

EMPIRE - BY CLIFFORD SIMAK
Spencer Chambers and Interplanetary Power owned the Solar System because they controlled the source of power. It fell to Russell Page and Harry Wilson to challenge that control if they had to cross the universe to do it.

NIGHT OF THE LONG KNIVES - THE CREATURE FROM THE CLEVELAND DEPTHS - BY FRITZ LEIBER
Two classic novellas set in the not too distant future from a classic master of science fiction.

ARMAGEDDON - 2419 A.D. - THE AIR LORDS OF HAN - BY PHILLIP FRANCIS NOWLAN
The two novels that introduced the world to that intrepid hero of the 25th Century, Buck Rogers. Buck Rogers must save the world from the clutches of the insidious Han.

Other Classic Resurrected Science Fiction
Edited by Greg Fowlkes

RESURRECTED MARTIANS
Classic Stories about Mars and Martians from the Golden Age of Science Fiction

RESURRECTED ALIENS
Classic Stories of Aliens and Alien Encounters from the Golden Age of Science Fiction

RESURRECTED FLYING SAUCERS
Classic Stories of Flying Saucers and Alien Invasions from the Golden Age of Science Fiction

RESURRECTED ROBOTS
Classic Stories of Robots, Cyborgs and Androids from the Golden Age of Science Fiction

RESURRECTED SPACE SHIPS -
Classic Stories of Space Ships from the Golden Age of Science Fiction

RESURRECTED TIME TRAVEL
Classic Stories of Time Travel from the Golden Age of Science Fiction

RESURRECTED DIMENSIONS
Classic Stories of other Dimensions from the Golden Age of Science Fiction

RESURRECTED FUTURES
Classic Stories of the Far Future from the Golden Age of Science Fiction

RESURRECTED MAD SCIENTISTS

Classic Stories of Mad Scientists and their Creations from the Golden Age of Science Fiction

RESURRECTED MONSTERS
Classic Stories of Monsters and Mayhem from the Golden Age of Science Fiction

The Fictional Detective
by Greg Fowlkes

Who killed Ezekial O. Handler?

A beautiful dame, a hard-boiled private eye − and a dead body.

It started like any other case. When a famous writer dies in a mysterious car crash, private detective Frank Slade is called in to find answers, but all he finds is more questions. Who killed Ezekial Handler? Who is Janet Nielsen and why is she so interested in finding out? Who is leaving the neatly typed clues? And as Slade tries to find answers to these questions he starts to wonder if the ultimate answer will threaten his very existence.

Read about it in
The Fictional Detective

Visit www.thefictionaldetective.com

About Resurrected Press

A division of Intrepid Ink, LLC, Resurrected Press is dedicated to bringing high quality, vintage books back into publication. See our entire catalogue and find out more at www.ResurrectedPress.com.

About Intrepid Ink, LLC

Intrepid Ink, LLC provides full publishing services to authors of fiction and non-fiction books, eBooks and websites. From editing to formatting, from publishing to marketing, Intrepid Ink gets your creative works into the hands of the people who want to read them. Find out more at www.IntrepidInk.com.

www.ingramcontent.com/pod-product-compliance
Lightning Source LLC
Chambersburg PA
CBHW070839250626
47159CB00003B/849